WOLVES OF ADALORE

BOOK 1 OF MARK OF THE HUNTER

Morgan Gauthier

Wolves of Adalore

Copyright © by Morgan Gauthier

Map by Gonzalo A. Mendiverry (IG: @gonzalom.art)

Cover and Character Artwork by Klára Dostrašilová (IG: @artzzofkae)

Edited by Ada Charlesworth

For more information visit www.morgangauthier.com

Library of Congress Control Number:

ISBN 978-1-7368282-0-5 (paperback)

ISBN 978-1-7368282-1-2 (ebook)

To my husband, Brad, who bestowed upon me a last name that looks cool, but no one knows how to pronounce.

It's "Go-Chay". You're welcome.

And to our three beautiful children, Remi, Archer, and Roux: Mommy loves you.

SALOME

NIABI

CRISPIN

Books by Morgan Gauthier:

Fantasy:

Wolves of Adalore (2021)

The Red Maiden (2022)

Contemporary Romance:

Aloha, Seattle (2021)

CHARACTERS

Northwind (North)
Niabi, Queen, Mistress of Shadows
Salome, Exiled Princess, The Hunter
Crispin, Exiled Prince
Gershom, Niabi's Second in Command
Pash, Commander of Shadows, Gershom's son
Ophir, Gershom's Brother, Pash's Uncle

Borg (West)
Zophar, Crispin and Salome's Guardian

Elisor (Andrago)
Tala, Niabi's Most Trusted Advisor, Oldest Friend
Leoti, Tala's Daughter, Niabi's Daughter-in-Law
Dichali, Niabi's First Husband (Deceased)

Gomorrah
Matildys, Queen
Cyler, King
Thanos, Prince, Ranalda's Twin
Ranalda, Princess, Thanos' Twin
Thrak, Cannibal Soldiers

Caelestis (Immortals)
Harbona, Seer

Numbio (South)
Osiris, King
Heru, Prince
Rayma, Royal Healer
Memucan, King's Advisor
Amunet, High Priestess

The Sisters (Blind Order)
Neempo, Sovereign
Penn, Master of Keepers
Balor, Master of Witnesses

Members of the Order (Rebel Force)
Oden, Leader, formally known as Lord Maon
Nubis, Stormcrag
Ziggy, Prostitute from Borg
Makeda, Manages *The Whispering Fox* Tavern

Stormcrags (Mountain Men Tribe)
Cato, Scout

Other Characters
Adonijah, "The Wanderer"
Odelia, Enchantress of the Swamp
Vilora, The Old Witch of Endor
Lykos, Prince of Northwind (Deceased)
Issachar, King of Northwind (Deceased)
Bilhah, Queen of Northwind (Deceased)
Diron, Captain of *The Golden Rose*
Anaktu, The Last Nephilim, Niabi's Iron Guard

Wolves of Adalore

Book One

PROLOGUE
NIABI – 12 YEARS AGO

The Gate of Tayborne was underutilized and forgotten by most Northerners. She knew it would not be difficult to infiltrate, even on her own. Her green eyes glistened in the moonlight as she scaled the forty-foot-tall, white stone wall. As she neared the top, she hugged the wall to ensure the guards would not see her.

She expected a small company of guards to be on duty, but there were only six. Six was foolish. Six would require little effort to kill.

Slithering to the cobblestone street, the hooded intruder strutted up to the soldiers huddled by a flickering fire in the bailey.

"Halt," their captain stepped forward. "Who are you?" The soldiers drew their swords and encircled her when she did not answer. "I will ask you once more," he growled. "Who are you?"

Again, she did not speak, but she stretched her arms wide, level with her shoulders, fists closed and unarmed. Confused, the soldiers lowered their weapons. Then she struck.

With the flick of her wrists, she launched twin daggers in opposite directions, slicing the necks of two guards.

Two charged her. She whipped two lightweight blades from the holsters on her back, closed her eyes, and waited for them to reach her. The first soldier to get close enough swung his sword, but she dodged his blow, and as she rose stabbed him through his chest in one swift motion. She opened her eyes as the second soldier lunged toward her and blocked the incoming blow with her second blade. He thrust his weapon again but was unable to keep up with her speed. Losing control of his longsword, she sliced through his neck, nearly decapitating him.

Two remained. Both trembled at the sight of the assassin covered in blood.

"Who are you?" the soldier's voice cracked.

"One the North wished to forget." Her raspy voice caught them by surprise.

"A woman?"

"A demon," spat the taller soldier. "Come closer, so I might send you back to hell."

Even though she wore a black mask covering the bottom half of her face, the guards could see her smirk as she sprinted toward them. The tall soldier braced himself. She was quick. Their weapons clashed loudly as they dueled. The other soldier jumped in to take her down, but she ducked, dodged, and tumbled to elude them. They stood on opposite sides of her, one in front, the other behind. She remained very still as they circled her. With a nod signaling to attack, both Northmen charged. She waited until they were near and when they swung their swords, she dropped to the ground in a front split and watched as they struck one another down.

She retrieved her daggers and opened the gate where her elite squad of warriors, the Shadows, was waiting. Marching in four rows, their black robes concealed their leather armor and their black masks made them look more like executioners than a rival army.

"That didn't take you very long." Tala the Andrago kicked over one of the dead bodies.

"The Northmen have grown weak hiding behind their white walls." She sneered. She caught a glimpse of the ivory stone White Keep perched on a hill in the center of the city of Northwind.

For a moment, everything was quiet; everything was peaceful. She closed her eyes. She inhaled the crisp mountain air and listened as the waves of the Ignacia Sea crashed in the harbor. The white stone buildings and cobblestone streets glistened under the moon's glow. It was always a magical sight; it was just as she had remembered.

"Just six?" Tala rubbed his clean-shaven, bronze face. He never wore a mask. He wanted his enemies to know exactly who was about to kill them. "Why just six?"

"He always did underestimate me." She wiped her blades clean against her black leather pants. "Give the signal."

Tala reached for the war horn that hung from his hip. "You're sure about this?"

"I have come too far to turn back now." Her eyes narrowed as the horn sounded. "Now to kill the King."

CHAPTER ONE
GERSHOM

Gershom glared across the room at the chubby astrologer clothed head to toe in a flowing robe more expensive than he could afford. The astrologer stared into the heavens, mumbling to himself and jotting down notes forcing the Second in Command to wait in great angst to be clued into his findings.

Although most Northerners no longer believed in the prophecies of the Old World, Gershom had been a believer in the stars and their messages since his youth. The dark bags underneath his eyes were proof of the nightmares he had been plagued with for nearly two weeks and he wanted answers.

"What do you see?" Gershom growled as he scratched his scraggly beard.

"I see… I see…"

"I grow impatient," Gershom egged the old man to speak. "What is it that you see?"

Now frightened, the stargazer dropped his quill and spat, "My Lord, I see that the stars have moved."

"And?" He edged closer. "What does that mean? Speak," he shouted.

The white bearded man stuttered, trying to find the right words, but ended up saying what Gershom had feared most. "My Lord, I see the time of the prophecy has come."

"What?" Gershom leaned forward, wondering if the astrologer would dare utter that report again.

"The Year of the Hunter has come," the wrinkled servant shrunk back.

Gershom slammed his clenched fist on the arm rest of his high back chair. "Who is he?"

The astrologer trembled where he stood. "I do not know, my lord. His face is hidden from me."

"Where is he?" Gershom motioned to the grand solid oak table in front of him. A map of the Ten Kingdoms of Adalore had been carved into the top and the faces of bears were etched into the feet. Rumor was when Gershom was around fifteen, he crossed paths with a giant black grizzly and fought it off with his bare hands. For this reason, he was known as the Bear and he adopted the creature for his House sigil.

The astrologer unfastened his necklace and suspended the gold chain with a purple crystal tied to the end over the table. He muttered an incantation as he circled the table and stopped over the forests in the Western Lands, which was mostly inhabited by peasants protected by King Benaiah of Borg.

"He is in the Western Lands, my lord."

"Which forest?"

"I do not know for sure, sire."

"Then what do you know, old goat?" Gershom fumed. But the astrologer's sudden silence confirmed his suspicion. There was more he was not telling him. "Is that all?" His question was met with silence. "Is. That. All?"

"No, my lord," his voice cracked.

"What else do you see?" he squinted; voice low.

"I sense great danger for you." The elderly servant shook.

"What kind of danger?" Gershom approached him; he could almost smell the astrologer's fear with each step he took.

"He knows who you are and what you have done. He will kill you if he is given the chance." He stepped back.

"Is there anything else I need to know?" His voice softened; he rested his enormous hand on the astrologer's bony shoulder.

"No, my lord," he smiled slightly.

"Good." Gershom snatched him by the neck and lifted him off the floor. The old man's feet dangled as he struggled to free himself from Gershom's tightening grip. Crazed, he choked his servant until he stopped flailing. "Then I have no more use for your service." He threw the stargazer's body to the marble floor and stepped over him as he marched to the door.

The Bear whipped the door wide open and stared at the two soldiers guarding the entrance. "Bring me my son!"

Gershom grumbled as Pash, a tall, muscular man with dark chestnut hair and brown eyes, who was slow to respond to the summons, entered the room. The Commander of Shadows was always armed with a long blade and looked exactly as Gershom did when he was younger, with exception of their hair and complexion. Gershom had sported both sides of his head clean shaven with light chestnut locks, now streaked with white, slicked back into a bun atop his head since his youth. Pash, on the other hand, made sure his shoulder length hair was in a traditional Northern bun at the back of his head. Hairstyling was not the only thing they disagreed upon.

Pash stepped toward the dead body lying on the floor, not at all surprised by the sight.

"You sent for me?" Pash asked, formal in his tone.

Gershom was hunched over the oak table. "It seems that the Year of the Hunter has come."

"Is that what he told you?" Pash motioned to the dead astrologer.

"You always were cynical of the prophecies," he hissed.

"No one has seen a Hunter in over two hundred years. Frankly, I'm not sure they are anything more than stories told to frighten children," he shrugged off his father's superstitions.

"Then make sure the stories aren't true. Find him," Gershom ordered, pouring himself another glass of wine.

"I doubt the Queen will approve the dispatch of her Shadows for such a purpose," he reminded his father of who was truly in charge. "You have bannermen at your disposal. Send them."

"If I thought my men could handle this situation, do you think I would have involved you in this?" His nostrils flared, eyes wide.

He and his son had not seen or spoken to one another in almost two months, and he was beginning to remember why that was the case. Whenever they found themselves together, Pash was quick to smugly remind him, that he was *not* the King of Northwind, although he acted as if he was. In actuality, he also had a master to serve: The Queen.

"I cannot do what you ask without her -"

"I am her Second in Command," Gershom shrieked. "Everything she has I have helped her build."

"Even if this man did exist, why should you believe he would come for you?" Pash made himself comfortable in one of the chairs and kicked his feet up on the table.

"Believe it or do not," Gershom pushed his dirty boots off the table, "but mark my words: he will come for me."

He had never appeared so unsettled and by the look on Pash's face, Gershom knew it was obvious. He honestly believed his life was in danger.

"If I dispatched some of Her Majesty's Shadows to find your marked man, where would you suggest they start their hunt?"

"The western forests."

Pash's eyes widened, "The West is all forestlands."

"That is all I know," Gershom huffed, slumping into his seat.

"You want my men to search hundreds of square miles of peasant-infested forestland for one man you think might try to kill you?" The commander shook his head and chuckled. "Would they not better serve you here, where I am sure you have far more people wishing you dead?"

Normally Gershom would fire back with a snarky comment, but he said nothing, and that was far more concerning.

"You actually believe your life is in danger?" Pash rubbed the back of his neck.

"Yes."

Pash poured himself a glass of his father's finest wine. "Tell me what I need to know about the Hunters?"

"You never did pay enough attention to the tales of the old world." Gershom scoffed, taking the decanter, ensuring his son would not have a second serving.

"Forgive me, father. If I could go back to being a boy, I would have paid more attention to your stargazers' myths than to my sword masters."

The Bear eyed his skeptic of a son with great irritation as he pointed to one of the astrologer's drawings of the constellation of the Hunter. "The mark is in the shape of Orion the Hunter. Do not ask me where it should be on his person for each Hunter has been branded in a different spot since Malachi the First walked over a thousand years ago."

"Of course." Pash shook his head after downing his drink.

"It isn't water, Pash," Gershom crinkled his nose in disgust. "One should enjoy a glass of wine from the Isles of Myr."

He rolled his eyes. "Does it really matter?"

"You know it does," Gershom hissed through gritted teeth.

"Are you going to tell me what I need to know or not?" Pash motioned for him to get back to business, stifling a chuckle as soon as Gershom turned his focus back to the table.

"There have only been five documented Hunters and only one is marked at any given time," Gershom continued, although he wanted to chastise Pash further for his attitude. "Malachi the First was marked on the palm of his right hand; Tolemy the Red, the middle of his chest; Raego the Mighty, his left forearm; Lor the Meek was marked on his upper right thigh and Polantis the Peacemaker on

21

the left side of his neck. Tale has it they were all marked for the same purpose: to avenge innocent blood."

"And you have spilled plenty of innocent blood, have you not?" Pash cocked his head to the side, knowing the answer to his question. "If there is a man who bears such a mark, he will be found." Swiftly saluting his father without allowing him to respond to his accusation, the commander left before he changed his mind.

With a new-found sense of relief, Gershom snapped his fingers alerting his guards to the body lying on the floor. "Do something with the astrologer."

CHAPTER TWO

SALOME

Salome quietly drew an arrow from her quiver and took aim at the doe roughly twenty yards in front of her. She held her breath, and was about to release her arrow, when a tree branch behind her snapped, spooking the deer. She turned around, weapon drawn, ready to strike whoever had sneaked up behind her.

"It's me, Salome, it's me!" Jacobi yelled with his hands held above his head, eyes nearly squinted shut.

She lowered her bow. "Jacobi, I could have killed you. You know better than to sneak around in these woods."

"Did you kill anything?" The stocky, rosy-cheeked baker asked with a touch of excitement.

"It escaped."

She gathered her belongings to move to a different spot. For months, he had mentioned how he wished he knew how to hunt, hinting she could teach him, but she had no interest in teaching him. Honestly, she had no interest in spending time with him. Yet here he was.

"Don't worry, Salome." He patted her back gently. "Your skills will improve."

She rolled her eyes.

He followed her as she walked farther into the forest. She was not sure what irritated her more; the fact he made waste of the hours she spent stalking her prey or his failure to recognize he was the reason she missed her mark.

She whipped around, causing him to stagger backwards. "What is it you want?"

"Just ensuring my lady is safe in the woods," he flashed a boyish grin.

"I am not your lady." She shook her head and pressed onward. "How many times must we have the same conversation?"

"Once more," he replied sweetly.

"You say that every time. Do you not grow tired of rejection?" She ducked from hitting her head on a fallen tree.

"I am a patient man, Salome. I will wait every day until you agree to be my wife."

She stopped. *There it was*, she thought. He finally made his true intentions known.

"You are a good man, Jacobi," she faced him, "but I am not the woman for you."

He rubbed his hands together, eyes fixed on his feet. "I may not be who you imagined being with, but I can provide for you and I can… I can protect you," he plead his case.

"Does it look like I need protection?" she asked, covered head to toe in weaponry.

"Well, you can protect me then," he said with a chuckle. She was not looking at him anymore. "Please, just give me a chance to make you happy."

"You know what would make me happy?"

"Tell me." He stepped toward her, a glimmer of hope in his blue eyes.

"Being left alone."

"You don't mean that." Her words stung.

"Go home, Jacobi."

"How many times will you reject me?" he snarled.

"How many more times will you ask me to be your wife?"

"Ten thousand more times if that is what it will take for you to say yes."

"Then my answer shall be 'no' ten thousand and one more times," her nostrils flared. "Now leave me to my hunting."

"I may be the only hope you have of marrying. No man wants a sharp-tongued woman as the mother of his children. Remember every time you reject me, you grow older," his voice cracked.

She had wounded him, and she knew it. But she was not willing to spare him the truth to protect his feelings.

"I grow older, yes, but not desperate." As she walked away, she could feel his teary eyes glued to her. If she had not said something then, she would have said something eventually. She had reached her limit.

Finding a different spot to wait for her prey, she hid herself in a bush and calmed the blood that boiled within her. Jacobi had spent the last two years buzzing around her. At first, she was polite in declining his unwanted advances, but even someone as patient as she was had a breaking point. The baker tended to overshare with anyone who would listen, and she was sure when she returned to the village, she would be on the receiving end of a few dirty looks.

"You didn't need to be so harsh with him." Crispin bit into his apple with a smirk. "I think you hurt his feelings."

Her older brother was everything a brother should be: Protective. Dependable. Annoying. Very annoying. They were extremely close, being eleven months apart. When she thought about it, she realized he was the only real friend she had. And she was okay with that.

In no mood to ask him why he had perched himself in the tree above her like a gargoyle, she continued to focus her gaze straight ahead. "I don't need to waste his time with false hope, nor allow his unwanted feelings to plague me a moment longer."

"Just admit it. You have no intention of marrying any man." He allowed one leg to hang from the tree limb, clearly not as zealous about the hunt as she was.

25

"Did you come to hunt or to irritate me?" She glanced up toward her impetuous brother.

"Both," he smiled widely, smacking as he chewed. "Do you deny it then?"

"Deny what?"

"You have no intentions of marrying." He brushed loose curls from his face.

"I would rather die alone this very second than marry Jacobi." She shuddered at the very thought of being the baker's wife.

"That's harsh, sister. I think he loves you," he pressed with a twinkle in his eye.

"He loves the thought of me." She refused to take the bait, knowing he was just trying to get a reaction out of her. "It's no wonder you never kill anything when you hunt, smacking your lips as loud as you do."

"Fishing is more my speed." He leaned back against the tree and closed his eyes.

"And yet you are not good at fishing either."

"I live for the day you meet your equal." His mouth twisted into a half-smile.

"If there is such a man, I will marry him the moment he outwits me," she snorted, hoping it would silence him.

She was seventeen. Ripe for marrying. In truth, she was getting to the age where people started to ask questions of why she was not already married or at least betrothed. When she thought about her options in the village, it was not something to be excited about. Of the available single men in the Tree House Forest, she had exactly three options. There was obviously, Jacobi the baker. Followed by the Elder's son, Yosef, who was the village drunk, though his father did his best to keep that quiet. And rounding out her potential suitors was Old Man Canon, who was just as his name made him out to be: old. She shuddered again.

"The Almighty One bless the man who wins your heart." Crispin snorted, throwing his apple core on the ground. He jumped down and twisted left and then right to crack his back. "I think I'll head back."

"Empty handed again, I see," she muttered.

He rolled his eyes and huffed, "There are matters that require my attention."

"And what matters would that be?"

"If you must know-"

"How about whispering?" she cut him off with a hiss. "Some of us are actually trying to be successful today."

He whispered loudly, "I said, if you must know, Zophar asked me to fashion some arrow heads for our training session this afternoon."

"Even your whispers aren't quiet." Salome shook her head, hiding a smirk. He always made her laugh. Not on purpose. He was himself, and that was enough.

"Well, I will see you at home when you have either killed something or have grown weary in your failure," he bowed with a sarcastic grin.

"Be careful walking home," she teased, "wouldn't want to shoot you by mistake."

Once he was out of her sight, she trudged deeper into the forest. If there were any deer within a few hundred yards, they would have heard Crispin and hidden themselves.

She prided herself on not only being an excellent hunter, but a knowledgeable tracker. Stalking a deer was far more challenging than waiting for a deer to cross her path. And the reward was just as exciting. Other than the obvious reason for hunting, she was most relaxed when she was in the woods. Her mind quieted; she was focused; she was in control.

She tip-toed, following the tracks until she spotted a buck in the distance. A majestic beast: the largest one she had ever seen. With her back against a pine, she inhaled sharply and nocked her arrow. She slithered around the tree and aimed at the deer. Ready to release her arrow, a strong gust of wind rustled the leaves around her and she heard someone whisper her name.

"Salome."

She missed. She swore under her breath.

"Crispin," she growled, looking for her brother, confident he had been the one calling out to her. But as her eyes scanned the trees, she did not see anyone.

Maybe she *thought* she heard her name. She had not gotten any sleep the night before. She had been having nightmares for weeks and forced herself to stay up by cradling her knees to her chest and biting her lip.

She turned where the buck was standing and sure enough, he was gone. She swore once more, gathered her belongings, and pressed on.

After she and her brother narrowly escaped the Green-Eyed Raven's invasion of Northwind twelve years ago, she spent most of her childhood perfecting her skills. Hunting, fishing, surviving. All she had ever known was survival. She knew what it felt like to be prey and swore she would never taste it again. She learned to be the hunter. Patience was her strongest virtue and tenacity was in her blood.

She threw her disheveled brown curls up in a messy bun, revealing a small, red circular birthmark on her right temple. She tightened the holster around her left thigh and tapped on her most prized weapon, a dagger with an ivory handle carved in the likeness of her family sigil: The White Wolf. Before it was hers, it had belonged to her eldest brother, Lykos.

"Lykos," she whispered his name.

As she walked, she eyed the six black lines tattooed around her left forearm. Each ring represented a member of her family who had been murdered the night the city was attacked. Before refocusing on her hunt, she whispered each of their names and said a prayer for their souls.

"Salome."

She heard her name clearly that time and unsheathed her knife, now uneasy. She no longer cared for the hunt. It was the deer's lucky day.

"Crispin?" She did her best to sound brave, but her voice trembled.

Her name was whispered once again, except this time it was louder. "Salome."

Her grip tightened around the handle of her knife, "Who's there?"

"Salome."

The voice was familiar.

A strong gust of wind knocked her off her feet. She held her breath. She wanted to run, she wanted to scream, she wanted to hide. But she was frozen.

A bright white light appeared in the distance. It was coming toward her. She squinted as it drew closer. She thought she saw a silhouette of a man but did not really want to find out.

Scrambling to her feet, she sprinted home, hoping whatever was after her would not be able to catch her.

CHAPTER THREE

CRISPIN

Crispin took maintaining his weaponry seriously. His knife, his sword, his bow and arrows; they were all an extension of him, a representation of what type of man he was. He was clean. He was orderly. He was strong. He was dependable. Lost in thought, sharpening his knife, he did not hear his guardian, Zophar, behind him.

"A rare sight indeed," Zophar leaned against the threshold of their tree house smoking his long stem pipe.

Crispin looked at his knife, his brow furrowed. "What do you mean?"

"Not that," he gestured toward the knife and exhaled a puff of smoke. "You hunting."

Crispin flashed a lop-sided grin, "And what is so remarkable about that?"

"You aren't what we call a morning person."

"Well, I happened to wake up early."

"You're not a very good liar."

Zophar had brought Crispin and Salome to the Tree House Forest as children. It was one of the most remote locations in the Western Lands that he could remember from his youth. Unless someone had prior knowledge of the lurking dangers of the dark forests, outsiders normally steered clear. The Westerner had aged well over the past twelve years. His blue eyes were still bright, and his red hair was wild as ever, but he was unable to elude the wrinkles that encircled his eyes.

Crispin clicked his tongue, "I'm a good liar, just not with you."

Zophar sat down next to him. "You had another nightmare."

Crispin was not surprised he knew. Whenever he had a nightmare, he would wake up screaming, dripping in sweat.

"Salome always goes hunting when she has a nightmare." Crispin tried to draw the attention away from himself.

"So, you thought you would do what she does?" he chuckled. "You know that hunting isn't your strength."

Crispin continued to sharpen his knife without looking up at Zophar.

"It's the same dream every time."

"What do you see?"

Crispin had not told Salome or Zophar what tormented him, but each time the nightmare visited him, the more real it became.

"I'm on some kind of battlefield and see a man staring at me from the other side." He stopped fiddling with his knife. "His hands are covered in blood. I try to draw my sword to fight him, but my sword will not budge. He charges; he swings his sword and..."

"And what?" Zophar gnawed on the tip of his pipe.

"Nothing." Crispin's voice cracked. "Nothing happens. I wake up."

A muscle in Zophar's neck twitched. "Hmm."

"What do you think it means?" Crispin glanced at him.

Zophar's eyes widened, and he sighed. "I am not an interpreter of dreams, Crispin."

"But you are the wisest man I know," he pressed, "surely, you have an opinion."

"Only a Seer can interpret dreams. Everyone in Adalore knows this." Zophar scratched his jawline. His bushy red beard could not fully hide the smile scars that extended from the corners of his mouth and nearly up to his ears. "All I know is that I am a soldier, nothing more, nothing less."

"You haven't been a soldier in twelve years." Crispin pointed at his belly. "Maybe there's a reason for that."

Zophar struck a match and relit his pipe. "Do I detect a hint of sarcasm?"

"Or truth?" he snickered, clasping one of his knees to his chest as he leaned back in his seat.

"Always the jokester." Zophar leaned back in his seat and rested his hands on his belly. "You know it's ok to miss them."

Crispin shifted his brown eyes to the ground. "What?"

"You don't speak of them -"

"Talking about them won't bring them back." Crispin had not talked about his family in years. He was six when they fled. Six when he lost everything. Six when he lost everyone, except Salome.

He ran his fingers through his short curly hair, beads of sweat dripped down his olive skin. "It's been twelve years..."

"Aye," Zophar sadly agreed, "twelve long years."

"Sometimes I wake up wondering where I am. I'm not supposed to be wasting away in this forgotten forest. I'm meant to be something more. Someone like my father was."

"Perhaps, if you got to know the villagers better -"

"This isn't my home, Zophar."

Crispin avoided getting close to most of the villagers as Salome and Zophar did. They had put down roots. He could not do that. If he befriended them, if he cared about them, if he, too, put down roots, he would then have to be content with staying. The Tree House Forest was as pleasant as the next village. It was quirky with its dozens of tree houses and wooden ramps and swinging bridges connecting each tree to the next. But it was not home. Northwind was home, even after all these years.

"What will it take to make you happy?" Zophar asked, with a heavy heart.

Crispin knew what Zophar was thinking. He had, after all, sacrificed everything to keep them safe and he had done everything in his power to make them happy. It was not his fault. In truth, Crispin would never be satisfied until he drove a knife through the hearts of those who had stolen from him.

"Seeing her dead body," Crispin growled. "That would make me happy."

"And what do you plan to do about it?" Zophar huffed, crossing his right leg over his left, a clear indicator he was uncomfortable. "Do you plan to march up to the gates of Northwind and demand your sister give up her crown? Do you intend to challenge Gershom to fight you for killing your mother and your brothers?"

"She is *not* my sister." Crispin's clean-shaven jaw tightened.

"Denying her does not change the fact she is your blood."

Crispin took a deep breath. There was a reason he never spoke of his family, his past. He had never met Niabi. She had been sent away from Northwind for an unspoken reason and by the time he was born, she was married to the King of Elisor. No one in Northwind spoke of her. It was as if she did not exist. That is, until she appeared twelve years ago and marched her army through the White City.

"Maybe I will challenge them," Crispin flashed a wry grin, shaking his thoughts free from his mind.

"They would strike you down before you had a chance to utter a word." Zophar exhaled a ring of smoke, noticeably impressed with its nearly perfect form.

Crispin just wanted the conversation to end. "I would welcome Death if it meant I tried to do something."

"Death would laugh at you," Zophar stifled a chuckle.

"I would welcome her like an old friend." Crispin stretched his arms wide, face turned up for the sun to shine upon him.

"May she be patient in her reaping." Zophar slid his index finger from the middle of his forehead down to the middle of his chest.

They sat in silence for a minute until Zophar said, "You don't plan on challenging them, do you?"

Crispin could tell by the tone in his gravelly voice there was more he wished to say. "If I did?"

"What good is it to your sister if you, too, are dead?" Zophar's eyes were fixated on him. His glare burned into his soul. "A lone wolf doesn't last long on its own."

Crispin mulled over his guardian's words, far too stubborn to admit he was probably right, so he changed the subject. "Are we still training today?"

"When your sister returns." He puffed another ring of smoke where he stood, pointing it out for Crispin to admire. "I'm getting better." He smiled proudly and walked across a swinging bridge to the main square.

Crispin shook his head, put his sharpened knife in its holster, and began crafting arrows. He enjoyed the work. He found he was quite good at carpentry, crafting, and whittling.

Toiling in silence, he was oddly caught off guard when a tiny hand tapped him on the shoulder. Only one person could ever sneak up behind him and that was a young, soft-footed nine-year-old village boy named Korah.

Korah always had a smile on his dirty face and had a knack for finding mischief. His father had died before he was able to walk, so his mother worked at the one-room tavern in the main square to support them. During the day, the red-headed boy would spend his time watching Crispin train. Crispin knew by the look in his eyes that he imagined himself being a great fighter one day; Crispin had the same look when he was that age.

Crispin smiled at his blue-eyed friend, "Korah, what mischief are you up to now?"

"Will you teach me how to fight today?" Korah asked the same question every day.

"I thought we made a deal to wait until your tenth year." Crispin continued fashioning his arrows.

"I turn ten in a few days. You could teach me early," the boy begged as he sat down.

Crispin could not hide the smile that crept across his face. "I suppose we can begin with a simple lesson."

Korah was stunned. "Really?"

"Really."

"What will I learn first?" Korah jumped up in excitement. "How to shoot an arrow? How to cut off someone's head? How to -"

"Today you learn how to fasten these arrowheads to their shaft." He handed the young boy several wooden sticks he had fashioned.

"No fighting?" He crinkled his nose; the corners of his mouth fell downward.

"A soldier is only as good as his weapon. Now, string." Crispin patted him on the back with soft encouragement.

The boy stared at the arrowheads then looked back up at Crispin. With a smile once again on his face, he began to string the heads.

"Is Salome hunting?" Korah asked.

"Aye, she is," Crispin nodded, focused again on his whittling.

"Do you think she will teach me one day?"

"And why would I not teach you to hunt?" Crispin's left eyebrow rose.

"Because she is really good." Korah answered honestly.

"Am I not?" Crispin chuckled; hopeful his reputation had not already proceeded him.

Korah's eyes shifted. "String," he muttered. "String."

Salome stumbled up to the treehouse, short of breath.

"What? No kill? Did the deer elude you again?" Crispin teased. She appeared unhinged, as if she were being followed. "Salome, is everything alright?"

"I'm... I'm fine," she stuttered, wiping sweat from her forehead.

"Zophar is waiting for us." Crispin watched her intently, knowing something was wrong.

"I will be down. Just need... I... Give me a minute." She marched up the front steps to the tree house.

"What is wrong with her?" Korah demanded, without looking up from his work.

"I am not quite sure." Crispin watched her race up the steps two-by-two.

"Women," Korah sighed.

"And what do you know of women?" He looked down at the boy with a grin.

Korah stopped his work and eyed his teacher. "What would you like to know?"

"Never mind all that," Crispin clicked his tongue and shook his head.

"Can I at least watch you and Salome spar today? Please?"

Korah had a lisp he was teased over regularly, but Crispin never treated him differently. After a while, he did not even notice it anymore.

"Do you not already watch from the tree you perch yourself in?"

"Maybe." Korah blushed and stared at his feet. "I just thought I could get a better view this time?"

"Finish stringing and then you may come," Crispin granted his request.

"Really?"

"String."

"String." Korah returned his focus to the arrowheads with a wide grin.

CHAPTER FOUR

SALOME

As she grabbed the knob to the door, she was soothed with the feeling of safety. Slamming the door behind her, Salome heard a stack of books fall off a nearby shelf.

"Great," she mumbled.

Frustrated, she gathered them from around the room, hoping Zophar would not find her rustling in his private collection. She stood up to restack a handful when she caught a glimpse of her reflection in the mirror on the wooden plank wall by the crooked door. She grimaced at the sight of the dark circles under her bloodshot eyes.

Her eyes.

How she hated looking at them. From a distance, her eyes were brown. But upon closer inspection, her left eye had green speckles scattered around her pupil. She was teased growing up over the deformity; children and adults alike claimed she was cursed by the different gods of the Ten Kingdoms. And, for as long as she could remember, she thought their whispers might be true.

She felt hot.

She cupped water from a tin bowl and washed her face. Her olive skin glowed in the beam of sunlight that poured through the circular window. Her mother was from the southern Isles of Myr, so, she and her older brother had darker skin than most Northerners.

Thankfully, the villagers could not place their origins based on their looks alone and did not care to ask where they had come from over a decade ago.

Putting the last of the books back on the shelf, she noticed a handwritten piece of loose parchment that did not belong with any of the texts.

"What is this?" Her curiosity got the better of her.

Zophar,

I hope you find your accommodations adequate in these troubling times. While not at all exciting or glamorous like the White Keep, the Tree House Forest is quiet, and the people are friendly.

I will find you again once the Year of the Hunter begins. Until that time comes, train them both well – their lives depend on it.

Keep them safe. Keep them hidden. Make sure they know the truth.

May the Almighty One be with you, my friend.

H

She had questions. Lots of questions.

"Who is H?" she whispered, turning the piece of paper to the back only to find it blank.

Zophar would not be pleased she had read the letter, but he would more than likely answer whatever questions she had about it. He had always been truthful as they rattled off a thousand questions a day when they were younger, especially about what happened the night they fled their home. They were well aware that the Green-Eyed Raven who had conquered their city was their sister, Niabi. They were also aware that Gershom, her Second in Command, had joined her to settle a personal vendetta against their father, King Issachar.

Was there another truth they did not know about?

Her thoughts were interrupted as she heard footsteps creaking up the front steps of their treehouse. She stuffed the note in one of the books, hoping Zophar would not notice they were not in their right order. He was extremely meticulous when it came to his collection.

He had books varying in subject matter, so she would not even begin to know how to organize them.

"There you are, Salome." Zophar walked in the door, Crispin right on his heels, and greeted her cheerfully. Too cheerful if she was being honest. "You have returned early from your hunt. No deer?"

"I will try again tomorrow." Her stance was awkward, but she was unaware of how uncomfortable it made them.

"Zophar and I are going to the training grounds." Crispin broke the momentary silence. "If you aren't up for it today -"

"And miss another opportunity to beat you? Not a chance." She forced a smile, this time fully aware of how uncomfortable they were. "I will see you out there." She hastily brushed passed them before they could ask her anymore questions.

The moment the door closed, Crispin crinkled his nose. "I told you she was acting strange. Did you see how she was standing there?" He imitated her ungainly posture. "What was that about?"

"You said she came home looking troubled?" Zophar rubbed his chin.

"Aye," Crispin nodded his head. "As if she were running from something. She was spooked for sure."

Zophar scanned the room.

"What are you looking for?" Crispin turned around the small living space. "Is something missing?"

"Everything appears to be in order." Zophar lied; he had noticed the books as soon as he walked in. "We shouldn't keep her waiting. She might suspect something."

Crispin grabbed the training weapons by the door, "You ready?"

"I will meet you down there," he motioned for him to leave. Once the door closed behind him, Zophar quickly organized his books and papers in their proper order. "That would have bothered me all afternoon."

Zophar headed for their make-shift training grounds without noticing Salome backed against the side of their treehouse. Her head was by the window overlooking the living space. She heard everything they said.

Of course, Crispin noticed her odd behavior.

She could tell them what had happened in the woods. But what exactly would she tell them? *That a white light chased her?* She felt ridiculous even thinking it.

No. She would not tell them anything. She had to put the whole ordeal out of her mind. After all, she might have imagined the whole thing. She was exhausted. Lack of sleep can have a strange effect on one's mind.

That's it. She thought, rubbing her itchy eyes. *None of that actually happened. I just need sleep.*

CHAPTER FIVE

ZOPHAR

Living in one of the outskirt tree houses made it easy for the trio to set up a training area less than two hundred yards from their front door. Weather permitting, they would trek through the woods to their practice arena to sharpen their skills in the art of war.

Zophar took his time getting there, rushing was no longer befitting his lifestyle. Around one of the mighty pines was a large stump he used as a seat, but as he circled the tree, he noticed someone was already there. Young Korah had made himself comfortable on his stump and Zophar was having none of it.

"What do you think you are doing?"

Korah shrugged his shoulders. "Sitting."

Zophar's nostrils flared. "That is my seat," he snorted.

The two of them stared silently at one another until Zophar waved his enormous hand for the boy to move. Korah jumped off allowing his elder to sit.

"But where will I sit?" Korah crossed his arms over his chest.

"The grass appears most suitable for a boy your age." Zophar motioned broadly to the ground next to him.

Korah eyeballed the old soldier and muttered incoherent nothings as he slumped down next to him.

"And what is that you are mumbling?" Zophar scrunched up his face.

"Nothing, sir," Korah faked a smile, "just sitting."

Guardianship had been thrust upon Zophar in desperate times. His duty was to protect the crown. His orders were to lead two of the royal children to safety. He swore he would raise them, protect them, provide for them. He had kept his promise. Although, he was unsure of how successful he would be caring for royal children, for many reasons. The attitudes. The lack of survival skills. The constant state of needing something. But over the twelve years of rearing them, he found he had been wrong about them. He had grown quite fond of them. With all their challenges and ever evolving phases, there were more rewarding facets to them than he initially realized. Their unconditional love. Their quickness to forgive. Their eagerness to learn. In a way, they reminded him of his two sons...

He grunted and shooed the memory from his mind. "Take your stances."

Salome and Crispin stood ten feet apart in the cleared area, armed with blunt swords.

Zophar knew them well enough to know that Crispin's heart was beating fast. Whenever a duel was about to start, his breathing quickened. Salome however, never appeared nervous. She inhaled and exhaled rhythmically, keeping herself grounded.

They lifted their weapons to their faces and took their stances.

"Begin." Zophar set his wolves loose.

Crispin charged toward his sister the second Zophar spoke. She stood her ground, waiting patiently for him to reach her. Every clash of their dull swords kept Korah on the edge of his seat. They were quick and skilled in their movements. They were everything Zophar had taught them to be.

Crispin's attack was fast and aggressive. His sword was an extension of his arm. Bold, fearless. He was an unstoppable force.

Salome was defensive by nature. She read her opponent, learned his fighting style, and used his strengths against him. She was patient, she was cunning, she was a predator, which made her extremely dangerous for impulsive fighters like her brother.

Breaking free from his sister's counterattack, Crispin circled around her with his sword extended, keeping her at a safe distance. Flashing a twisted grin, he declared, "Impressive, Salome, you almost fight as well as a man."

"Funny, I was thinking the same of you," she fired back, smirking as Korah laughed. "I think the boy might agree with me."

"Whose side are you on?" Crispin gave him a once over. "Remember who is going to train you when you are old enough."

"And who will correct that training when he is through," she poked, causing Crispin to laugh.

"Enough talk," Zophar stifled a chuckle, demanding order. "Resume your starting positions."

The brother and sister waited for Zophar to release them again. The Westerner paused; he was unsure which one of his pupils would end up the victor that afternoon.

"Begin." He sounded, kicking one leg over the other.

This time, Crispin resisted the temptation to lunge toward his sister and waited for her to initiate.

Salome hurled her sword over Crispin's head. He carefully watched her weapon glide through the air and once it was close enough, he lifted his free hand and caught her sword.

He grinned. He was now armed with two blades, but when he looked for his sister, to his horror, she was nowhere to be seen.

"Salome?" He whipped around, but she was not there. "Where is she?" he asked Zophar and Korah.

"She is -"

Zophar covered the eager boy's mouth before he could reveal her position.

With Crispin distracted, Salome quietly jumped down from a nearby tree. She crept up behind him, just like prey in the forest and put her dagger against his throat.

"Yield," she hissed in his ear.

Crispin dropped his weapons. "Is this even allowed?"

Sharpened blades were banned from training sessions, but to Crispin's dismay, Zophar stated, "You took your eyes off her and it cost you this duel. Let that be a lesson to you, Crispin. Next time it could cost you your life."

Zophar beamed with pride. He had trained plenty of women in his homeland of Borg, because women, like men, were both expected to fight in the king's army. But he had never had a student like Salome. She did not have a soldier's mindset. She had a hunter's mindset. Instead of seeing an enemy, she saw prey, and he knew years ago she could be deadly, if she wanted to be.

"I have not had two better pupils." He patted Salome on the back. "And I love seeing you beat Crispin," he whispered in her ear and grinned.

"I can hear you, Zophar," Crispin chimed in.

Salome laughed and tossed him his sword. "Best two out of three?"

Crispin smiled and took his stance once more.

CHAPTER SIX

NIABI

Niabi's green eyes scanned the city from Her Majesty's Tower as crowds of adoring citizens lined the cobblestone streets from the main gate to the White Keep steps.

Six months she had waited for his return. The White Keep seemed empty without him. In the blink of an eye, her small defenseless child had grown into a mighty warrior fit to rule the North. She had raised Rollo to fear nothing; to fear no one. He was her pride and joy, her saving grace.

Cheering from the crowd drew her attention to a nearby street where she spotted him. She ran to the mirror and brushed long strands of black hair from her face and tucked them into her intricately braided updo. Now presentable, the slender queen rushed hastily down the spiral staircase and through the castle to greet him at the front steps. Rollo was home; she could now stop worrying about him.

The White City was buzzing with excitement, not only for Prince Rollo's return from visiting the Andrago of Elisor, but for his Name Day Celebration. At his mother's request, Rollo spent six months learning the customs, history and traditions of his late father's people, the Andrago. Although Dichali had died a couple of years after he was born, Niabi wanted her son to know the former King of Elisor and to keep Dichali's memory alive in Rollo's heart.

The Andrago, also known as the Horse Lords, lived in the Valley of Elisor west of the Tayborne Mountains. They were the most respected tribal nation in the Ten Kingdoms and were famous for their incredible and elaborate braids, which showcased their bronze skin and high cheek bones; physical traits they all shared. Unlike other nations, they did not build stone walls around their city, but respected the land and lived off what they could hunt and gather.

The horn of Northwind echoed throughout the city as the royal caravan approached the White Keep.

Riding alongside the green-eyed prince was Tala, Queen Niabi's most trusted advisor and oldest companion. Tala had known Rollo's father from boyhood and the only signs of his age were the crow's feet creasing the corners of his dark brown eyes and streaks of white in his black hair. Sworn to protect Rollo from infancy, he rarely left the prince's side.

Rollo waved at the crowds who welcomed him home. "I had hoped for a quiet return before the festivities."

"You of all people should know your Name Day will be celebrated for at least a week, especially after your long absence." Tala the Andrago flashed a warm smile at the prince. "Your mother will be very excited to see you."

"Perhaps now that I have returned, she will tell me how my father died."

Tala sighed. Every day they were with the Andrago, he heard nothing but Rollo's plea to know more about his father's death. "Dichali's death was tragic for our people, but your mother, well... she never recovered."

"I don't understand the secrecy. I have a right to know," Rollo huffed. "I know it was you who instructed the Lords of Elisor not to tell me the truth."

"As your mother wished." Tala was unmoved. "After your eighteenth year has been celebrated, I am sure she will tell you what you wish to know. Until then, let it be."

46

"And if she doesn't tell me?"

"I have it under good authority that she will."

"But if she doesn't," he persisted, "swear, you will."

"My Prince -"

"He was my father, Tala. Please!" Rollo held his breath.

"If after all the festivities have ended, and she has not told you the truth, I swear I will." He held up his hand, putting an end to the matter.

The people cheered as Rollo turned into the royal courtyard. Once he dismounted his steed, his eyes travelled up the steps until he saw the familiar face he had been looking for: his mother.

"Mother!" The tall, lean prince bowed, bringing his right arm across to his left shoulder.

Niabi hugged her son, relieved he had returned to her safely. "Oh, how I have missed your face." She cupped his well-defined jaw in her thin fingers. "My heart and my soul, how you have grown."

She was stunned by how much his features had developed and how he had transformed from boy to man in just six months.

"And you have grown far more beautiful since I have been away." His kind eyes danced.

"Tala, how did he do?"

Tala's chest puffed up. "Dichali's blood runs through his veins."

Niabi smiled and squeezed Tala's hand. "Get some rest, dear friend, for tomorrow, we celebrate."

Tala bowed and left them to walk through the gardens.

The mother and son walked arm in arm as the attendants scurried around them to finish decorating.

"Are you excited for tomorrow night?" Niabi asked, with her eyes glued to him. Six months without him had been unbearable. She had not spent so much as one day apart from her son since he was little.

"Of course, I am," he flashed his boyish grin. "I know you have gone through a lot of trouble to ensure I enjoy my celebration."

47

"Soon it will be your responsibility to entertain the Lords and Ladies of the North." She was relieved at the thought.

He shook his head, "Not for many years."

She stopped and tugged at his arm. "That is what I wanted to speak to you about, Rollo."

Her tone was odd.

"Is something wrong, mother?" he grasped her hand tightly.

"All is well, my son." She patted his hand reassuringly. "Tomorrow night, I plan to announce your coronation."

By the look on his face, she could tell he was surprised.

"But that would mean..."

"I am abdicating the White Throne." She nodded her head, a smile on her face. "It is your time to lead our people."

"I... I don't believe I am quite ready."

She tenderly tucked loose strands of black hair behind his ear. "You will always have me here to support you."

"Mother, this is your kingdom."

"My time has come to an end." Niabi wrapped her arm around his and forced them to continue their stroll. "I have accomplished everything I set out to do. I made a promise years ago when you turned eighteen, I would let you rise and take your place at the table. It's time."

"I still have so much left to learn."

"Good kings are ready to rule, great kings are ready to learn." She kissed her son's cheek, sensing he was overwhelmed. "You will have to appoint your Second in Command tomorrow. Do you have someone in mind?"

"Yes," he said without a second thought, "Tala."

She beamed. "A wise choice."

Niabi noticed Leoti standing in the gardens and dipped her head toward her.

"I believe there is someone else who wants to welcome you home."

Tala's daughter stood with a shy smile. Her hip-length black hair, full lips, and round brown eyes were gifts from her late mother.

Her honesty and calm demeanor were all Tala. Leoti was two when Rollo was born, and they had been promised to one another since that day. For them, it was not political. They were in love and everyone could tell.

"Don't just stare at her," Niabi gently pushed him forward. "Go to her."

Rollo made his way down the garden path until he stood in front of her. She curtsied.

"Prince Rollo, it is good to see you." Her soft voice soothed anyone who heard her speak.

"My Lady," he kissed her tattooed hand. "Would you care to walk with me?"

She wrapped her arm around his. "I would be honored."

Niabi watched with fondness as they strolled through the gardens and remembered what it was like being with her late husband. Her heart always quickened when she looked at Dichali. He was everything she was not. He was calm, patient, forgiving. Not a day went by that she did not think of him.

"They make a handsome couple," Pash said.

She turned to face Pash who was standing next to her. "They do," she nodded. "I didn't see you in the courtyard when my son arrived."

"My apologies, my Queen. I had matters that required my attention."

"Is something wrong, Commander Pash?" She was good at reading people and noticed he seemed rattled.

"Nothing I need to bother you with," he forced a smile. "You must be relieved he is home."

His change of subject had not gone unnoticed.

"As his mother, I am relieved. As his Queen, I am proud. My son is now a man."

"The people worship him." He nodded, hands gripping the balcony railing. "He will make a fine king one day."

"Of that I have no doubt." She rested her hand on top of his. "Walk with me. There is an important matter I wish to discuss with you."

"Is something troubling you, my Queen?" he followed her.

"I have decided to announce my son's coronation, as I plan to step away from my duties as Queen."

His voice cracked, "You plan to abdicate?"

"I will recommend to my son he appoint you to be his Iron Guard." She watched him carefully to evaluate his reaction.

"Forgive me, my Queen, if I sound ungrateful, but I think my skills would be best used remaining with the Shadows." He motioned toward the silver masked Nephilim who lurked in the background. "Perhaps, your Iron Guard would be better suited to guard our future king."

Anaktu the Nephilim, the Queen's Iron Guard, was the last of his kind; born from the fallen Immortals, who had been banished from the City of Caelestis hundreds of years ago, along with the mortal men they had imprisoned. To most people, the Nephilim were mere fables, but all who knew of him knew the truth. He, too, was immortal but was cursed to a life of misery. Niabi saved him from his captors, and to repay her kindness, he swore an eternal oath to protect and serve her. A promise he had kept for two decades.

"Anaktu will stay in my services." She faced Pash, unwilling to accept anything less than his agreement. "There aren't many people I would trust with my son's life."

He hesitated. "If I accept, what will become of my position among the Shadows?"

"They rode before you and they will ride after you are gone. That is the way of the Shadows."

"But my men -"

"Are not yours to begin with." The fiery response startled him. "Or have you so quickly forgotten who their true master is?" Without giving him a chance to speak, she grabbed his arm. "Accept when Rollo appoints you." She released her tight grip and her gaze softened. "I will rest easier knowing he will have you by his side when he bares the crown."

His eyes narrowed. "Are you worried something will happen to him?"

"He is the only true Northern heir left. That alone places a target on his back."

His forehead creased.

"I have a certain reputation in the Ten Kingdoms that my son does not have. There may be some who wish to challenge him, oppose him." Her eyes bore into his soul. "So, when my son appoints you as Iron Guard?"

"I will accept." He had no choice but to agree.

CHAPTER SEVEN

ROLLO

"Remember, don't take the blindfold off until I tell you to." Rollo held her long fingers tightly as he led her down the side of a rocky cliff.

"Where are we going?" Leoti asked.

The sounds and smells made it obvious they were not near the White Keep. The waves crashing indicated they were either near the docks or the white cliffs to the north of the harbor.

"How much farther, Rollo?" she giggled in anticipation.

"We're almost there. No peeking." He gently pulled her forward and positioned her in front of him. He untied the blindfold. "You can open your eyes."

Leoti opened her eyes and was shocked. They were not on the white cliffs nor by the docks. They were in a cavern with a circular hole at the top where the stars were twinkling brightly. She took her shoes off to feel the sand between her toes and allowed the water to envelop her feet. Turning toward him, she was surprised to see a basket of her favorite foods sitting atop a blanket. Torches surrounded the cavern interior just enough for them to see one another, but not inhibit the view of the stars above them.

"You did all of this for me?" She tucked her hair behind her ears with a smile.

"I hope you like it." He took her hand in his.

"I never knew this place even existed. How did you find it?"

"I used to come here a lot as a child," he admitted sheepishly, knowing as the sole heir he was not supposed to leave the White Keep unsupervised. "It's my favorite place in Northwind."

"It's beautiful."

"Sit with me." He guided her to the blanket where she sat between his outstretched legs. She could feel his heart beating against her back once he wrapped his arms around her.

"I missed you." She squeezed his arm.

"I missed you too, Leoti," he kissed the side of her head. "I have something else for you."

"What else could you possibly give me?"

He handed her a small book filled with dried flowers. "I know violets are your favorite and I knew they wouldn't make the long trip back from Elisor. But I wanted you to have a piece of your home."

She flipped through the pages. "You remembered?"

"I just wish you could have been there with me. They are far more beautiful in the valley than in this book."

She clutched it tightly against her chest. "I love it. Thank you."

He positioned himself to face her and took her hands in his. "You don't like it here, do you?"

"Why would you think that?" her eyes narrowed.

"Northwind and Elisor are different. I could only assume you prefer one over the other."

"It is different here, but I've lived here for ten years now." She shrugged. "I've grown fond of it in my own way."

"You're lying," he said softly.

"No, I'm not," she shook her head.

"Your nose twitches when you lie," he pointed out.

She touched her pointy nose and blushed. "I... I didn't know that."

"I think it's cute," he smiled warmly.

"I do miss Elisor." Her eyes met the ground, admitting what he suspected. "But I know where my duty lies."

"That's what I wanted to talk to you about." He pulled a simple turquoise beaded necklace from his pocket.

Her jaw dropped. "My mother's necklace. I haven't seen it since I was a little girl."

"I asked for your father's blessing."

"His blessing?" She stared at him wide-eyed. "For what?"

"I know our parents arranged our marriage when we were children. It has always been expected of us." He took a deep breath. "But I'm asking for myself now. Will you be my wife?"

"And if I say no, would I be free to return to Elisor?"

He was not expecting her to respond that way. "If that is what you want," he stammered. "Then yes. I only want you to be happy."

She smiled. "I am happiest when I'm with you."

His eyes lit up, he breathed deeply. "Are you saying yes?"

"Yes, Rollo," she caressed his cheek. "I love you."

He leaned in and kissed her forehead. "You nearly made my heart stop, woman."

She kissed his lips, "You're stuck with me."

He ran his fingers through her hair and whispered, "I'm ok with that."

CHAPTER EIGHT

ADONIJAH

Travelling south toward the forests of the Western Lands at top speed, four Shadows on horseback left a cloud of dust behind them as they began their search for the Hunter. On one side of the dirt road were stretches of fields and on the other side of the road were unending acres of forestlands. Any villager who caught sight of the black riders immediately took refuge in their humble homes and prayed they were not the ones the mercenaries were sent to find.

Unlike the other frightened peasants, a hooded figure perched high in a pine tree waited for the four Shadows to pass his hiding spot. As soon as the last rider approached, the cloaked man jumped down, landed on the mercenary's horse, and stabbed him in the chest.

Ditching the body, the vigilante rode toward the other three mercenaries undetected. Approaching the next Shadow, he stood up on the horse and leapt onto the next one. The black rider did not have a chance to react before the vigilante snapped his neck and threw him from his mount.

He was noticed by the third Shadow who threw a knife at him. Being quite skilled with knife throwing, the cloaked attacker caught the incoming dagger and quickly returned it, stabbing the masked soldier in the neck.

One Shadow was left, and he was tackled to the ground.

The Shadow drew his sword while his mysterious enemy held two knives, one in each of his fingerless leather-gloved hands. Barreling toward the unknown figure, the last remaining Shadow swung his weapon with great force. Avoiding the incoming blow, the vigilante slid beneath the soldier and sliced the back of both his knees, rendering him incapable of escape.

The rogue fighter made his way to the survivor as he tried to crawl away. Stepping on his black cape made it easy to turn him on his back. He ripped off his black mask, but it was not him.

"I seek a Shadow who wears a mask to hide his disfigured face," the vigilante stated his purpose.

"We all wear masks," the Shadow hissed.

Dropping a knee on the wounded Shadow's chest, the hooded victor leaned in closer. "You see my dilemma then. More of you will die until I find the one I seek."

"I do not know who you seek."

Adonijah put a knife to the Shadow's throat. "Oh, but I believe you do know him. It is said, he is seven feet tall with burn scars all over his body and is missing an eye. We common folk know him as the 'Nameless Rider'."

"Who are you?" The Shadow squinted, trying to get a good look at the face hidden in the darkness.

"The last man you will ever see." Adonijah slit the Shadow's throat.

Rising slowly, his hooded face still a mystery, he retraced his path to unmask the three deceased Shadows. Coming up empty handed, he disappeared deep into the forest, leaving their bodies to rot on the main road.

CHAPTER NINE

ROLLO

Rollo splashed water on his face then patted himself dry with a nearby towel. Hunched over the bowl he looked into the mirror that sat against the wall and stared silently at his reflection. He had not slept much. His mind had been flooded with a thousand thoughts. But there was one question that tormented him.

Was he ready to be King?

Consumed with his thoughts, he did not hear the knock at his chamber doors. It was only when Tala spoke, he returned to reality.

"It is time, Prince Rollo." Tala stood in the threshold with his hands clasped behind his back.

Rollo stared at the Andrago in the mirror. "I don't know if I can do this, Tala."

"Entertaining the Lords and Ladies of the court was never your mother's favorite obligation either."

"It's not that." Rollo rubbed his forehead.

Tala shut the door. "Then what troubles you?"

Rollo retreated to the bench at the foot of his bed and sat down. "I am not ready to be king."

The Andrago joined him. "Your father thought the same thing the night before he took the crown."

"I wish I had known him," he sighed. "Maybe I'd understand myself better."

"Dichali was the most patient and humble man among the Andrago," Tala smiled fondly. "And believe me, he had no reason to be. Even in our youth he was skilled with all kinds of weapons. We knew he was meant for greatness."

"But?"

"He didn't want to wage anymore wars." He leaned back and crossed one leg over the other. "He wanted a family and desired more than anything for the Andrago to live in peace. Marrying your mother was supposed to fulfill both dreams."

"Did it?" Rollo's eyes were fixed on him.

"For a time," he nodded. "During those few years, I had never seen him happier. He and your mother shared the same spirit. And he loved you more than anything. He would be proud of the man you have become."

The Prince rubbed his hands together and stared at the floor. "You think so?"

"I know it." Tala patted him on the back reassuringly. "He may be gone, but his spirit lives on in you. He will guide you during this next phase of your life."

"Will you be there too?"

He nodded. "Whenever you need me, I will be there."

"I told my mother I plan to appoint you as my Second." The prince squirmed, unsure of what he would say. "I'm hoping you will accept."

"It would be my greatest honor." He embraced the prince tightly, wiping a tear from his eye. "You will make a great king. It is in your blood."

"I still have so much to learn."

Tala pulled away from him and rested his hands on his shoulders. "A good king is ready to rule; a great king is ready to learn."

"My mother said the same thing to me yesterday." He was confused.

58

Tala's mouth twisted. "They are your father's words."

Rollo shifted his weight. "You still won't tell me how he died?"

"I still have a week of celebrations before I fulfill my promise," he smirked, smoothing his clothes as he stood. "I will give you a few minutes to finish up." He bowed and left the room.

Rollo breathed in deeply as he rose from his seat and opened one of the wooden drawers near his bed. Inside was a piece of paper, a sketch of his father.

He stared at the drawing then looked at his reflection in the mirror. Other than his green eyes, one would think it was a drawing of the same person. His mother drew it shortly before she gave birth to him. She kept it in her room until he was eight years old and only parted with it because Rollo begged her for it. He wanted his father to watch over him as he slept. He dragged the tips of his fingers across it.

"It's in my blood." He whispered Tala's words under his breath. "It's in my blood."

There was a soft knock on his door.

"Come in." He placed the sketch back inside the drawer and closed it.

He thought Tala had returned but was pleasantly surprised to see Leoti standing there instead. Her braided hair was adorned with pearls and her thin lips were painted a dark red. He had never seen her in a billowing gown before. She preferred simple dresses and even pants when she could get away with it. The off-shoulder white dress she wore left him speechless.

"You look incredible." He could not tear his eyes off her.

She ran her hands over her braid, "Your mother gave these pearls to me while you were away. She said they were from the Isles of Myr."

He took her hand and kissed it. "It's my Name Day, but I have a feeling all eyes are going to be on you."

"Stop it." She nudged him.

"It's true." He grinned, intertwining his fingers with hers. "The Almighty blessed me a thousand times over with you."

She kissed his cheek. "I need you to do something for me."

"Anything," he whispered.

"Would you help me with this?" In her hand was the turquoise necklace.

"Of course." He fastened it around her dainty neck and kissed her bare shoulder. "How would you feel about getting married next week?"

"Next week?" She turned around wide eyed. "So soon? Is that even possible?"

"Not soon enough if you ask me." He held her in his arms. "If I could marry you tonight, I would."

"You are too romantic for your own good, Rollo." She tapped the tip of his nose with her tattooed index finger.

"I'm serious." His eyes twinkled. "Being away from you for six months made me realize I want you by my side. I need you by my side."

"What would your mother say?" Her left eyebrow lifted. She was teasing him. She already knew the answer.

"You know my mother loves you as if you were her own flesh and blood. She's been praying for this moment since the day I took my first step." His giggle always put a smile on her face.

"And I love her like a mother." Her gaze fell to her feet.

"What is it?" He lifted her chin.

"I wish my mother could be here."

"I know you do." He embraced her again. "Our loved ones may be gone, but their spirits live on in us."

"And who told you that?" She wrapped her arms around his waist.

"This wise old man I know," he shrugged with a sheepish grin.

"Oh, is that so?" She rolled her eyes. "Which wise old man do you speak of?"

"Your father."

"Ah, I should have known," she chuckled with a sarcastic sigh. "He tells me that every night."

"Let's hope he's right."

Her gaze caused his heart to race.

"Why are you looking at me that way?" He brushed a loose strand of her hair from her round face.

She stood up on the tip of her toes and gently kissed his lips. "I love you," she whispered. "And I *would* marry you tonight if we could."

"Why don't we then?" Just by the tone of his voice she could tell he meant it.

"What about the party?"

"I suppose we will be a little late." His smile sent a warm sensation down her spine. "Should I send for the Elder?"

She nibbled on her bottom lip, failing to mask the smile that stretched across her face. "I think you should."

The Andrago Elder arrived shortly after being summoned and found the young lovers on the balcony. He bowed and touched the middle of his forehead with his index finger and floated it down to the center of his chest.

"Prince Rollo. My Lady. How may I be of service?" The wrinkles etched into his skin enfolded his narrow eyes, but his smile was as genuine as any.

"We wish to be married." Rollo patted Leoti's arm wrapped around his.

"My blessings, Prince Rollo," he nodded in approval. "When would you like the marriage ceremony to take place?"

"Now." He barely waited for the Elder to finish the question.

"Now?" He rubbed the back of his neck. "This is rather unorthodox. Royal weddings are planned well in advance."

"Please." Leoti's silky voice eased him.

The old man touched his chest with a tight-lipped smile. "Who am I to deny two souls becoming one?"

Standing on the balcony as the sun set, the Elder had them hold one another's hands as he wrapped them in red silk. Together, they recited the traditional vows of the Andrago.

You are my shelter,
You are my warmth.
You are my now,
You are my always.
You are my breath,
Until we breathe our last.
From this day forward,
You are mine and I am yours.
Forever my spirit,
Forever my soul.

"May the Almighty bless you." The Elder grasped their hands in his. "May the Almighty keep you."

CHAPTER TEN

PASH

The Commander of Shadows made his way down the white stone hallway toward the queen's quarters. He was to escort her to the party, although he did not like public celebrations. He was a man of action and few words. Chatting with Lords and Ladies was never his strong suit but put a weapon in his hand and he would be noticed.

After a glass of wine and a good night's rest, Pash had come to terms with his promotion to Iron Guard. It was not a title he had desired, but he was a soldier, and obeying orders was what he did best.

"Pash." Gershom skulked around the corner and motioned for his son to approach him.

"Father," he greeted him with a sigh.

"What word from the West?" Gershom whispered.

"Nothing has been reported."

"They need to hurry their search," Gershom was visibly displeased, "my life is in danger."

"I will be ordering them to return immediately." Pash tried to walk by his father, but he grabbed his arm.

"What do you mean?" he hissed. "They haven't found the Hunter."

"And they won't," he jerked his arm back. "You will have to take your concerns up with the new Commander of Shadows. Perhaps, he will oblige."

"I grow tired of your games, Pash," the Bear growled. "I have told you how important this mission is. As Second in Command, I order you -"

"You don't know, do you?" Pash was giddy.

"Know what?" his eyes narrowed.

"The Queen plans to announce her abdication tonight. Prince Rollo will be crowned within the week."

Gershom shrunk back. He placed his hand on the wall for balance as his breathing quickened. "You're lying."

Pash shook his head; he was amused by his father's reaction. "She told me yesterday and informed me I will be the new king's Iron Guard."

"But..." Gershom rubbed his forehead. "I am her Second in Command."

"Not for much longer I'm afraid." He did not even try to hide the smirk that crept onto his face. "I have reason to believe that the prince intends to appoint Tala the Andrago as his Second."

The Bear furrowed his brow, his pale skin flushed.

Pash knew what he was thinking. His father had never liked Tala. It was bad enough to be stripped of his title, but for that title and all the power that came with it to be given to a foreigner was more than his father could swallow.

"Niabi can't do this to me." Gershom paced. "We made a deal."

Pash shrugged. "She is the Queen. She can do as she pleases." He brought his right arm across his chest with a slight bow. "I have matters that require my attention. Enjoy the party, Father."

"She won't get away with this," he muttered. "No one undermines the Bear."

CHAPTER ELEVEN

SALOME

As night shrouded the Tree House Forest, Salome, Crispin, and Zophar were scattered around the living space completing their own tasks. Zophar puffed his favorite hand-crafted pipe, while Crispin carved a small block of wood into the likeness of a wolf by the fire.

Salome was obsessed with cleanliness in their tight living quarters and spent her evening organizing the small space as she saw fit. Maintaining the house was a peaceful task for her and kept her mind from wandering into troubled waters. But as routine as their evening seemed, there was an unexpected knock at their door.

"Were we expecting a visitor?" Crispin eyed the others.

"Not that I am aware of," Zophar shook his head and kept on smoking.

Salome walked to the door armed with a knife concealed behind her back, and slowly opened it. Before her stood a tall, clean shaven man with long platinum blonde hair under his hood and hypnotizing grey eyes.

"May I help you, sir?" she asked.

"The question is not what you can do for me, but what can I do for you?" The cloaked figure returned her question.

Confused, she tightened her grip on her knife. "I'm afraid I don't understand."

"You need not be afraid of me. The weapon you hold is not necessary, I mean you no harm." He spoke with such a gentleness that she believed he indeed was no threat.

"How did you know about the -"

"I am a Seer. I have come to speak with you and your brother," he interrupted. The old man's demeanor spurred Crispin to make his way toward the front door.

"I'm sorry, you must have the wrong house. We don't know a Seer." She attempted to close the door.

"Ah, but the Seer knows you, Salome," he smiled warmly, stopping Crispin dead in his tracks.

"How do you know my name?"

Zophar leapt to the door, battle axe in hand, "Who goes there?" He ripped the door wide open. "Harbona?" He took a step back. "Is it really you?"

"Zophar, my old friend," Harbona entered the house and embraced him.

The siblings stood in confused silence. For as long as Zophar had been their guardian, he had never entertained visitors.

"What is going on?" Crispin furrowed his brow.

"Crispin, Salome, this is Harbona the Seer," Zophar introduced the foreigner.

"How do you know each other?" Crispin's nostrils flared.

"I was one of your father's advisors many years ago." Harbona leaned his walking staff against the wall and made himself comfortable.

"You knew our father?" The prince shifted his weight.

"Oh, yes. I know all of you very well," Harbona smiled, knowing he was looking upon the heirs of Issachar. As he removed his hood, the banishment brand around his right eye made Salome realize she had seen him before.

"I know you," she took a step forward, visions of him walking around the White Keep with her eldest brother flashed before her eyes. "You knew Lykos."

"Yes" he nodded. The corners of his eyes crinkled. "Your brother was one of the finest men I have ever known."

"It has been far too long, my friend." Zophar patted the Seer on the back.

"I have kept my eye on you from afar to ensure your safety." Harbona's tone changed.

"You are here for a reason then." Zophar's breathing quickened as he glanced at his wards.

"I am afraid so," he confirmed.

"They know where we are?" The old warrior exhaled a puff of smoke, hoping to take the edge off.

"The time has come to reclaim Northwind." His eyes lit up. "The Year of the Hunter has begun."

"Year of the Hunter? What are you talking about?" Crispin scoffed. "There hasn't been a Hunter in over two hundred years. And even if that were true, what has that got to do with us?"

"*You* wrote the note," Salome figured out who 'H' was in Zophar's letter.

Harbona nodded. "What do you know of the Hunters?"

"Stories our mother told us – the first was Malachi over a thousand years ago. He was given the mark of the Hunter to avenge the deaths of the innocent." Salome recited all she could remember. "I'm afraid I don't remember much more than that."

"Have you ever wondered about the discoloration of your eye?" Harbona pointed a thin finger toward her.

"What about my eye?" Her shoulders tightened. *What a bold question,* she thought to herself.

"You believe you were cursed? That there is nothing more to the pattern the dots create?" He leaned forward, staring at her eye.

"If it's a curse handed down by some unknown god, then there's not much I can do about it." She shifted her weight, now defensive.

"What are you trying to say, Harbona?" Zophar set his pipe down on the small wooden table.

"You were not cursed, Salome." The Seer stared at her, even though he could sense it made her uncomfortable. "You were marked by the Almighty."

"Marked?" Crispin straightened from the wall he had been leaning against. "Are you saying -"

"She is the Hunter?" Harbona finished his sentence. "Yes."

"Me?" Her eyes darted around the room.

"You," the Seer repeated himself.

"Aren't Hunters male?" Crispin stepped toward the group. "There's never been a female Hunter."

"The Almighty does not choose his servants based on whether they are male or female. He chooses the heart," Harbona's eyes shifted back to a silent Salome, "and your heart has been chosen." He rested his back against the narrow wooden chair. "The Year of the Hunter has begun, and Gershom knows this. He fears this. He has dispatched a company of the Queen's Shadows to search these forests for the Hunter."

"So, he doesn't know who the Hunter is?" Zophar was only slightly relieved. "Does he know which village to find her in?"

"No to both," Harbona shook his head, "but we cannot stay here. It is no longer safe."

Crispin could not stop gawking at Salome's discolored eye. For years he teased her. He too believed she was cursed by one of the gods but now...

"Have you always known?" Crispin's tone was equally threatening as it was fearful.

"Of course not." She crossed her arms. "You don't actually believe any of this, do you?" Looking around the room she could sense she was the only one who had any doubt. "This is nonsense," she hissed like a cornered animal. "I am not a Hunter! I'm just... just me. I don't know what you want from me. I am not who you seek."

"Salome, listen to me." Crispin rested his hands on her shoulders. "We can avenge our family. Once I kill Niabi and Gershom, we can finally return home."

"As noble as that sounds," the Seer chimed in, "I am afraid that is not your destiny."

"You just said it was the Year of the Hunter; the time to take back our city. Are you now saying that is not the case?" Crispin's brow furrowed; he appeared as irritated as he was confused.

"Only the Hunter will avenge the blood of the innocent." Harbona sat stoically at the table with his thin fingers intertwined. "I believe you had a dream that needed interpreting?"

By the look on Crispin's face, he was clearly thrown by the sudden change in subject. How could he have possibly known about his dream?

"Tell me your dream and I will tell you what it means. Maybe then you will believe me." The Seer's piercing grey eyes did not shy away from him.

Crispin flipped a chair around and straddled it directly across the table from him. "I am fighting in a great battle in an open field outside of Northwind when I come face to face with a man."

"Gershom." Harbona identified and motioned for him to continue.

"He is mocking me, blood dripping from his hands. I reach for my sword to fight him, but it will not budge."

The Seer nodded his head as he stroked his chin, "You will indeed come face to face with Gershom during a great battle. In that moment, you will have a choice. Either you attempt to kill him and forfeit your life, or you leave him untouched and live to rule your people as King of the North. Taking Gershom's life is not your destiny. Your path is to forge the way for the Hunter."

Silence engulfed the room. Tension was thick and frustrations were at an all-time high until Salome spoke.

"Are you saying Crispin will die if he tries to do what is right?"

"Listen to him." Zophar's voice was raspy. "I've learned from years of experience to heed Harbona's words."

"You are afraid." Harbona saw right through her.

"Wouldn't you be afraid if you were me?" She was not normally one to pace around the room, but that evening was different. She could not sit still; her body would not allow it. "How can you be so sure about this?"

"Why do you think you happened to escape the night your sister attacked?" Harbona asked.

The question caught her off guard. *What did he mean by 'happened to escape'?*

"From the day you were born, any Immortal who looked upon your face knew of your destiny. Even your mortal brother knew. Your brother believed. Your brother understood his duty to ensure your survival no matter the cost."

"Lykos knew?" There was a lump in her throat. His face flashed before her eyes. She closed them, rubbing her hands against her forehead. She could hear the screams. She could smell the sulfur from her city burning. She could feel the fear as if she was reliving that night all over again.

"I know you are afraid, Salome." Harbona grasped her hand in his, snapping her out of her flashbacks. "Don't let your fear hinder you from fulfilling your destiny."

"I am just one person." Her palms began to sweat, and she struggled to breathe.

"But you are not alone."

She ripped her hand from his. "I cannot do what you ask of me." She darted up the creaky stairs.

She sat with her knees to her chest on the roof of the tree house in complete silence, gazing at the stars in the night sky. They had always brought her comfort in the past but staring at them now only stressed her.

There he was: The Hunter.

Sparkling brightly, mocking her.

Why me? That was the only question she had and knew no one would be able to give her an answer that would satisfy her.

"I remember when we were younger all you ever dreamed about was being the North's first female warrior." Crispin interrupted her thoughts when he sat down next to her. "To have songs written and tapestries woven depicting your heroic conquests and countless victories against our enemies." He tried to hide it but could not help but stare at her discolored eye. "We all made fun of you and as it turns out, you're the only one of us meant for glory."

"Save your flatteries," her nostrils flared. "Say what you actually came here to say."

He took a deep breath. "We've spent years training, waiting for the day we could face those who stole everything from us." He leaned toward her; the tone of his voice more serious than sentimental. "Would you have us miss our opportunity due to your fear? Our family -"

"Is dead," she interrupted, the sharpness in her tone stung. "Nothing we do will ever change that. The North has forgotten us."

"If you really believe that then what was the purpose of Lykos sacrificing himself to save us?"

"For us to survive."

"For us to live." He rested his hands atop hers. "We owe it to him to do more than waste away in this forest."

"The North is not our home anymore," she whispered. "This is our home, and these are now our people. Why can you not see that?"

"Other than Zophar, you are the most tenacious person I know. You've never once backed down from a fight," he rubbed his temples, desperate to understand her hesitation. "What are you so afraid of?"

"I cannot lose you too." She touched his face, fighting back tears. "Have we not lost and suffered enough? How much more must we sacrifice?"

71

He moved away from her. "You don't believe we could defeat her."

"Why do you think we can? Because an old man with a staff told us we could? Because of this," she pointed to her marked eye, blood boiling.

"Because I believe in you."

"That is not enough."

"Why not?"

"Because," her voice cracked, "I do not believe in myself." She had never admitted that out loud before. She always carried herself in a confident manner, but she was rattled and could not hide anymore.

"Don't think for one moment you will be safe by doing nothing. Those who stand by and watch lose their lives the same as those who fight to keep theirs." He touched her hand. "I know you are afraid but know you will not fight alone."

She withdrew her hand. "Touching words from one who will not carry the burden that is being forced upon me."

"Salome, please -"

She scrambled to her feet, nostrils flared, "All you've talked about for years is killing our sister -"

"She is *not* my sister," he nearly shouted as he too jumped to his feet.

"Denying our blood does not make it less tainted." She stepped up to him. "Does it not anger you to know, you trained for years to challenge them, and you will never be able to touch them and live?"

"Does it not anger you to know, you are the only one who can do what is right and you would rather waste away in this forest?" He squared his shoulders up to her, staring down at her. "We all have paths we must follow."

"There lies our problem," she scoffed, not backing down. "You wish to fight them, but if you do you will die. I do not want a war, yet if I do not go, my life is forfeit. It seems the Almighty is playing a cruel game and we are nothing more than pawns."

72

"I would gladly be a used pawn in order to make a difference."

"I am no one's pawn!" Her eyes narrowed.

"Then take your place and fulfill your destiny!"

"I want no part in this." She retreated down the wooden steps and locked herself in her room, ensuring no one would bother her for the rest of the evening.

CHAPTER TWELVE

NIABI

The Great Hall was filled with Lords and Ladies of the royal court who lined up to have but a moment with the young prince to wish him well on his Name Day. With Leoti by his side, Rollo stood taller and looked more confident. He looked ready to be king.

The royal trumpets blared bringing the room full of guests to a hush; their queen had arrived with Pash and her Nephilim Iron Guard following closely behind. She might have intimidated all who stood before her, but none could deny how radiant she looked that evening. In a form fitting dark green dress with a long train trailing behind her, her shimmering white crown was accentuated by the crystal embellished neck and waistline. Her raven black hair raised in an up-do exposed her bare back as she glided through the room of dignitaries.

Rollo met her in the middle of the Great Hall, kneeling before her with one arm crossed over his chest. As he rose, he extended his hand, inviting his mother to dance with him. The music began to play as mother and son shared the first dance of the evening.

"You look beautiful," Rollo whispered in her ear and smiled.

"A mother never did have a better son." She noticed the twinkle in his eyes. "Something is different about you tonight. What is it?"

"Why do you say that?" The slight tilt of his head confirmed her suspicions.

"I am your mother, Rollo. I have seen those dancing eyes before." She stroked his cheek. "You remind me so much of your father. He would be so proud of the man you are. Oh, how he loved you."

The shakiness in her voice made him hesitate before asking her what he really wanted to know. "Will you tell me how he died?"

Her smile faded, "Now is not the time for such melancholy stories."

"I want to know," he pleaded. "I need to know."

She was visibly unwilling to speak on the matter but humored him. "Your father was assassinated shortly after you turned two. The same blade was meant for you as well, but I made sure you did not suffer the same fate."

"Who killed him?" he urged her to give him details.

"All those responsible for Dichali's death have been dealt with." Her answer was sharp and by the tone in her voice, she was done answering his questions.

He furrowed his brow. "Why won't you tell me the truth?"

"Perhaps some truths should remain in the past." She maintained a smile and nodded her head toward the onlookers. As a royal, maintaining a certain appearance was vital.

"What are you afraid of me knowing?" He was not interested in what the Lords and Ladies thought of him and pressed further.

"There are things I have done that I am not proud of," her eyes narrowed, and her lips tightened. "If you knew the truth, you would see me as most Adalorians do: as a monster."

"You are my mother." He gripped her hand tightly. "Whatever you did, it wouldn't change how I see you."

"I wish I could believe that," she sighed. "I want you to know and remember me for who I am now. Not what I was."

75

Rollo was just as stubborn as she was. "If you don't tell me the truth before the week is through, I will deny my birthright, I will refuse the crown, and I will never sit on the White Throne."

Her mouth dropped. "Rollo, don't be -"

"How am I to be king if I do not know my own history," he interrupted. He softened his tone. "Nothing you have done would ever change my love for you. All I want is to know what happened to my father."

She could see learning from the Andrago had indeed impacted him; he was bolder. "Before your coronation, I will answer any question you ask of me. But not tonight. Tonight, we celebrate you." She caught Leoti's eye and noticed her blush. "Now what is it you have to tell me?"

The sudden change in subject threw him. "What do you mean?"

"Like I said before," she tilted her head toward the Andrago maiden. "I have seen those dancing eyes before."

"I can never hide anything from you," he smiled as his eyes met Leoti's. "I married Leoti tonight."

Her eyes widened; that was not what she was expecting to hear. "Married?"

"Married by an Andrago Elder at sunset."

The Andrago believed that by reciting marriage vows at sunset, it signified the death of two individuals and the birth of one spirit.

"I promise we will have a northern ceremony as is customary for northern kings but -" He realized her eyes were glossed over. "I hope you are not angry, Mother."

"Angry? How could I be angry?" She whispered with tears in her eyes and kissed his cheek. "My son, I couldn't be happier. You two now share the same spirit."

"You're really not upset?"

"All I ever wanted was for you to be happy with someone the way I was happy with Dichali."

"I am happy." The corners of his eyes crinkled as he smiled at his new wife. "She means everything to me."

"Then stop talking to me and dance with her." She nudged him in Leoti's direction.

Rollo kissed his mother's cheek and bowed. "My heart and my soul."

"My moon and my stars." She squeezed his hand and watched with a warm smile as the newlyweds danced. The way they looked deeply into one another's eyes reminded her of Dichali. It was as if no one else in the room existed.

Tala approached her, offering her a glass of wine. "It's almost time."

She guzzled half the glass. "Then maybe I will stop worrying about him."

"Are you sure you wish to abdicate so suddenly?"

"I swore an oath and I intend to keep it." She could not take her eyes off her son. "He looks so much like him, does he not?"

"Spitting image." Tala nodded his head, taking a sip of wine from his glass.

"My heart breaks that he is not here."

"We will see him again when Death comes for us." Tala touched his forehead and dragged his finger down to his chest.

"May she be patient in her reaping." She mimicked the same motion.

"They make a fine couple." Tala's chest puffed up.

"It seems," her velvety voice caught his attention, "that we are now family, my dear friend."

His sideways glance was filled with confusion. "What do you mean?"

"My son just told me he married your daughter before coming to the party," she grinned. "Married by the Andrago Elder at sunset."

His gaze settled on the couple. His mind was flooded with memories of Leoti as a child. She had grown up so quickly and now she was a married woman. Married to the future King of Northwind. "It seems like yesterday I was holding her for the first time."

"Our babies aren't babies anymore." She rubbed his back with a fond smile. "She will make a fine queen."

Her eyes caught sight of Gershom who had just slithered into the room. By the look on his face, she knew someone had alerted him to her plans. Once he spotted her, he weaved through the crowd toward her.

Tala's brow furrowed, "He looks like he has something to say." He had never cared for Gershom, and he had not bothered to hide his disdain for him.

"He knows." She finished her glass of wine and sighed.

"You didn't tell him?" His eyes bulged.

"Since when do I have to inform anyone of my intentions?" she snorted.

He placed his hand on top of the handle of his sword. "Let's hope he remembers he is in the White Keep and not in one of his favorite brothels."

Gershom reached them with fire in his eyes and throbbing temples.

"Lord Gershom," she greeted him with formality. "Have you wished my son a blessing on his Name Day?"

"Word has reached my ears that you intend to abdicate the throne," he growled.

Niabi noticed Tala's grip tighten around the handle of his blade and motioned for him to stand down. "You have heard correctly. I do plan to abdicate tonight and within the week have my son crowned King of the North."

"How can you give up the crown after everything we did to secure it?" He spat every word through clenched teeth.

"Surely you did not believe I would rule forever."

"What about my position?" He fidgeted. "We made a deal."

"You know the tradition of northern kings. My son will appoint his own Second." She lifted her chin. "Do not fret, Lord Gershom, you have more than enough money to live comfortably for the rest of your days."

"But our agreement -"

"Has been fulfilled!" She cut him off with a hiss. "You have prospered as my Second. When I step down, you shall too."

"Your son is not ready to be king."

She was silent. The look in her eyes was one Tala had not seen in years. She was no longer standing before them as Niabi, Queen of the North. The Green-Eyed Raven awakened within her. She flashed the tip of a hidden knife in the left sleeve of her gown.

"If you care even an inkling for your tongue, Lord Gershom, I suggest you remain silent and do as you are told." Her eyes narrowed and her speech slowed. "Remember it is *I* who rule the North, not you."

Knowing she never made idle threats, and aware Tala was more than eager to strike him down, he crinkled his nose and retreated to an unoccupied corner of the room.

Tala watched him intently. "He may end up being a problem."

"You know how we deal with problems, Tala." She refocused on her son who had once again started to greet people in the room. "Do not worry about Gershom. He has always been a man of many words with little action." She patted his arm. "Congratulate your daughter on her marriage. I am sure she wants you to know the good news."

Tala bowed and left the queen with her stoic Iron Guard, Anaktu.

A voice yelled from the crowd. "Speech, Prince Rollo, speech."

Applause echoed throughout the Great Hall as Rollo made his way to the small platform to appease his guests with a toast.

"I am honored to have you all here tonight to celebrate my name day. Over the past few months, I have come to appreciate you, my people, more than ever before. I spent the last half of this year with the Andrago, learning the ways of my father and all I could think about was when I would be able to return to my home. Now that I have returned, I am ready to be the leader I was born to be and lead us into the future." The guests applauded and hung on every word he spoke. "One day, I will bear the crown and responsibility my mother now carries, and I promise you, I will do all I can to ensure our people thrive, even though at times, I do not feel that I am ready to be king." The Lords and Ladies seemed uneasy with his confession. "Someone very wise told me that a good king is ready to rule while a great king is ready to learn. I am not perfect but this I can guarantee, I am ready to learn." The crowd once again erupted in applause. Rollo lifted his goblet. "And now, I would like to raise my glass to the people of the North and my mother, Queen Niabi for... for a..."

Something was wrong. Rollo started to sway from dizziness and his eyesight started to blur. His heart raced so fast, he thought it would burst from his chest. Dropping his goblet, the prince stumbled off the platform.

Niabi pushed through the crowd to get to her son as he clutched his chest. "Rollo!" She screamed, catching him as he collapsed to the floor. Tightly holding him in her arms she said, "Rollo, speak to me. Rollo." He continued to gasp for air. The queen looked around the room. "Someone bring the healers!"

"My heart," Rollo wheezed. "Mother, my heart..."

"Stay with me, Rollo, stay with me," she rocked her son in her arms.

Leoti dropped to her knees and grabbed his hand, tears streaming down her face. "Rollo."

He touched Leoti's face and forced a smile. "I love you."

"Don't!" she cried. "Don't leave me."

He weakly reached up and touched his mother's face, "My heart and my soul." His eyes closed.

"Rollo?" Niabi whispered in a panic. "Rollo?" He was gone. Pash knelt beside her.

"Get them out of here," she demanded.

"Everyone out," Tala barked. "Everyone out." Noticing Gershom was the first to leave, Tala peered down at Pash, who tried comforting their queen.

Three healers arrived and scurried to the prince's limp body, but it was too late for them to save him. All they could do now was take his body to prepare him for a traditional Northern burial. One of the healers knelt and grabbed Rollo's arm which was met with Niabi's wrath.

She unsheathed the dagger hidden in the left sleeve of her dress and chopped off his hand. "The next one of you who attempts to touch my son will beg for Death before I have finished with them. Get out!"

Terrified, the healers scrambled from her sight, leaving only Pash, Leoti and Tala in the room while Anaktu guarded the entrance. Leoti rocked back and forth holding Rollo's hand in hers, sobbing uncontrollably.

"For eighteen years I did everything in my power to protect my son," Niabi choked. "As a parent, that was my first priority, and I failed." She brushed the hair from his face, tears streaming down her cheeks. "Tala, Pash. I need you both to make the necessary burial arrangements following the traditions of our ancestors."

"It will be done, my Queen." Tala wiped his face clean.

"She lied to me," Niabi muttered.

"My Queen?" Pash eyed her.

"Leave me."

Pash knelt in front of her with Rollo's body between them, "We must prepare him."

Her lip quivered when she realized she would have to release her son and accept that he was gone. "He never should have gone before me. A mother should never have to bury her child."

Pash gently rested his hand upon hers, but she withdrew.

"Forgive me, I meant no offense."

Her eyes were filled with a pain so palpable it caused him to tear up. Niabi gently kissed her son's forehead and released him from her tight embrace. She stood up and reached for Leoti's hand and squeezed it.

Tala wrapped his arms around his daughter and escorted her out of the room.

Niabi left the Great Hall, swearing she would never set foot in that room again.

Niabi entered her chambers and headed to the stone hearth that sat in the middle of her room. She reached up to the right sconce and pulled it down. The stone hearth spun, revealing a dark room only she knew about. Since she had not used the room in years, dust had covered all the ancient texts and wooden furniture in the secret space. The grieving queen wiped clean the only book that sat out on the table and began flipping through the brittle pages. Once she found the incantation she was searching for, she pulled out her dagger and walked over to a pedestal filled with water. She ripped the left sleeve of her dress which revealed a black blotch that had the appearance of a spreading poison creeping up her arm. She took her dagger and sliced her left hand allowing the black blood to drip into the basin.

"Show me her face."

The blood swirled around the water until the image of an old woman was visible. Her wild white hair and weathered brown skin did not scream villainous, but Niabi knew her for who she truly was: The Old Witch of Endor. Niabi hunched over the bowl.

"Show me where she is hiding."

A beam of light rose from the bloody water and floated to the map of Adalore that hung on the wall. It illuminated a small area in the Black Forest. The Black Forest was now known to be inhabited by less than desirable folk that would not hesitate to skin you for your worldly possessions. Although these woodland dwellers were menacing, they would be no match for Niabi and her men.

"Anaktu," Niabi yelled for her nine-foot-tall bodyguard to enter the secret room.

She kept her eyes fixed on the reflection of her enemy. Her blood still dripped down the side of her hand, staining the floor.

Gritting her teeth, she gave the Nephilim his orders, "Bring her to me *alive*."

Anaktu, who never spoke, crossed his right arm across his enormous chest and left his master in the dimly lit room.

Enraged, she threw her dagger at the map of Adalore hanging on her dark stone wall, piercing the very spot the witch now inhabited. She screamed from the depths of her soul, releasing a sound she had never heard another human being utter before. She grabbed books, vases, trinkets, whatever was nearest, and smashed them against the walls and floor. She fell to the ground, exhausted; her heart was broken.

CHAPTER THIRTEEN

CRISPIN

As the sun crept above the horizon, the usual routine the villagers carried out was interrupted by the sound of pounding hooves coming from the dirt path leading to the Tree House Forest. Every Adalorian's nightmare was now upon them. A troop of Shadows had trotted into their community and that only meant one thing: they were looking for someone, and they would not leave until they were completely satisfied with the results of their interrogation.

Kicking in door after door, the Shadows herded and dragged all the frightened villagers into the main square. Pushed into one group, Korah caught sight of Crispin and rushed over to him.

"What is happening?" The young boy grabbed Crispin's arm in great distress as the Shadows encircled the villagers.

"I don't know. Stay close to me. Everything will be alright." Crispin did his best to ease the young boy's nerves but knew if Shadows were in their village, it was more than likely going to end poorly.

He saw when Zophar and Harbona were ripped from their beds, but Salome was not with them. She was not in the house at all.

Once the last tree house was emptied of its occupants, the leader of the Shadows stepped forward to address the crowd.

Neth was a man of average height with broad shoulders and a sinister appearance. Although not as tall as the other Shadows, he was still an intimidating specimen and people feared the mere sight of him. His commanding presence brought the crowd to a hush before he had even uttered a single word. Once all eyes rested on him, he spoke.

"Lord Gershom, Second in Command of the Northern Lands, has issued a warrant for the arrest of one who bears the mark of the Hunter. Anyone who gives us any information toward the capture of this criminal will be handsomely rewarded." Neth waited for the quiet members of the village to speak up with the information he sought. "You have ten seconds, then my offer is void."

One brave villager finally spoke up. "Sir, we do not know anyone who bears such a mark."

Neth shot the most hateful expression in the villager's direction. "I know he is here in this forest. This is your last chance before I take my investigation further." An eerie silence fell upon the group. "Have it your way."

Neth snapped his fingers and ordered his men to sift through the terrified crowd and grab the first young boy they could find. They dragged the squirming child forward to the dismay of the crowd. Women screamed as Korah was thrust before Neth who now had his muscular hand on the young boy's shoulder. Crispin had tried to grab Korah before he made it to the front of the crowd, but one of the Shadows punched him and bloodied up the side of his mouth.

Neth unsheathed his dagger, alerting the villagers to impending doom. "The blood of this boy stains your hands." Without hesitation or remorse, he slit Korah's throat and dropped his body on the ground.

Blood curdling screams erupted from the crowd.

Crispin attacked the nearest Shadow, taking his weapon and running the soldier through with his own sword. Noticing the one villager fighting back, Neth ordered his men to bring Crispin before him, but before they could subdue him, Crispin managed to kill two more Shadows.

Zophar was restrained from helping his young ward by Harbona who was standing in the back of the crowd.

"Let me go, Harbona," Zophar cried, fearing Crispin would suffer the same fate as Korah.

"Trust me, my friend. Trust me." He refused to relinquish his hold.

Crispin was forced to his knees before Neth who leaned toward him, "You will pay for your rebellious act, peasant."

"You killed an innocent child," Crispin spat. He did not feel fear. He only felt anger, hatred, and a thirst for blood.

"And you killed three of my best men," Neth returned the sentiment.

"Best? If you say so," Crispin mocked. His eyes burned as he fought back tears.

"The penalty for attacking the Shadows of the North is death." Neth lifted the same blood-stained knife he killed Korah with and pointed it against Crispin's throat. "Any last words?"

"Go to hell."

Neth had every intention of slitting Crispin's throat but was shot down by an arrow from above. The two mercenaries that held Crispin on his knees were also swiftly struck down.

Crispin jumped up, grabbed a nearby sword and charged the two remaining Shadows. It felt like an out of body experience. Almost slow motion in his mind. All he could hear was the beating of his own heart, his rapid breathing. He sliced off the first Shadow's leg, then slit his throat as he fell to the ground. The last Shadow threw a knife at Crispin, but he dodged it, rolled toward him and stabbed him in the abdomen. Crispin did not stop pushing the sword until the tip pierced through his back.

Salome jumped down from the rooftop with bow in hand and ran toward Crispin who was kneeling next to Korah's lifeless body.

"Crispin?" She stopped when she saw the boy's neck had nearly been severed from his body. "They killed him? He was just a child."

"Gershom knows no limits. Kill or be killed." Crispin carried Korah's body to his mother, Marta, who had not stopped wailing since her son had been taken from her. The villagers mournfully took his body away to prepare for burial.

Crispin wiped tears from his eyes as he watched his young friend being carried away. "Today, he turned ten." He walked back to the tree house and wiped his bloody hands against his pants.

Salome tried to follow him, but Zophar grabbed her arm. "Let him go."

CHAPTER FOURTEEN

SALOME

The villagers gathered again that evening to mourn the death of the young boy who had brought them so much joy during his few short years. Korah's body was carried out on a white sheet held by four elders. They escorted his pale and cold body down a path that led to a wooden platform. Laying him down carefully, the elders wrapped his body in the linen sheet, as was their burial custom. Korah's mother, Marta, was given a lit torch and she walked slowly toward her son's plat. As she faced her dearly departed, tears streamed down her cheeks. She laid the torch underneath his wooden pallet, allowing his spirit to be released to join their ancestors.

After the villagers watched the wooden pallet burn to ashes, they returned to their homes silently. Crispin, was the quietest of them all and retreated to his rooftop hiding spot, hoping to be alone for the rest of the evening.

Salome followed him up the creaky stairs and stood behind him in the doorway. "I know how much you cared for him."

Her comment was met with silence, which she expected. With an inkling of hope, she waited to see if he would respond, but he remained quiet. She turned to leave, knowing it was probably best to leave him to his own thoughts until morning, when he finally spoke.

"They were looking for someone with a mark." His words were filled with resentment.

She was surprised. "A mark?"

"No one knew anything except the people in this house and we said nothing." Crispin wiped the guilty tears from his face. "Korah's death was punishment for our silence." Salome touched his shoulder, but he wiggled away from her grasp. "Where were you? You saved me but not that innocent child."

"I know you're angry and you're hurting, but you cannot blame me for Korah's death. I would have done anything to save him. You know that, Crispin."

"All I know is he died today and nothing I do will bring him back. That is now my burden to carry."

"Crispin -"

"Leave me." His voice was icy.

She could not bear to see him this way. He was the strong one. He was the one who wiped tears from her face. She could not even remember the last time she saw him cry. "Listen to me."

"There is nothing you can say that will bring me peace." He refused to look at her.

"I am not suggesting peace," her tone changed.

"Then what are you suggesting?"

"That we kill them."

"Kill who?" He finally looked up at her.

"Niabi and Gershom stole our homeland. They sit at our father's table. They have taken everyone we love from us." Her eyes were filled with fury. She was ready. "No one else dies."

"You changed your mind?" Shivers ran up his spine at the thought of finally having her on board.

"Too much innocent blood has been spilled. Knowing what I know now, seeing what I saw today, I cannot turn a blind eye to this evil any longer. If a fight is what our sister seeks, then a fight is what she will get."

Their attention was suddenly drawn to a large mob of angry villagers stomping toward their front door. Armed with pitch forks and torches, they murmured amongst themselves. It appeared they had found someone to blame for the Shadows' unwelcome visit.

Zophar opened the front door to address the crazed mob of tree dwellers with Harbona by his side. "Friends, what is the meaning of this?"

Tiron, one of the elders of the village, spoke on their behalf. "Those Shadows came here only after that man came to our village." The elder pointed an accusatory finger at Harbona. Salome and Crispin worked their way to the front door just in time to hear Tiron say, "He is responsible for Korah's death."

The angry mob echoed their support for Tiron's words until Zophar was able to calm them down long enough to hear what he had to say. "I assure you, Tiron, this man is a man of peace."

"The death of a child is your definition of peace, Zophar?" Tiron continued to fuel the fire.

"We have lived here for twelve years without a problem -"

Tiron interrupted Zophar. "Until now. You must leave this village immediately. You are not welcome here any longer." The crowd cheered in agreement with his decree of banishment.

"Now, wait a minute -" Zophar's pleas fell on deaf ears.

"Look what you have done to our village," Tiron riled the community further.

Crispin stepped forward. "We saved this village. Those Shadows would not have stopped with Korah."

"Leave now before you bring death to us all." The villagers masked their fear with angry shouting.

"Do you really believe they would have let us live in peace had we not interfered?" Crispin shouted.

Zophar rested his hand on Crispin's shoulder, "Let it be. They are not going to listen."

"Leave! Leave us! Go now!" the mob shouted at them.

Salome turned to Harbona. "What will happen to them if we leave?"

Harbona was hesitant, "More Shadows will come."

"They will kill more of them?" She had a lump in her throat thinking of their future.

"Yes," he pressed his lips together, "more of them will die."

"We must warn them," she insisted, panic in her voice. "They must leave the forest."

"They will not listen," Harbona warned.

"You have seen this?"

"If I say yes, would you believe me?"

Salome asked, "Is there any hope one will listen?"

"There is always hope," the Seer nodded his head with a sad smile.

She pushed her way to stand before the men and women she had come to love and earnestly pleaded. "My people of the Tree House Forest, we received but a glimpse of the North's growing evil. The Shadows will return and once they see their men are dead, they will kill more of us. We must all leave this place and find homes elsewhere. It is the only way to survive future attacks. Please, think of your families. Save yourselves."

Though the mob had fallen to a hush, Tiron stepped forward once again and growled. "We are *not* your people. You and those men never belonged here in the first place."

"Please, you must listen -"

"It is because of you, my son is dead."

Salome was interrupted by the voice of a grief-stricken woman in the back of the crowd. Marta, Korah's mother, made her way forward.

Crispin stepped in front of his sister. "Marta, what happened to Korah was not her fault."

"She saved you," Marta scolded with a tear-stained face. "Why did you not save my son? Or do you only aid those who matter to you?"

"Marta, please -"

Marta refused to allow Crispin to speak. "She is just as guilty as the man who killed my son. She is a murderer with blood-stained hands."

"Leave this forest and do not return. You have brought nothing but pain and suffering to us all." Tiron capitalized on furthering his plan to banish them.

Salome was wounded. *Murderer? Blood-stained hands? Was that really what they thought of her now?*

Zophar wrapped his arms around her and escorted her inside. "Come, Salome."

Crispin followed them inside while Harbona addressed the angry mob one last time. "The Shadows will return, and they will not be diplomatic when they arrive."

"And why should we believe you, old man?" Tiron spat at Harbona, inciting the villagers to cheer.

"Heed these warnings or do not. The choice is yours." Harbona reentered the treehouse, leaving the crowd to disperse.

Salome sat by the fire, shocked by how quickly their community turned on them. She never expected the sweet men and women she had grown up with to reject them so viciously. Crispin cloaked his arm around her hoping to raise her spirits, but she shrugged him away.

"Salome -"

"Why will they not listen? They will die," she interrupted her brother.

"You have done all you can do; now you must let them go." Zophar drank his hot tea, his eyes fixed on the fireplace in front of them. "You cannot save those who do not want your help. We must prepare to leave before more Shadows arrive or our angry neighbors return for another round."

Salome focused her gaze upon the Seer. "Did you see their reaction?"

Harbona's eyes were filled with a warm kindness. "Yes, but I also saw if you did not warn them, you would have regretted it. Your hands and conscience are clean."

"Then why is my heart so heavy?"

Zophar lit his pipe and began to fill the small gathering room with smoke. "Where are we to go now?"

"We will make way to my house in The Hollow. From there we will plan our next course of action," the Seer assumed control of their future endeavors. "Take only what is important. Leave everything else."

"When do we leave?" Zophar asked.

"Tonight," Harbona answered to Salome's surprise.

"You would have us flee as cowards in the night?" she scoffed, unwilling to follow his orders.

"If you do not leave tonight, you will die here. Pack your things quickly. There is not much time." Harbona spoke with such conviction that no one dared to ask him anymore questions.

As quietly as they could, the fugitives packed their important possessions with great haste, saddled their horses and stood outside their humble tree house for presumably the very last time.

Zophar had tears in his eyes, which was a rare sight for a man born in the city of Borg. He stroked his red beard with a heavy sigh and mounted his chestnut steed.

The four travelers somberly rode out of the Tree House Forest. Zophar followed closely behind Crispin and Harbona, who took the lead positions in their caravan, but noticed Salome was no longer riding beside him. He turned and saw she had stopped right outside the village, taking in one last look of the place she had accepted as her home. He rode up next to her and looked with fondness at the village they had both found comfort in.

"I will miss it as well," he broke the silence.

"You trust Harbona?" she whispered.

"With my life." He did not hesitate.

"I hope he is right," she wiped a tear from her cheek. "This will be harder than I thought it would be."

"You feel like you are leaving your home behind?" He glanced over at her, barely making out her features in the darkness.

"I feel as if I am leaving myself behind and being forced to become someone else entirely." She admitted with a quiver in her voice.

"Trust in the Almighty One's plan, Salome." He patted her arm, hoping to comfort her.

"What if he is wrong? What if I am not who you think I am?"

"From the first day I met you, I knew you were more than just a princess. I noticed how strong and brave you were as a child and the warrior in me, saw the warrior in you. I think it's time you remembered who you are."

Salome continued to wipe the tears that streamed down her face as she stared at her home. She turned toward Zophar, knowing what she needed to do.

"What is your decision?" he asked her.

"We ride."

CHAPTER FIFTEEN

NIABI

Every Northerner lined the main cobblestone street in Northwind to honor their departed prince as he was carried to his final resting place. Since the founding of the White City over a thousand years ago, every member of the royal bloodline had been buried in the mountain crypt just outside the kingdom gates. The carved tombs had only one way in and out and the one gate was heavily guarded day and night. Even Niabi's family members were given honorable burials according to the traditions of her people, all except her father, whose remains were burned.

The one royal she had not planned to bury was her own son. Rollo was her world, her light, and now she had to escort his lifeless body through their city to the Mountain of Kings. Her black gown boasted an eight-foot train and in keeping with northern tradition, she wore a sheer black veil to cover her face. The veil gave the queen a sense of privacy as she grieved the loss of her son as well as maintain a powerful image with her people. Her white crown sat upon her head as she marched down the street next to her son.

Rollo rested on top of a white golden plat, dressed in his favorite royal robes and furs; his crown was perfectly placed upon his well-groomed hair. The sword she had given him when he turned twelve rested on his chest. Even on his plat, he looked like a king.

Following closely behind the queen, Leoti, Tala, Pash and Gershom kept a steady pace. As the funeral procession progressed through the grieving city, citizens threw flowers on the path, paying their last respects.

A young little girl with loose brown curls dashed out of the crowd with a flower of her own, wishing to place it atop the prince's body. Her mother screamed and cried for her daughter to return before it was too late, but the young child did not listen. Instead, she pressed on and unexpectedly bumped into the queen. Niabi stopped, halting her entire entourage. A hush fell upon the citizens, knowing it was forbidden to touch a royal.

Niabi bent down and lifted her veil, revealing her tear-stained face. "Is that for Prince Rollo?" She pointed to the flower in the young girl's hand.

"Yes, my Queen." The brown-eyed girl's knees buckled as she stood before her.

Niabi extended her hand and led her to the plat that was being pulled on wheels by four armored horses and allowed her to honor the prince. Wide-eyed, the six-year-old respectfully placed her offering upon Rollo's chest and bowed before her queen.

Her face still unveiled, she once again took the girl's hand and escorted her back to her panic-stricken parents. With the girl now embracing her loving mother and father, Niabi whispered, "Your daughter is very kind."

Niabi locked eyes with the girl's mother. Pity. That is what she saw in the peasant woman's eyes. It hurt. She never wanted to be pitied. When someone wronged her, stole from her, harmed her, she would enact her revenge. She would protect and defend herself. But for the first time in quite a long time, she felt powerless. Vulnerable. Small.

Now mindful of all the eyes glued to her, she covered her face and continued her journey to the mountain.

Once the entourage arrived at the mountain crypt, six soldiers, including Pash and Tala, carried the plat down the dark hall to Rollo's burial plot. His body was placed in a white stone casket and would be covered with a statue of the prince once Niabi left the tomb. The soldiers disappeared so she could say her final goodbye.

"Tala, wait." She leaned over Rollo's body and cut several strands of his black hair, grabbed the sword on his chest and handed them to her friend. "See to it my son receives an Andrago burial, so he may ride with his father, until I meet them again."

"It will be done." Tala clenched the items tightly. "I will return as soon as I can."

Alone, Niabi placed her dainty hand upon the casket and cried. Feeling weak, she dropped to her knees and kissed the side of the coffin.

"I never should have had to bury you, Rollo," her voice cracked. "I never should have had to bury my son."

She wiped the tears from her eyes, a fire raged inside of her. She rose to her feet, grabbed his cold hand, and kissed it.

"I swear on the blood of our ancestors that I will avenge you, my son. Those responsible for your death will curse their mothers for bearing them. They will beg Death to take them, but she will wait, for I bend my knee to no one, not even her. The Ten Kingdoms will remember why they fear the Green-Eyed Raven."

⋖――――⋗

Eerily silent, Niabi reclined in the White Throne as she drank her wine. She had not moved from her seat since her son's funeral and refused to see any member of her small council. Matters of importance would have to wait until she dealt with the old witch, she had sent her Nephilim to capture. Hatred boiled in her heart and the only memory she mulled over was the day she met the hag.

It had been nearly twenty years since Niabi wandered farther than she should have from her camp. Nagrom, the black stallion gifted to her by Dichali on their wedding day, became anxious as he

97

trotted through the dark and mysterious forest, compelling her to stroke his neck, attempting to ease his nerves. They continued to trek through the spooky woods until they happened upon an old cabin with smoke rising from the chimney. With rain fast approaching, and no idea how to find her way back to camp, she reluctantly rode up to the house, fearful of what lurked behind the door.

Her horse was uneasy, and his body language hinted they should not stop.

"We are lost, Nagrom. Maybe they can help," she insisted with a false sense of bravery.

She dismounted her horse and cautiously walked to the cabin door. The stallion neighed and stomped his feet to prevent his mistress from continuing, but she kept moving forward despite his warning. Once she stood at the wooden entrance, she knocked, and the door opened. She did not see anyone, so she pushed the creaking door wide open to reveal a large room with furniture scattered around.

"Hello? Is anyone here?"

She entered the small cabin with trepidation. There was a stone hearth built from the floor all the way to the ceiling. A crackling fire roared while a large boiling cauldron hung above the flames and the aroma of myrrh filled the one room cabin. Two windows flanked the stone fireplace which allowed dim lighting to spotlight the long pine table in the center of the space. A rug was placed underneath the table which was surrounded by four high back pointed chairs. A large double door cabinet stood to the left wall and a small cot sat against the opposite corner. Quilts rested upon the single bed making the cabin very cozy.

Even though her eyes saw the innocence of the home, her heart was racing with the unshakable feeling of evil. She was soaking in her surroundings when the door suddenly slammed shut. Niabi could hear Nagrom whining outside urging her to return to him. She felt she was being watched, but no one was inside. She spun in a complete circle and still saw no one. Nagrom's wails did not cease. He stomped his hooves onto the ground demanding her immediate attention. Fear washed over her as she decided to heed her horse's warnings, but as she tried to open the door, she realized it would not budge. Terror set in as she pulled as hard as she could, but still failed to escape.

"What is your hurry, child?" A raspy voice behind her asked.

She whipped around and saw a petite white-haired woman standing near the fireplace. She had a ladle in her hand and began to stir the liquid in the cauldron.

"I did not mean to intrude. I was lost and needed direction," Niabi's voice trembled as she tried to explain her presence.

"Are you afraid of a little old woman, girl?"

"I am not afraid," she lied.

"Everyone fears something, Niabi. Why not be what they fear?"

Niabi suddenly realized her horse was not making noise. She looked out the front window and saw he was standing quietly.

"Your horse is fine, dear."

"How do you know my name? Who are you? What do you want?"

The old woman faced her. "My name is Vilora, but most Adalorians call me -"

"The Old Witch of Endor," she finished her sentence fully aware of the danger she found herself in.

"I see you have heard of me," the wild haired hag smirked.

Niabi's fear paralyzed her. All she could do was watch the witch. Everyone grew up being told stories about the Old Witch of Endor. How she was cursed from birth, scorned by her family, and rejected by her people. She had been sent to the smallest of the five islands that comprised the Isles of Myr. Consumed with anger, she used her darkness to sink Endor, killing every inhabitant. Niabi did not know exactly how Vilora escaped the Isles of Myr unscathed, or how she came to be hiding in a one room cabin in the foothills of Elisor, but what Niabi did know, was that the witch was not friendly to unexpected guests.

"Tell me, girl, what stories did they frighten you with?" She poured two bowls of what she had brewed in her cauldron and made her way to the table.

"That... That you were cursed from birth..." Niabi stopped. The witch's eyes were not filled with the evil she expected. They told a painful story, and in that moment, she pitied her.

"Go on, girl. What else have you heard?" Niabi remained silent. "Sit down," the witch instructed her timid guest. "I said sit down. Are you hard of hearing?" Vilora scolded.

Niabi obeyed and sat directly across the table from Vilora. She passed the young woman a steaming bowl filled with an unidentifiable stew. She looked at it and slowly stirred the mush attempting to recognize what she was offered to eat.

"What is the matter, girl? Have you forgotten your manners when offered food?" Vilora stared at her with icy blue eyes.

"Forgive me, I did not mean to offend you," Niabi said softly.

"If I wished you dead, I would not use poison. That is a coward's weapon."

Niabi realized she no longer feared for her safety. The witch was right. If killing her was her mission, she would have already taken her life. Niabi took a spoonful of the mush and swallowed it quickly. It was actually good.

"What is this?" Niabi asked, extremely curious about the odd colored stew.

"Human liver," Vilora burped.

Niabi choked as she did her best to spit out the mouthful she just consumed. The witch laughed which angered her. "What is the meaning of this?"

"Hush, girl. I spoke in jest. It is rabbit stew," Vilora continued to cackle as Niabi calmed down.

"It's not...?"

"Human? No, foolish girl," she chastised. "I may be many things, but a cannibal I am not. I leave that atrocity to the Thrak."

Niabi exhaled a huge sigh of relief as she took another bite. "It is good."

Vilora gazed at her visitor until she noticed.

"Is something wrong?" Niabi asked, taking another mouthful of food.

"What is it that you seek?" The witch's eyes twitched.

"What do you mean?"

"No one finds me unless they are meant to. So, tell me, what do you seek?" The elderly woman finally showed a hint of uneasiness.

"I... I found you by chance. I was... I was lost," Niabi stammered.

"Lost or not our paths have crossed for a reason."

"You do not truly believe that, do you?" Niabi did not believe in superstitions.

"Do you mean to tell me that there is nothing you desire?" Vilora squinted as she slurped from her spoon.

Niabi hesitated as she thought once more about the question posed to her. Slowly, she looked up at the nervous witch. "There is something I used to desire."

"Tell me, child." She leaned forward, sauce dripping down her chin.

"I wanted my father's throne. I wanted his kingdom, his crown. I wanted the North." Her response was chilling.

"To have your father's crown means he and all who would oppose your reign must die," the old witch explained rather callously.

"I know." Niabi had clearly thought about this before.

"You know all this, yet you do not seem bothered. Why is that?" Vilora realized she was not dealing with an ordinary woman.

"If you had the opportunity to exact revenge on those who shunned and banished you, would you take it?" Niabi turned the tables on her hostess, appealing to her emotions.

Vilora smiled. "I did take it. And I paid the price for it. Are you willing to do the same?"

Niabi was silent. She had not thought about her father in a long time; her desires had changed.

101

"No child of your womb will sit on the White Throne of Northwind until all other usurpers have been vanquished. But I warn you, you will pay a heavy price for victory and an even heavier price for failure," Vilora prophesied.

"I do not have a child."

"You carry him with you as we speak."

The young royal was surprised. "You mean to say that I am with child?"

"A son."

She rubbed her abdomen, "I am going to be a mother?"

"Born of both wolf and hawk blood." Vilora nodded her head. "He could sit on the White Throne if you choose."

Niabi mulled over her words. Northwind was envied by most Adalorians. Some would say it was the most powerful of all the Ten Kingdoms. To have her son sit on the White Throne...

"But you said it yourself," Vilora continued, "your desires have changed."

Niabi nodded, her eyes were glued to her bowl as she stirred the liquid aimlessly.

"Unless that was a lie," the witch watched her carefully.

"I am a different person now." Niabi snapped from her daze. "I love my husband, his people, and now I am to bear him a son." She once again rubbed her stomach. "Our son will bear his father's crown when the time comes."

Vilora shrugged, "And if that is not your son's destiny?

"What do you mean by that?" Niabi frowned, "What do you know?"

"Just a question, dear, just a question."

Niabi found herself deep in thought again. She was the first born of the Northern King. Northwind was her birthright, her son's birthright.

She shook her head. "I am a different person now," she mumbled.

Vilora slurped stew loudly, bringing Niabi back to the one room cabin. Niabi pushed the bowl away from her.

"If I claimed my birthright," Niabi enunciated each word, "what must I do to ensure my son's reign?"

Vilora's smile was unsettling. "Once more you will lose, then no one will forget your name."

Niabi looked confused, "What does that mean?" Vilora cackled which angered the green-eyed beauty. "Answer me, witch. Do not speak to me in riddles," she snapped.

"When the time has come, you will meet the one known as The Bear. But I warn you, do not underestimate him."

"Who is he?"

"That is all I can tell you."

Frustrated by the witch's lack of explanation, she asked, "Will you tell me how to get back to my camp?"

Vilora pointed outside. "Follow the path you were on, and you will find your camp."

"I was already on that path, and it did not lead me home," Niabi reminded her.

"No, but it led you to me. Now do not argue with me, girl. Just follow the path."

Niabi stood up quickly, slicing her left hand on the wooden table where she was sitting; some of her blood spilled onto the floor of the cabin. She opened her mouth to argue with Vilora when suddenly she was standing alone on the path with no evidence of the witch or her cabin.

"That is not possible!" She turned in a full circle looking for the hag, but she was gone. Her eyes rested on Nagrom, who stood quietly waiting for his mistress to return.

That was the first and last time the Green-Eyed Raven saw the Old Witch of Endor.

The queen was jolted from her trance when the throne room doors opened and Anaktu entered. She stood up, her black robes flowing behind her as she marched toward him. Her glistening crown sat gracefully upon her raven black hair that was pulled back in a loose braid. Deprived of sleep for days, she finally had a spark of hope.

"You found her?" Anaktu nodded without uttering a single word. "Take me to her."

She followed the Nephilim down the dark and ominous hallway that led to the damp and cold dungeons. Throughout the corridor echoed the screams of the tortured prisoners that had been held captive for various crimes against the crown. Niabi was unmoved by their pleas for mercy and continued onward to her most coveted prize. As she turned the corner, they came to a door at the end of the hall.

She peered around the small, windowless cell until her eyes fell upon the old, shriveled up witch who was chained to the wall.

Crumbled on the cold damp ground, Vilora opened her eyes and saw the young girl she had met years ago. She was now the most powerful Queen Adalore had ever known.

"I heard stories of the last Nephilim," Vilora sparked the conversation. "I never expected to see one with my own eyes."

"Leave us."

The giant obediently closed the door behind him. Two torches lit the dark, foul smelling, prison cell as the two powerful women stared at one another.

"How did you find me?" the witch asked.

Niabi lifted her left arm and pulled her sleeve back, "We have more in common than you know."

"My magic!" Vilora was surprised to see the discoloration of her arm.

"You know why you are here," Niabi stated matter of fact.

"I am your prisoner," Vilora lifted her shackled arms. "Perhaps, you should enlighten me of my crime."

Niabi squinted and hissed, "You dare test me, Vilora?"

"I assure you I do not know -"

Niabi lunged toward her, inches from the witch's face. "I did everything you told me to do, and you still took my son from me."

"You did not eliminate all usurpers that would oppose your reign. That was the price, and you did not pay it," Vilora remained calm.

"None of my siblings survived."

"I told you not to underestimate him," Vilora shook her head.

"Who?"

The witch smirked, "Two children slipped through the Bear's fingers that night."

With one swift move, Niabi unsheathed her dagger and put it against the Old Witch of Endor's throat. "Lie to me again, and I will cut out your deceitful tongue."

"The Witch of Endor does not lie." Her raspy voice irritated Niabi.

"They are all dead." She enunciated each word through gritted teeth.

"Did you see their bodies?" Vilora asked, knowing the answer.

Niabi thought back on the day she conquered her father's city and realized she had not seen her siblings' bodies. Nor her mother's. Per their agreement, Gershom would handle her five brothers, sister, and mother, while she took on her father. Gershom had the bodies cleared out before she even had a chance to see them. In truth, she did not want to see them. Her quarrel had never been with them; just her father. But for her to be queen, they had to go. He assured her they were dead. He swore to her.

Surely Gershom had held up his end of their deal. But if he had, Rollo would not have died.

"Crispin and Salome live. And because they live, Rollo no longer could." Vilora knew exactly what she was thinking.

Niabi lowered her weapon. Her eyes burned. *He had betrayed her.* She had given him power, wealth, a home, and he repaid her with lies.

Vilora kept her eyes glued on Niabi. "Am I free to go?"

The Green-Eyed Raven composed herself and stared so deeply into Vilora's eyes that it made the witch uncomfortable. Instead of releasing the old woman, the queen walked to the prison cell door and rapped on it three times.

"You cannot keep me here forever, Niabi," the witch hissed.

"Do not fret, Vilora," she smirked. "Soon I will have no more use for you, and you will meet the executioner's blade. Consider yourself fortunate to still be breathing until that day comes."

Niabi slipped out of the cell and had Anaktu lock the door behind her. "Bring Gershom to me."

———

Niabi strummed her fingers on the armrests of her throne, waiting for Gershom to arrive. She eyed the door, rarely blinking, focused on the man who had betrayed her. Two soldiers stood guard on either side of the wide doors as their queen waited for her unsuspecting prey. The throne room doors opened, and Gershom entered escorted by the Nephilim.

The Second in Command confidently strutted toward Niabi, unaware of the lion's den he had just stepped into. "My Queen." He knelt before her.

"Save your pleasantries for someone who cares for them."

Gershom rose. "Is something wrong, my Queen?"

"You tell me." Her bloodshot eyes narrowed.

It was evident he was confused. He noticed Anaktu was standing in front of the door with two soldiers by his side. Panic began to stir inside him when he realized he was most likely in danger. "What is the meaning of this?"

"For twelve years, you have lied to me," she seethed. "I gave you power, wealth, and a kingdom to call home and you repay me with betrayal."

"Niabi, I have never lied to you."

"You will address me properly or your head will be brought to me on a platter." She slammed her fist down on her armrest, launching a thunderous echo throughout the vast room.

106

"Apologies, Highness," Gershom tripped over his words, unsure of what to do to appease her.

"Give me one reason I should not gut you like a pig," She slowly rose from her throne, fire raging in her eyes.

"My Queen, it has been a stressful week. Prince Rollo's death was an unexpected tragedy and you have been searching for the reason it happened. But I assure you, I have always been your faithful friend and ally."

"You speak as if we are equals and we are not." She stepped toward him. "We had a deal. I fulfilled my promise and you failed to hold up your end of the agreement."

"I have done everything you have commanded of me." He held his ground.

"You let two of my siblings escape the night we took the city."

His eyes shifted, "I swear I killed them all."

"Do you truly stand before me and deny it?"

"My Queen -"

"Stop lying!" Niabi's menacing glare struck fear into him.

Gershom knew his best chance of survival at this point would be to beg for forgiveness. "By the time we realized they had escaped, it was too late."

Furious with his confession, Niabi backhanded him, drawing blood. "Your betrayal has cost my son his life and you will pay dearly for it. Anaktu!"

The silent giant stepped forward, ready to obey any order she gave him.

Gershom's eyes darted back and forth between the monstrous Nephilim and the dangerous woman he called Queen. Falling to his knees he pleaded for mercy. "I swear I will find them."

"Finding them will not bring my son back," she shouted.

"Let me right my wrong, my Queen."

"Begging does not become you," she snarled at the pitiful soldier she once thought mighty. "I see now that you are weak, and I have no more use for you."

He stood in reckless boldness. "I am not weak!" He pounded on his broad chest. "The blood of the bear runs through my veins. Where are your wolves? Homeless, nameless, forgotten. The Bear has already conquered the Wolf."

Niabi raised her hand, halting Anaktu from coming any closer. She took another step toward her prey, thirsty for blood.

"You may think the bear is mightier than the wolf," she hissed, "but how many wolves have you seen dancing for peasants at their master's command?" Her words seeped from her mouth like a smooth poison. "The wolf is slave to no man; he lives and dies by his own choosing. It is time you knew your place."

Gershom stood in frightened silence.

She lifted her right hand exposing the long scar on her palm. "You know as well as I that I cannot kill you. Bring Crispin and Salome to me alive. If you fail me again, I promise you will beg for Death to take you before I am through with you."

"I will not fail you. I will send every man in my charge to each corner of Adalore if that is what it takes." He crossed his arm over his chest and rose to leave but Anaktu blocked his path.

She tilted her head, the corners of her mouth turned up. "Surely you did not believe you would leave this room unscathed."

Terror overtook his face.

Niabi nodded her head cuing Anaktu to force Gershom to his knees. She glided toward him; her freshly sharpened dagger clutched in her left hand.

"We swore a blood oath -"

"I never swore I wouldn't harm you." She knelt before him and touched his cheek with the tip of her blade. "Everything comes at a price."

She sliced his left ear off. Her hands were covered in blood as she held his severed ear. Anaktu released Gershom, who was screaming, from his clutches.

"Perhaps now you will learn to listen and obey. Get out of my sight, before I take your other ear."

He clawed his way out of the throne room holding the hole where his ear used to be, tears streaming down his scarred face.

Niabi handed Anaktu the ear, "Take care of this."

CHAPTER SIXTEEN

NUBIS

When his watch ended, one of the guards from Niabi's throne room ditched his armor in the barracks and made his way to the docks. The dark alleys were packed with seedy characters and promiscuous women looking to earn their keep. Soldiers were known to frequent the area during their free nights to drink themselves into a stupor and hopefully, wake up next to a wench they never intended to see again.

However, Nubis was not like the other footmen in the queen's service. Originally born in Fennor, known to most Adalorians as the City of Bones, the Stormcrag tribesman had journeyed to the White City of Northwind several years earlier to serve the man who had saved him from a rival Mountain Men tribe, called the Krazaks.

The Krazaks were a brutal and bloodthirsty tribe who smeared ashen clay on their bodies and adorned themselves with the bones of their fallen enemies. Black and red war paint was always splattered on their skin; and they were ready for battle at a moment's notice. Both men and women wore their hair in braids; the longer the braid, the more battles they had won. Now in control of the Throne of Skulls, their sole purpose was to annihilate any member of the Stormcrags and fashion their skulls into prized helmets.

Being a Stormcrag was Nubis' greatest honor and safely kept secret. His kin were fur wearing, tattooed survivalists who spent their time killing Krazaks and Gomorrian Thraks, while guarding the sacred temple known as "The Tears of the Gods". Although his people all dyed their hair and painted their bodies in shades of blue, purple, and white, he had no choice but to maintain his shaggy black hair in a traditional northern bun and hide his blue ink tattoos. In contrast to the Krazak's long braids, Stormcrag men had two distinct beard braids to boast of their many victories, though he no longer participated in this tradition.

Boasting an impressive six-foot six-inch frame, Nubis never had any trouble with his soldier brethren. Though he had sworn an oath to protect the queen and fight her enemies, he had not come to serve her, but rather to spy on her and report his findings to his underground commander. With Niabi's feeble support of the Krazaks stopped, his people could once again assume control of the City of Bones. If that meant he would spend the rest of his natural born days in a foreign land fighting in an underground northern rebellion, then he was inclined to do just that.

As he turned the corner, he saw his destination: The Whispering Fox. Known around the Kingdoms of Adalore to be one of the most dangerous taverns, Nubis never feared for his safety because he was amongst his fellow rebels. Slipping in the bar unnoticed by the celebratory ruffians, the well-groomed, dark bearded insurgent carefully made his way down a steep, creaky staircase into the candlelit basement where he found him.

"You have news?" the voice in the darkness sounded out.

"Aye," Nubis stepped forward. "Prince Crispin and Princess Salome live. Gershom is searching for them now."

"Two of the royal children escaped?"

"Yes, my lord."

The underground warlord, who was masquerading as a tavern owner in the unsavory brothel district, stepped into the light. Oden, who was previously known as Lord Maon, now donned a thick long braid down the center of his back and rings on nearly every one

111

of his fingers. For years, he had remained secluded in order to protect himself from the vicious, tyrannical queen who killed his king. Before the invasion, he had been King Issachar's Second in Command. Now, Oden was responsible for orchestrating The Order, a guerrilla brotherhood. No one truly knew if the rebellion existed or if they were just a hopeful legend, but the handful of members that were bonded in blood knew one day their band of assassins would overthrow the queen and all who followed her.

"Are you positive of their names?" Oden had to be sure.

Nubis nodded his head. "The Queen named them herself right before she sliced off one of Gershom's ears."

"She sliced off his ear?"

"Aye, said it was punishment for his betrayal. Said if it weren't for him, her son would still be alive."

"Rollo would be alive?" Oden said each word slowly, eyes closed.

"That's what she claimed. I don't know what she meant by it," Nubis shrugged. "And by the looks of it, neither did Gershom."

"She blames him for Rollo's death and let him live?" He scratched the stubble on his chin.

"She said he knew as well as she did, she couldn't kill him."

"See what you can find out." Oden paced. "Clearly, we are missing key information about her and Gershom's history."

"From what I know, the Nephilim was away from the city for a week on the Queen's bidding. Once he returned, she went to the dungeons and then summoned Gershom to the throne room."

Oden's eyes twinkled. "Who did she see?"

"No one knows." Nubis leaned against the wall, arms crossed over his broad chest. "According to the records, there is no one in that cell. Whoever it is, is meant to remain a ghost."

"We need to find out who she saw down there." Oden rubbed his hands together.

Nubis had seen that look before. He knew Oden's mind was racing trying to piece the puzzle together.

"In the meantime," Oden scattered pieces of paper on his desk and reached for his quill, "we must send word to the others. We need to find King Issachar's children before Niabi or Gershom do."

"They could be anywhere," Nubis reminded him with a scoff. "How do you expect to find two people who have gone twelve years undetected?"

"I still have many knowledgeable friends in Adalore who owe me a few favors," he smiled. "Seems it is time I pay them a visit."

"Are you sure it is safe for you to leave the city? Someone could recognize you."

"And how would that make me look to our brethren?" Oden shook his head. "Not burdened in issuing orders but too frightened to do my part in our fight. I would rather slit my own throat, than have The Order believe me to be a coward."

"At least have someone accompany you." Nubis knew Oden had not left the city in nearly six years and Adalore was a much more dangerous place than before.

"Where I am going, I must go alone." The commander shuffled around the room looking for his satchel. "If I do not return, you know what you must do."

"Aye."

"Good. Now go. There is much to be done."

CHAPTER SEVENTEEN

SALOME

"How much farther, Harbona?" Crispin huffed childishly, thoroughly exhausted from their journey.

"Not much farther." Harbona kept his eyes on the path.

"What is this place called?" Salome was in awe of the mystical forest they had entered.

"This is the Hollow." Harbona also admired the woodland he called home.

Wisteria trees in full bloom lined the dirt path and swayed in the light breeze. It almost seemed as if they were whispering as they rode by. Hypnotized by their airy song, she stopped to listen, convinced she could hear them calling her name.

"Do they speak?" She stopped the Seer dead in his tracks.

"You can hear them?" he asked.

When she saw their expressions, she realized they did not hear what she heard. "You don't hear them?"

"No, child." Zophar was wide-eyed.

"Not many can," Harbona chimed in.

"What does that mean? Not many can?" Crispin stared at his sister as if she had a contagious disease.

"It means they have something to say, and she should listen." The Seer stated. "What are they saying?"

"Just my name," she confessed sheepishly.

"Has this happened to you before?" Harbona pressed.

"Once."

"When?"

"Before you came to our village," she confessed. "I was hunting, and I heard my name. At first, I thought it might have been Crispin, but I was alone."

"Is that all that happened?"

The way Harbona looked at her, she felt like he already knew the answer. She could lie, but if the Seer did know, there would be no point.

"A bright light started to approach me," she felt silly admitting it, "but I ran before it could get to me."

"Sounds like dark magic to me," Zophar puffed.

"What would the trees want with me?" Salome pondered aloud.

"The trees are a mysterious bunch, but you needn't fear them." Harbona tried to ease her nerves.

"Needn't fear talking trees?" Crispin balked. "Am I the only sane one here? Trees are trees, nothing more."

"Trees are living beings," the Immortal countered. "Perhaps they speak to those who will listen."

"Maybe I just need some rest," Salome diffused the situation as best she could. "Do we have much farther to go?"

"We are here." Harbona pointed toward a wooded bend. The weary travelers saw a house carved in the hollow of a large Angel Oak tree.

The siblings had never seen anything quite like it. There was a yellow door and windows of different shapes and sizes scattered around the trunk and branches. Once they dismounted their horses, they walked into the warm and inviting house. Countless books and parchments were strewn throughout the main room. A narrow staircase, carved in the tree, spiraled to the second and third levels of the home. Harbona ignited the fireplace logs and set a cauldron above the flames to make supper.

"Please, make yourselves comfortable," their generous host smiled. He had not had visitors in years, so this was a pleasant day for him.

Salome and Zophar perused through all the Seer's books, while Crispin gazed at the weapons mounted around the small hovel.

"Why so many weapons?" Crispin questioned, genuinely intrigued. "What is it you fear?"

"Nothing at all, young Prince," he grinned.

Zophar's eyes fell upon a large book whose cover was made of solid gold. "Do my eyes deceive me? Is this the Book of Malachi? It is said this book was given to him by the Almighty One himself."

"Who exactly was this Malachi?" Salome walked toward her mentor, fascinated by the rare find.

"Over a thousand years ago," Zophar recounted, "a king rose to power and united all the citizens of Adalore. King Greygor was loved by the people and ruled them for ten years before his own brother, Phlias, consumed with jealousy and believing he was the mightier of the two, gathered his band of ruffians and attacked his brother's castle, Oakenshire. After overthrowing King Greygor and seizing control of his kingdom, with malice and pure hatred in his heart, Phlias murdered his younger brother and slaughtered all who opposed his illegitimate reign. Seven years passed and after numerous failed assassination attempts on Phlias' life, the Adalorian people accepted no one would be able to defeat the tyrant king.

In their darkest hour, The Almighty One heard their cries and sent a Seer to a poor farmer named Malachi, the youngest of seven brothers. Anointed to be his chosen warrior, he was marked with the symbol of the Hunter and was bestowed a golden sword forged by the Almighty himself. Having great favor, Malachi quickly gathered an army of peasants and noblemen alike to dethrone Phlias. Nearly two years after his encounter with the Almighty One, he came face to face with the vile self-proclaimed King of Adalore.

A duel ensued, both men were bloodied and bruised, but Malachi was the one who drove his golden sword through Phlias' chest, finally ending the evil reign his people had endured. The people demanded Malachi be their new king. But he knew one man should not have that much power and instead, spent the remainder of his life helping to establish the Ten Kingdoms of Adalore.

It took nearly fifty years for all Ten Kingdoms to be established, but once his task had been completed, the Almighty One called him home. Leaving his golden sword, this book, and a letter, he ascended into the heavens on a chariot of fire."

"How did you come to possess such a book?" Crispin asked suspiciously.

"Malachi entrusted me to protect it." Harbona poured himself a cup of tea.

"Wait, you are saying you were there?" He nearly choked on the question.

"Oh yes," Harbona's eyes twinkled, "I was there."

Crispin rubbed his temples. "But... But that would mean you were alive... over one thousand years ago."

"Yes," he nodded.

"You were the Seer who found Malachi," Salome chimed in once she put the pieces together.

"Yes, I was." Harbona smiled fondly remembering the victories he and Malachi achieved together.

"That is not possible." Crispin refused to believe the man who stood before him was over a thousand years old.

"Anything is possible, Crispin, if you only have faith." The Seer poured another hot cup of tea and offered it to the confused prince.

Crispin declined the beverage. "How old are you?"

"You would not believe me even if I told you."

"Are you immune to death?" Crispin asked, sounding like a little boy with a hundred questions.

"It is simply not my time yet; my work is not finished," the old man graciously answered as he sat in his favorite leather chair.

"And what of the sword?" the prince pressed. "Do you have that as well?"

He shook his head, sipping his tea. "Malachi entrusted another with its protection."

"Who -"

"Enough questions for now." Harbona offered him the tea again. "Eat. Rest. This is just the beginning of a long road ahead."

CHAPTER EIGHTEEN

LEOTI

Nestled between the winding Ameyalli River and the evergreen lined farmlands, the Kingdom of Elisor was comprised of thousands of lodgings made of wood, animal skins, and colorful woven tapestries. The city was unique because it was the only Adalorian capitol that was not enclosed by stone walls.

Tala, followed closely by his entourage, approached his homeland with a heavy heart. The citizens of the city stood outside their homes with streaks of black paint below their eyes down to their chins; a traditional gesture to pay their last respects to the prince they had only recently come to know and admire.

Although Rollo had spent most of his life in Northwind, as soon as the Andrago met him six months earlier, they knew his spirit was kindred to their own. As a descendant of both the Wolf of Northwind and the Hawk of Elisor, Rollo would receive a traditional farewell before his prized possessions were laid to rest next to his father's grave. The Andrago believed the father and son who had not gotten to know one another in life now had the opportunity to know one another in death.

Feeling their eyes fixated on her during the entire ceremony, Leoti maintained a fair distance from the women in the community. The last thing she wanted was to be pitied. Death had come for her mother and now her husband. The female elders would assume she was cursed – and maybe she was. She could only imagine what they were thinking or saying about her in the privacy of their homes.

Her eye caught sight of a familiar face. The color had faded from her eyes, but they were still warm and kind. She struggled to her feet, grabbed her walking stick, and hobbled her way to Leoti with a sense of urgency. Leoti stopped and waited for her.

"It has been a long time, sweet girl," Nokoma's smile caused her eyes to shrink into wrinkles. "I have prayed for years I would one day see you again. I just wish it hadn't been under these circumstances."

Leoti stared at the ground, smudging the black paint under her eyes while attempting to hide her tears. "I have thought about you often."

Nokoma lifted Leoti's chin. "May the Almighty be the wind that lifts you up. May the Almighty be your comfort during this heartache. May the Almighty be your light in this darkness."

She grabbed the old woman's hand in hers. "I believe the Almighty has forgotten me."

"He loves all of his children, Leoti, especially during their times of trouble."

Leoti's eyes burned as she fought back tears. "Why did this happen?" her voice cracked.

"When my sweet Tallulah passed into the next world, I asked Him the same question," she sighed, forcing a smile.

"And what did He tell you?"

Nokoma wiped a tear from Leoti's cheek. "She had served her purpose. It was time for her to rest."

Leoti whispered, "I don't really remember her."

Nokoma cupped her chin in her wrinkled hand. "Granddaughter, you may not remember her, but she lives on in you. And if she were here today, she would wrap her arms around you and remind you how loved you are."

Her eyes shifted to those hovering around them. "They think I'm cursed, don't they?"

"Why should you care what they think?" Nokoma snorted. "Only the weak lose sleep over the opinions of others."

"Perhaps I am not as strong as I once thought I was."

"Shedding tears does not make you weak, Leoti. Showing emotion does not make you weak. Taking time to be alone to heal does not make you weak." She grabbed her granddaughter's hand tightly. "What makes you weak is letting the whispers of lessers cause you to forget who you are."

Leoti lifted her head and met her grandmother's gaze.

"To the lessers you say, 'I am Leoti, daughter of Tala and Tallulah. The blood of the Andrago flows through my veins. The spirit of the doe guides my path. The Almighty breathes life into my soul. And when Death comes for me, I will greet her as an old friend, ready to start the next adventure.'"

Leoti straightened, confidence rushed through her. "May the fire that burns within you, fill me." She rested her forehead against her grandmother's.

"Who are you?" Nokoma whispered, eyes closed.

"I am Leoti," she whispered back.

CHAPTER NINETEEN

TALA

Nearly a week had passed since arriving in Elisor, and Tala had spent most of his time sitting on the banks of the river. He had not been persuaded to eat or sleep since he arrived. All he desired was to be left alone to grieve in his own way.

As she did every afternoon, Leoti brought him lunch, hoping he would finally break his silence.

"I brought you something to eat."

His eyes did not waver from the water rushing downstream. Instead of returning to her grandmother's, she sat down next to him. She closed her eyes and inhaled deeply. Together they sat in silence for close to thirty minutes before Leoti spoke.

"Rollo gave this to me the night he returned." She stoked the small book of pressed flowers. "Does the pain ever go away?"

"No," he sighed. "You just learn how to live without them."

"I never thought I would lose my best friend." She flipped through the pages with care and admired each flower pressed in its pages. "I will never understand why he was taken from me."

Tala's weight shifted and he cleared his throat. "Before Rollo was born, Niabi happened upon a witch who told her if she claimed her father's throne, she would have to ensure none of her siblings would survive to challenge her reign. If they lived, her son would never sit on the White Throne."

She was taken aback. "I... I thought she was happy with the Andrago," she stammered.

"She was," he affirmed. "She abandoned her birthright and the hatred she had for her father was forgotten once she realized how deep her love for Dichali was. With Rollo growing inside her, she was reborn. But once she lost Dichali..."

"So, when Dichali died, she decided to go back north?" Her furrowed brow caught his attention.

"There is much you do not know of that night, Leoti."

"Then what happened that night?"

"Rollo always asked me to tell him about how his father died." He stared at the ground. "He never did learn the truth."

"Why all the secrecy?"

"That is how Niabi wanted it." He rubbed his hands together and leaned forward. "She didn't want Rollo to know her as the Green-Eyed Raven."

"Then tell me," she pressed.

He hesitated. He had kept that night a secret for years. The Andrago did not like discussing how someone died; they only shared memories of how they lived. But he needed to tell someone; he needed to tell her like he should have told Rollo.

"When Niabi's father, King Issachar, heard she had given birth to Dichali's son, he was terrified the child would attempt to claim the White Throne when he came of age. Issachar would have rather died than have any child of Niabi's claim the North, so when Rollo turned two, he ordered all three of them to be killed."

"Her own father?"

"The night they were ambushed in their tent, Niabi had to make a choice to save either Dichali or their son."

Her swallow was audible. "What happened to those assassins?"

"Niabi tortured them." Tala's eyes were glassy, as if he were watching it happen all over again. "They lasted longer than I thought

123

they would, but they finally told her who had sent them. Her hatred for her father pulsed through her veins once again and she swore that very night, covered in Dichali's blood, that she would avenge him."

"I still don't understand what that has to do with Rollo's death," she rubbed her forehead. "Niabi conquered the North. Her siblings are all dead. No one should oppose her reign."

Tala pulled a letter from his breast pocket. "I received this message this morning." He handed it to her to read aloud.

She ran her fingers over the broken seal of the Green-Eyed Raven. "Why would she not use the Northern crest?"

His eyes shifted and his fingers twitched. "This sigil strikes fear into the hearts of Adalorian men that the Northern crest does not."

She opened the parchment and read the message aloud:

'"My friend, truths have been uncovered since you left the city. Gershom, whom I once trusted, has betrayed me. He did not fulfill his oath the night we took the North and two of my siblings escaped. My Shadows are hunting them, and Gershom has suffered for his misdeeds. I need you to return as soon as you receive this. The Green-Eyed Raven."'

Leoti gave the letter back to her father. "What oath is she talking about?"

Tala folded the paper and put it in his pocket. "Niabi and Gershom made a pact before attacking the city. Gershom was to kill all her siblings and in return he would be her Second in Command. He let two escape him, which means he signed Rollo's death warrant."

Leoti's nostrils flared. "He should be executed."

Tala bobbed his head. "I agree."

"She said he has suffered for his misdeeds." Leoti mulled over the words of Niabi's letter. "Why would she let him live?"

"Niabi and Gershom swore a blood oath that neither would die by the other's hand."

"You mean she *can't* kill him?" She was so enraged she nearly screamed.

"She forfeits her own life if she breaks a blood oath."

"Dark magic." She spat on the ground.

Tala patted her hand in an effort to calm her down. "Anger and blind desperation often lead us to make foolish and rash decisions."

"Do you think Gershom planned this so he could take the crown for himself?" She could tell by her father's silence that he was deep in thought. "If he let them go willingly, then he plotted his usurpation from the beginning. If they escaped as he claims, then he had twelve years to right his wrong, but he did not. Either way, Niabi has no heir. Gershom could take the throne as her Second, in the event of her death."

Tala's eyes widened. "And upon his death, his son Pash, would be the rightful heir."

"Treason," she hissed.

"It seems they are both far more clever than I gave them credit," he snarled.

"When you return to Northwind, I am going with you."

His eyes softened. "I thought you wanted to stay in Elisor to mourn?"

"I will mourn Rollo the rest of my days." She clutched the book to her chest. "I will heal once Gershom and Pash's heads sit on spikes at the main gate of Northwind."

Tala heard something in the tone of her voice that sent a shiver up his spine. "What are you suggesting?"

"There are many ways to kill a man, father." The fire in her eyes scared him. "Most look like accidents."

"Leoti, he is still Second in Command. His death would demand an investigation." He shook his head. "It is too risky. What if you are caught?"

"Then I will see my love sooner than planned."

125

Tala watched the river flowing and grasped his daughter's hand. "It seems like a lifetime ago that I married your mother at this very spot."

"What does that have to do with any of this?" She was caught off guard.

"Whenever I am angry, confused, lonely or in need of guidance, I always come to this spot. I may not be able to touch her, but I can feel her here with me. We buried Rollo's body, but his spirit is still with you."

"You always say that," she brushed him off.

"You are just like you mother." He looked at the necklace that hung from her neck. "She was much like this river. Calm, steady, and at times, wild and dangerous. What she would have given to be here with you now."

"I don't remember much about her," she admitted, fingering the necklace.

"You were four when she passed on." He wiped his eyes and whispered, "I should have been here."

"You were at war."

"Had I known what I know now..."

"What would you have done differently?" She rubbed his shoulder. "You did what needed to be done. You avenged Dichali."

"Yes, I avenged Dichali," he nodded. "What would Rollo say if he knew of the plotting in your heart?" His words were gentle and kind and humbled her. "What would your husband say?"

Her eyes stung as she fought the lump in her throat. "It's not fair."

"It isn't," he wiped her cheek.

"Did you ask Niabi the same thing when Dichali died?"

"If I had, Rollo would still be alive." He stared at his feet. "Do you plan on assassinating them?"

She turned toward him, and they locked eyes. "I cannot promise I won't have a hand in their deaths."

He knew he could not stop her. And a part of him did not want to. "Be mindful of your steps. They are predators, always anticipating an attack."

"Every predator has a weakness."

By the ferocity in her voice, he knew her mind was made up. "We ride at dawn."

CHAPTER TWENTY

VILORA

The Old Witch of Endor's long white hair wafted as she was ushered through the back hallways of the White Keep. Not knowing whether she was safe, or her time had finally expired, Vilora held her head high, unwilling to abandon her pride.

"Where are you taking me?" she asked the Nephilim.

Anaktu stomped down the corridor without acknowledging his prisoner. He had his orders and interacting with her was not on the agenda.

"Are you silent because you choose to be or because someone cut that demon tongue from your mouth?" He was unmoved by her words, which was the expected reaction. "How long do you think she will be able to keep you alive?" She kept a watchful eye on the Nephilim. "She saved you once, yes, but what happens if she no longer lives?"

The giant swung around to face the witch who had spoken against his savior. Without any visible fear, Vilora stared deep into the black eyes of the monster, unmoved by his threatening stance.

"How unusual," one of her eyebrows lifted, "the monster has feelings."

As swiftly as he had turned toward her, he rotated once more to continue forward. Vilora had a way of finding one's weakness and using it to her advantage. Her purpose with the Nephilim was still a mystery to her, but she knew now how to control him.

Interrupting her plotting, the giant stopped in front of Niabi's royal chambers. Still in shackles, the witch slowly glided into the lavish quarters alone, amazed at the grandeur the girl she had met in the woods almost two decades ago now enjoyed.

"You were right," Niabi's voice echoed throughout the luxurious suite.

"About what?" Vilora peered around the room looking for the queen.

"He did lie to me." The Green-Eyed Raven stepped inside from her balcony with a small box in her hand. "Now he will know his place." She revealed Gershom's severed ear as a trophy.

"Why am I here?" Vilora was not impressed.

Floating across the room, Niabi proudly placed the prized box on a nearby shelf surrounded by other similar containers.

"You have been honest with me, and for that, I believe you are owed a debt of gratitude. What is your price?"

"What I desire, you cannot give to me," the witch shrugged off the rare and generous offer.

"Try me."

The sorceress invited herself to sit in the nearest chair. "Remind me again of the story you were told of the Old Witch of Endor."

Niabi smirked as she poured herself a glass of red wine. "Are you so old you have forgotten your own history, Vilora?"

"Indulge me, my Queen."

Now seated comfortably in her high back chair, Niabi's eyes danced with delight at the thought of playing the witch's game.

"The Old Witch of Endor,
How frightening is she.

The Old Witch of Endor,
How did they not see?

Her heart black as night,
Her eyes cold as ice.

With hatred so fiery,
That even her family,
Knew not the devil's wife in disguise.

Banished in fear,
All who were near,
Paid the deadliest price of them all.

The Isle of Endor,
Sunk deep in the sea,
Forevermore cursed for the dead.

The Old Witch of Endor,
Feared and hated by all men.

The Old Witch of Endor,
Worshipped and loved by all hell.

The Almighty grant you mercy,
If ever you see,
The Old Witch of Endor indeed."

"Does that sound about right?" Niabi sipped on her wine with girlish delight.

Vilora nodded her head, "You asked what my price for honesty was?"

"Tell me, what does the Old Witch of Endor desire?"

"I desire my sister's heart."

Niabi was stunned by the request; she never considered Vilora even had a family of her own. "Why do you need me to help you with that? You are the Witch of Endor, get it yourself."

"When I was a young child, my parents noticed a dark gift in me. They desperately tried to heal me, but you cannot fix what is not broken," Vilora recalled the beginning of her tale. "After my parents died, my sister became queen and fearing me to be a threat to our people, banished me to the Isle of Endor. Needless to repeat, you know what I did in retaliation for my sister's betrayal."

Niabi sighed. "I grow weary of your ramblings."

"My sister bore three daughters and each of them had a unique position. The eldest, Zara, is the heir to the throne and commander of the royal fleet. Damaris, the youngest, was christened as the virgin high priestess and she cast a spell, preventing me from ever returning home. Her middle daughter was the most beautiful one of them all," the old woman continued, not deterred by Niabi eyeing her. "My sister married her off to ensure a strong alliance with the mainland remained intact. Her name was Bilhah."

Niabi stared at the witch in complete disbelief, "You mean to tell me, your sister is Queen Nym of the Isles of Myr?"

"Your grandmother's heart is my price; nothing more, nothing less."

Vilora gave Niabi a moment to sift through all the information she revealed to her. The Old Witch of Endor was more than just a song parents would frighten their children with; she was her great aunt, her own flesh and blood.

"If I do this," Niabi leaned back in her seat, one leg crossed over the other, "you must also help me."

Vilora scoffed. "I thought this was your generous offer for my honesty."

"If your price for honesty is for me to have my own grandmother's heart ripped from her chest and given to you on a silver platter, then I will require more from you." The queen was prepared to make another deal.

"What is it you want?" She was intrigued.

131

Niabi spoke in a low voice. "You know how to raise someone from the dead, do you not?"

Vilora's eyes widened. "No one resurrects the departed. Kill or be killed, but do not bring back those who walk beyond the grave."

Niabi rose from her seat, grabbed a large leather-bound book from her shelf, opened it, and placed it on the table in front of Vilora.

"This is the Resurrection Spell," the queen continued, ignoring Vilora's reservations. "I know you have enough magic to complete the ritual. What I do not have is the Heart of the Righteous."

"You are mad to think you can save your son," she shook her head. She could not recall if anyone had ever successfully performed the Resurrection Spell.

"We can help one another," Niabi's eyes softened. "After all, we share the same blood."

"You said it yourself," Vilora smirked as she leaned back in her seat, "you do not have the Heart of the Righteous."

"No," she admitted with a grin. "But I know where I can find one." The queen bent down before the old woman and freed her from her heavy iron shackles. "I will give you your sister's heart if you give my son back to me. Do we have a deal?"

Vilora gazed into Niabi's eyes, sensing the danger they held. She knew there was a chance she would not be able to complete the Resurrection Spell and would face the queen's wrath, but her own deep-rooted desire for her sister's heart far outweighed her fear of Niabi. She nodded. "We have a deal."

CHAPTER TWENTY-ONE

THE NAMELESS RIDER

The leader of the newly arrived group of Shadows ordered the dwellers of the Tree House Forest to be gathered for questioning. He was a burly man with a prominent jaw. The left side of his face had a deep scar that ran from his eye to his chin. Burn marks covered most of his body, but nothing was more chilling about him than his one, icy blue eye that was visible through his black mask. He never allowed anyone to know anything about him, not even his birth name, Pert. To keep his identity a mystery, he preferred being known as the Nameless Rider. He was a heartless man who slaughtered men, women and children. And anyone seeking revenge was added to his long list of victims.

One by one, villagers were brought before him to be questioned about what happened to his slain Shadows. He sat quietly peeling an apple with one of his many knives as the next peasant was thrown at his feet.

Jacobi was terrified of the disfigured warrior sitting in front of him, yet all he could do was hope he would not be the next villager to be added to the pile of dead bodies the Shadows had accumulated that morning.

"Name?" the Nameless Rider asked in a deep and raspy voice.

"Jacobi, sir," the baker whispered as loudly as he dared.

"Jacobi," the Shadow repeated, which sent chills down the young villager's spine.

"Yes, sir." Sweat dripped down his forehead.

"What is it that you do here in this hellhole?"

"I am a baker, sir."

"A baker."

"Yes, sir."

"You seem to be an honest peasant. Is that a fair statement?" the Shadow swallowed an apple slice whole.

"I try to tell the truth."

"I am seeking the truth about what happened here. Would you care to tell me what happened?"

Jacobi lifted his eyes from the Shadow's feet to the tip of his mask. "They were killed, sir."

He chomped down on another slice, "That part is clear, Jacobi. What I do not understand is how seven of my brothers were slaughtered in this... village."

"The one in charge murdered a child, so Crispin killed some of your men until they subdued him," the whimpering villager spoke quickly, hoping to appease the assassin.

"If they subdued him, then what happened to the other men?"

"His sister, Salome, killed them. She is an excellent marksman," he continued answering any question posed to him.

"You mean to tell me that two peasants killed my men? One being a woman?" The broad-shouldered man leaned forward, smacking another slice of his juicy apple.

"Yes, sir."

"Is that the truth, Jacobi?"

"Yes, sir, the truth. That is all I know," the trembling villager wiped sweat from his brow.

"I will determine if that is all you know."

134

"Of course, sir."

"Which tree house is theirs?" The masked leader stood up; his seven-foot-tall frame towered over everyone in the entire village.

Jacobi pointed to the tree house the Northerners had occupied. "That one there, sir."

The Nameless Rider peered down at the compliant peasant. "You have been most helpful." He turned to one of the Shadows standing nearby and pointed at the tree house, "Bring the villagers who live there to me, *alive*."

"They are not there," Jacobi chimed in. "They left."

"They *what*?" he growled.

"We did not want them here any longer because of their crimes against the North and we told them to leave."

The Shadow grabbed Jacobi by his throat and lifted him off the muddy ground. "This is why people like you are not worthy of touching the ground we walk on. Fools! Where did they go?"

Jacobi gasped for air. "I do not know."

"Where are they?" He tightened his grip around the villager's throat.

Tears streamed down Jacobi's face. "I tell you the truth, sir, I do not know where they have gone. I swear on my very life."

In a rare moment of what appeared to be mercy, the blue-eyed soldier released Jacobi from his death grip allowing him to fall back to the ground. He knelt in front of the baker, looking directly into his fearful eyes, "Would you be able to describe them in great detail?"

"Yes, sir," Jacobi rubbed his neck, knowing he barely escaped death.

"Good. You may be of some use to me after all, Jacobi."

"I will do whatever you say," the baker bowed.

"Tell me one more thing, Jacobi the Baker." He dropped his apple core at his feet. "Who was it who told these criminals to leave?"

In anguish knowing he was about to betray his neighbor, the baker lifted his face and stared at Tiron. The elder was waiting to be questioned; blood trickled down his head from the blow he had suffered that morning. "That man there."

Not bothering to look in the elder's direction, the commanding Shadow hissed, "Bring him to me."

"What do you intend to do with him?" Jacobi questioned without thinking.

"What will happen to you, if you disappoint me."

Frightened, Tiron was dragged up to the platform and thrown before the Shadow. "Please, my lord," the bald man pleaded. "I will tell you all I know, please do not harm me."

"Name."

"Tiron."

"Tiron." He repeated. "What is it you do here in this hellhole?" He rattled off the same questions.

"I am a farmer by trade, but I am also the elder of this community." Tiron attempted to look brave as he answered the seemingly harmless questions.

"A farmer by trade but also the elder of this community." He echoed in almost a whisper.

"Yes, sir."

"It has come to my attention, Tiron the Farmer, that you ordered a family who lived in *that* tree house," he pointed at Crispin and Salome's home, "to leave the village immediately following their attack on my men. Is this true?"

Tiron peered at Jacobi hoping to get a read of the situation, but the baker kept his eyes glued to the ground. "I did."

"You ordered them to leave?"

"Yes, my lord. We can't have murderers in our village."

"And where did they go?"

"I do not know." Tiron dripped sweat.

"You do not know?"

"No, sir."

"Thank you for your honesty, Tiron the Farmer."

"You will let me go?" The elder was elated.

"I will tell you what I am going to do," the Nameless Rider smirked. "You take this sword," he pointed at his own weapon, "and if you can beat one of my men in combat, you will be free to go."

Trembling head to toe, Tiron begged the Shadow, "Please, sir, I do not know anything about weapons."

"Are you refusing my generous offer?"

"No, my -"

"Then pick up this sword and fight."

Tiron glanced at his neighbor with tears in his eyes. "Jacobi?"

"What is Jacobi the Baker supposed to do for you? Fight in your stead?" The Shadow turned his focus to the shriveled Jacobi. "Is that what you want to do, Jacobi the Baker? Do you want to offer yourself in his place?"

Jacobi shook his head. "No, sir."

"I suspected as much." He shook his head. "You cannot ask a coward to fight for another coward."

"Please -"

"Tiron the Farmer, what do you intend to do?" the Shadow interrupted his pleas. "Will you fight for your life and die like a man? Or will you lay down and die like a gutless pig?"

With every villager watching, Tiron slowly reached for the Shadow's sword.

"Go on," the Nameless Rider motioned him off the platform. "Down there where we can all watch."

The elder shook as he walked to the open square where he was met by one of the Nameless Rider's men with two curved blades in his hands. Knowing this was going to be his end, he lifted the blade and swung with all his might toward the soldier. With a sidestep, the Shadow evaded his weak attack and in one motion, sliced the elder's head from his body.

The Shadow Commander snickered as Tiron's head bounced on the ground. "This hasn't been a total waste of a day after all." Turning his gaze once more toward Jacobi, he asked, "Does anyone else have any information that might prove valuable to us?"

Hoping to spare what remained of his village, the baker quickly said, "No, they do not know anything more than what I have told you."

"Good. I have grown quite tired of this village." The Nameless Rider stood up and stretched. "We ride out. You are coming with us, Jacobi the Baker."

Relieved he did not have to stay to face the judgment of his fellow villagers, Jacobi welcomed his prisoner status.

"Kill the others, burn what's left of the village," he ordered four of his men to finish the job. "The rest of us ride out."

"Wait!" Jacobi was horrified. "I told you they didn't know anything else. Why kill them?"

The Nameless Rider cracked his neck, "Why not?"

"Please, sir, please -"

"You can stay and die with them if it pleases you or you can ride with us to find these murderers." He mounted his horse as the villagers began to scream in terror. "I need an answer, Jacobi the Baker. What is it going to be?"

Unwilling to die with the rest of them, Jacobi hopped on the horse offered to him and left the village he had always known as home.

"You get used to it."

"To what?" Jacobi asked.

"The screams of those about to die. Most nights I won't even attempt to sleep until I have heard it." He smiled.

CHAPTER TWENTY-TWO

NIABI

Smooth and calculated, every movement of her lean body was precise. Armed only with her two silver daggers, Niabi floated across the floor, a vision of fire, effortlessly sparring with three of her fiercest Shadows. Donning her black leather ensemble which afforded her the opportunity to wear pants, greatly increased her range of motion. Flexibility was her greatest strength. Roundhouse kicks, splits, and a wide array of flips were reasons why she was so deadly in combat. She had been trained by the Andrago and Myridians and her skills were no match for the structured battle techniques of other warriors in Adalore.

Her knives glistened in the beams of sunlight that poured into the courtyard as she swung her weapon at her approaching attacker. With a swift punch to his gut and cut across his face, the assailant stepped aside and allowed his two partners to advance. Both Shadows charged their queen, weapons drawn, instructed to strike if given the opportunity. As they drew near, Niabi sprinted toward them and slid in a front split between them, slicing the back of their nearest knees as she passed them. With two of them incapacitated, she turned her focus back on the Shadow with a cut across the left side of his chiseled jaw. He clutched his long blade and gritted his teeth, knowing he would suffer a similar fate, if he took his eyes off her for one second.

Circling one another, the last two standing warriors stared deep into one another's eyes. Once she spotted a hint of fear in his gaze, she pounced, flipping her daggers around her fingers. Blocking blow after blow, he continued to step backwards until his back hit a large column. Now knowing he had no choice but to charge her, he pushed off the wall and sprinted toward her. Niabi turned and ran across the courtyard until she reached a different column, ran up the side and backflipped over the Shadow chasing her. Landing on her feet, she pinned her opponent to the column with one of her daggers pressed against his neck and the other poking his left ribcage. He dropped his weapon, yielding the duel. She released him from her grasp.

Pash had slipped in undetected and watched as his queen sparred with the three Shadows for her daily training. Her knives were extensions of her two hands making her certifiably the most treacherous Shadow of them all.

It was in fact, Niabi, who originally banded the brotherhood together. Every member tattooed the symbol of the raven on top of their left hands to honor their master.

Having ravaged the three mercenaries, Niabi stood tall among the men scattered in the courtyard.

"You let my father live," Pash alerted Niabi of his presence. "Why?"

Her fierce green eyes peered up and down the commander's muscular body as she waved the other men out of her sight. "Does that surprise you?"

"Forgive me, my Queen, but you are not known to be merciful," he spoke boldly, standing between two large columns.

She smirked as she sheathed her two daggers and picked up a sword. "Spar with me. I could use the practice."

He walked down the steps into the sparring grounds and drew his sword. Both warriors took their stances as Niabi rubbed her weapon up and down the commander's outstretched sword. Circling one another, they began their duel.

"I let him live because he still serves a purpose," she exhaled, whilst landing powerful blows.

"And once he is no longer of use to you?"

"You know exactly what will happen."

"What will happen once you have tired of me?"

She dropped to the ground and knocked him off his feet with a low sweep kick. As he fell to the ground, she pressed her knee into his chest with her sword pinned against his neck. "Do you think I will grow tired of you?"

"You tell me, my Queen."

"I am cold," she softly breathed, "but I am not unfeeling."

"You took his ear," he pointed out.

"He is fortunate that was all I took," she spat.

His voice softened, "What do you intend to take from me?"

She gazed deep into his kind and gentle brown eyes as she kept him solidly pinned against the white stone floor. Leaning in, she kissed him, making her intentions known. Pash pushed the blade from his throat, spun her around and pressed her against the stone floor, furthering their passionate kiss.

"I thought you no longer cared for me," he whispered in her ear.

She ran her slender fingers through his long chestnut hair and admitted, "I do care for you, Pash."

"Then why have we not shared a bed in weeks?"

She pushed Pash off her and stood up, "You know why."

His eyes followed her as she retreated. "I loved him too, Niabi."

She kicked her sword up in the air and grabbed it. "Again."

Pash jumped to his feet, "Why do you push me away when you need me the most?"

"I do not *need* anyone," her eyes burned, nostrils flared.

He was unmoved by her menacing glare, "You are the strongest woman I have ever known but being strong does not mean going through life alone."

She threw his sword for him to catch, "Spar or leave."

"Niabi -"

"Is it not enough that I have told you I care for you?" she croaked, throwing her hands in the air. "Why do you push me?"

Pointing out the windows that surrounded the courtyard, he took a step toward her, "They may be afraid of you, but I know who you truly are, and I cannot abandon you to your own undoing."

"I entered this world alone and I will leave it alone, nothing you do or say will prevent that," she placed her sword on the rack. "You would do well to remember that I am still your queen, Commander, and I will be the one to determine my fate."

CHAPTER TWENTY-THREE

MARTA

Shrouded in a long black cloak, Marta weaved in the dark and foggy forest hoping to find the Hidden Tavern on the river. With rain eminent, she knew if she did not find the dock master within the next few minutes, she would be lost in the swamp until morning if she managed to live through the elements. Her heartbeat hastened as she continued to fumble her way down the path, lit only by a small lantern.

"Halt! Who goes there?" A gruff voice echoed in the fog.

"I seek the dock master, sir. I fear I am lost," her voice trembled in angst, hoping she had not stumbled upon a troubled fellow.

As the fog cleared, a weathered man with long stringy hair stepped toward her with a lantern held above his head. With a tired sigh, he motioned her to step forward. "Fear not, woman. You have found the dock master."

She squinted her eyes and saw the boat that would take her to the Hidden Tavern bobbing alongside the creaky dock. The bar was secretly located in the middle of the swamp and the only way to get there was to ride in the dock master's boat. Relief overtook the wary woman when she stepped into the small vessel and silently rode down the river.

After nearly ten minutes, he pointed in front of him. "There she is."

The large wooden structure built on sturdy poles stationed in the middle of the lake was exactly as everyone had described it. Excitement swept over her as they docked. She would soon see the man she had travelled for days to meet. As quickly as she dared, she climbed the flimsy ladder to the wooden platform and made her way to the front door.

Once she heard all the rough and raspy male voices behind the door, she hesitated, but took a deep breath and walked inside. Deep in their beer drinking raucous, none of them noticed the newcomer, or the fact that she was a woman.

The bar keep was passing by with four large pints of ale when she stopped him. "Excuse me, sir, I am looking for someone."

"What's his name, ma'am?" he asked in great irritation.

"I am not sure," she answered sheepishly.

"You came all this way to meet someone you don't have a name for?" he chuckled, now amused.

"What I meant to say is I do not know his birth name."

"What name do you have, and I will tell you if he exists." His arms were beginning to shake holding the overflowing pints.

She leaned in and whispered a name she did not wish anyone else to hear.

The dirty bar keep's eyes immediately widened, and he looked toward the back, dark corner of the tavern. "That is the man you seek, but I warn you, he is not known to be an agreeable man."

Before she could ask him any other questions, he hobbled away from her, as if he did not want to be associated with her. She marched to the corner table where the dark hooded figure was seated. She could not see his face, but noticed he was smoking a small pipe and had fingerless leather gloves on both of his dirty hands.

"Sir, I am in need of your skill set," she blurted before she had a chance to change her mind.

"That depends on who is asking," a gravelly voice responded from beneath the hood.

Korah's mother uncovered her head. "I am a mother who was robbed of her son. I seek revenge."

"I assume since you know of my services, you know required fees," he ignored her passion and remained focused on business.

"I do not have much, but what I do have I will give you." She took a small coin purse from under her black cloak and placed it on the table.

The hooded figure did not even examine the purse. "That is not nearly enough to tempt me, woman."

"It is all I have. Please, sir, I beg of you to have mercy on a mother who has lost every person she has ever loved," she choked back tears.

"And why should I pity you above the rest?" He was eager to hear her answer but was surprised to see her rise and grab two wanted posters from the wall next to them.

"Where did these come from?" She inspected the wanted posters the Shadows had been posting throughout Adalore over the last day.

"Everyone knows the work of the Shadows, woman."

She handed him the wanted posters with Salome and Crispin's renderings printed with a reward. "The two responsible for my son's death slaughtered seven Shadows a few days ago in my village and there is a hefty reward for their heads."

He was now intrigued and leaned forward, still not allowing his face to be revealed in the light. "What are you suggesting?"

"If you kill them, you can keep the reward money. I will be satisfied knowing my Korah was avenged, and you will have your payment and then some. What say you? Do we have a deal?"

He exhaled a puff of smoke and pushed the coin purse toward her as he stood up. Disappointment set in. She believed he had turned her down but was shocked to see him fold the posters and put them in his cloak pocket. "I will take care of them for you."

"Oh, thank you, sir!" Marta grabbed the mercenary's hand and kissed it only to have him yank his hand away from her.

"We are finished here."

Marta smiled coldly as she watched her savior leave.

CHAPTER TWENTY-FOUR

GERSHOM

Just as the sun rose above the horizon, Gershom, and a handful of his most trusted personal guards, disembarked their small vessel and walked to the center of the uninhabited island of Petram. The tiny island was one large slab of rock off the eastern coast of Northwind. Thousands of years ago, Petram was used as a sacred place for ceremonial sacrifices. Gershom held this secret place in high esteem, believing in the ancient rituals of the Adalorians of old. Knowing the island now frightened people away, he used it to conduct private meetings which ensured his secrets would remain exactly that: secrets.

As he reached the middle of the rock island, Gershom spotted a short, elderly man with wrinkles that stretched across his dark skin sitting on a stone slab once used for sacrifices. The bald old man with a slight hunch in his back, stroked his well-manicured white beard, waiting for Gershom to sit down next to him.

His bony fingers reached across his chest and touched his left shoulder. "My Lord," his wheezy voice hissed from his dry lips.

"Memucan." Gershom returned the magician's greeting, observing the armored crew the old man had brought with him. "Why so many guards?"

"One can never be too careful, my lord." Memucan rubbed his weathered eyes, which had faded to a light blue color due to slight blindness, in angst. "Why have you summoned me?"

The Second in Command made sure no one would be able to hear their conversation. Being satisfied their guards were at a decent distance, Gershom turned his focus back to his companion. "What do you know of the old tales and prophecies?"

"Which tales and prophecies are you referring to?"

"Tell me what you know of the Hunters." Since Gershom now only had one ear, he had to situate himself properly, so he could hear what Memucan had to say.

"What we all know. There is only one marked as the Hunter and he is charged with avenging the blood of the innocent. Of course, there has not been one for over two hundred years." The magician stared at the earless warrior. "Most Adalorians no longer believe in such tales. Why do you?"

"He is coming for me." Gershom had never been surer of anything in his entire life. "The stars have spoken, and his time has come."

"Even if that were true, why would such a warrior come for you?" The sorcerer, who was rarely interested in anyone's tale, was now intrigued.

"When I was a child, I wandered away from my house and found myself lost in the woods of the Black Forest. I crossed paths with a fortune teller, and she told me of my fate."

"And what did she tell you?"

His chestnut brown eyes were filled with fear, "She told me that if I allowed myself to be seduced by the Mistress of the Night, I would betray my closest friend and the penalty for my sins would be the Hunter's blade buried deep in my heart." He rubbed his calloused hands together, staring toward the sun rising above the horizon. "According to the stars, he has come of age, and unless I find him first, my life is forfeit."

Memucan rubbed his chin, "Was that all she told you?"

"That was all she said, then she sent me on my way."

After a moment of silence, the wrinkled old man squinted his fading eyes. "What would you have me do?"

"I need to find him," Gershom hesitated, unsure how the next portion of his request would go over with Memucan. "And I need to find two of Issachar's children."

"You mean to tell me you let two of his heirs escape you?" he wheezed. "They could be anywhere in Adalore! They will not be easy to find."

"I recall helping you track down the elusive thief that stole your illegal book of dark magic." Gershom had no problem in reminding him of the favor he owed him. "I am now asking you to help me find those who threaten me."

Memucan realized the position he was now in and had no other choice but to agree to Gershom's terms. "I will see what I can do." He rose from his seated position and used his short wooden cane to help him limp back to his side of the island to board his awaiting ship. "Whatever happened to the thief?"

"He still rots in my dungeons." The fur wearing warrior stood up and flashed a sinister grin. "You know, I had nearly forgotten he even existed."

Memucan smirked, crossed his feeble arm across his sagging chest and hobbled away. Gershom knew he could count on the old man and although he had many enemies, foreign and domestic, he was determined to prove the fortune teller a liar.

CHAPTER TWENTY-FIVE

NEEMPO

On an island in Narrow Bay, between the Southern and
Western Lands, stood two tall towers connected by an enclosed two-
story bridge near the top of the dark stoned structures. Simply known
as 'The Sisters', the self-sufficient fortress was home to citizens from
every corner of Adalore, making it the only city to welcome diversity.
However, there was a reason for the mixing of the races; every single
inhabitant was born blind and sent in their infancy to live out their
days amongst their own kind.

Adalorians born without sight had one of two gifts and were
separated according to their gift and sent to their respective towers
upon arrival. Witnesses were responsible for recording events,
prophecies, and visions. Their recordings were stored in the largest
library of the known world. Keepers were warriors who, although
blind, used their heightened senses to fight those who would attempt
to steal documents or treasures from the Blind Order. As a people,
they avoided picking sides in the wars of Adalorian kings and
remained neutral in order to keep accurate accounts of history. Both
sects were faithful to their studies and disciplined in their everyday
lives, so when it came to their city's defenses, they were superior to all
who opposed them.

Oden, formally known as Lord Maon, had just arrived at the remote monastery, and was escorted through the gothic hallways by four Keepers to meet with the Sovereign in his study. In order to be the Sovereign of The Sisters, one had to be equally gifted as a Witness and a Keeper, which was rare. In fact, it was only when one Sovereign died that the next would be revealed.

The present leader of the Blind Order was fifteen when he was appointed the youngest Sovereign in the order's history, and he had now been in power for twenty-five years. Neempo was tall and slender with straight black hair and his alabaster skin was spotted with freckles across the bridge of his thin nose. Like most of the citizens of The Sisters, his narrow almond eyes were glossed over, but he tied a red cloth around his eyes to set him apart as the leader of the blind.

Oden cheerfully greeted his old friend, who he had not seen in nearly a decade. "Time has been good to you, my friend, you don't look like you've aged a day."

"And you carry heavier burdens than you did before." Neempo's swift and graceful movements through the circular room located in the middle of the two-story bridge showed his lack of eyesight did not hinder him in any way. "What do I owe the pleasure of your visit?"

The Sovereign sat in a low back wooden chair and Oden sat in an identical chair across from him.

"Whispers from my little birds have led me to believe there is a storm coming for the North."

Neempo smiled, "You speak of Issachar's children."

"So, it *is* true. They did escape." The reports Oden had received were now confirmed.

"Prince Lykos's last selfless act was to see his siblings survive." Neempo weaved his fingers together as his smooth voice shared what information he knew. "But that is not why you have come to see me."

Oden never could disguise his true motives for journeying to The Sisters. "Rumor has it that the Year of the Hunter has begun. It seems Gershom is afraid of this news and has dispatched some of the Queen's Shadows to find the Hunter before he can pose him any threat."

"And afraid he should be."

Oden's eyes danced with delight, "Where can I find him?"

The Sovereign shook his head, "I am sorry, but I cannot answer that."

"Neempo, please! I must find him before Gershom does," Oden pleaded. "I need your help."

Neempo poured two cups of tea. "The Sisters does not concern itself with the trivial pursuit of Adalorian crowns. We solely exist to keep honest records and maintain order in our own city. You know this."

"Would you sit idly by once again to the suffering of the innocent?"

Although insulted, Neempo did not allow his voice to show any resentment. "What happened in the North twelve years ago was not due to our neutrality. Issachar was given report by his Seer, and he chose not to heed this warning, ultimately paying a heavy price."

Oden accepted the cup Neempo extended to him. "You do not understand -"

"I know how much you loved Bilhah, and I realize this is more personal for you than for most, but my people will not involve themselves with this matter." He could sense Oden's heavy heart just by listening to him breathe. "Issachar's children are the key. Find them and they will lead you to the Hunter."

"I don't know where to even begin to look for them." Oden rubbed his bloodshot eyes. "No one does."

"Perhaps looking *for* them would not be wise. But thinking of where they might be headed..." Neempo smiled, knowing that clue would be enough for his companion to figure out.

Oden rose with a newfound determination. "Thank you, Neempo."

"Go," Neempo embraced Oden as he bid him farewell. "They will need your help sooner than you realize."

"I will find them." Oden patted him on the back.

"And perhaps," Neempo chuckled, "don't wait another ten years before visiting with me again."

"Take care, my friend."

Once the door closed, Penn and Balor, masters of the two sects of The Sisters, entered from the adjoining room, having heard the entire conversation.

"You trust him?" Originally from the Andrago, Penn was the first female Master of Keepers and in keeping with the ancient custom, wore a black wrap around her eyes as their counselor. Her snub nose and full lips were prominent when the wrap was tied around her bronze face. Although, she had not spent much time in Elisor, she maintained tradition by intricately braiding her long, silky black hair.

"He has a good heart." The Sovereign sat back down in his chair to finish his tea.

"You did not answer the question," Penn pressed, sitting down.

"And he does not need to. He is the Sovereign." Balor's black skin was an instant indicator he was from the southern city of Numbio. Well into his sixties, his short white hair and manicured beard matched the white eye wrap he wore as Master of Witnesses. Sporting a wooden cane due to an injured hip, he limped toward the younger leaders.

"I beg forgiveness," Penn recanted. "I meant no offense."

"There is nothing to forgive, Master Penn," Neempo spoke softly as the masters sat with him.

"Will he find Issachar's children?" she persisted.

"When he is meant to." The Sovereign poured tea for them. "Why not speak on what troubles you?"

"War is inevitable," Penn spoke freely. "We will be forced to choose a side."

"We have never involved our people in Adalorian wars," Balor protested, stirring honey in his cup. "If they are bent on destroying one another, we should not take part."

"I have endured many sleepless nights as of late, Master Balor, due to disturbing visions," Penn was unmoved and did not accept tea. "Sovereign, we *will* be forced into this war." She felt his breathing pattern slow. "You have already foreseen this?"

"I have." Neempo admitted.

"So, war is coming for us." She leaned forward.

"We are a peaceful kingdom, neutral on these matters," Balor once again voiced his disapproval. "How else would the records of the Ten Kingdoms be accurate and impartial?"

"What good are your records if our halls are desecrated?" she argued.

Balor scoffed, "Our people are not trained for battle."

"Your Witnesses may not be," her nostrils flared, "but my Keepers certainly are."

"A haughty assumption from a soldier who has never engaged in true battle," Balor scratched his upturned eyebrows. "The blind fighting those with sight is ridiculous."

"Sight can be deceiving, Master Balor," she shot.

"Say we do send the Keepers to war," Balor sipped his tea, "what happens if you should fail?"

"We won't," Penn furrowed her brow.

"But if you do," he pressed.

"Failure is not a word I even comprehend," she pounded on her chest twice. "We were bred for this."

"Forgive me," Balor shook his head, "but I remain unconvinced."

"Do I question your Witnesses on the accuracy of their accounts? No. That is their purpose, their gift." Penn rested her hand on Balor's. "When war knocks on our door, for Death will come, we shall be ready to face her, sword in hand."

"Master Penn, Master Balor," Neempo set his teacup down on the end table. "Our neutrality has kept our people safe for hundreds of years, but I am afraid that is no longer an option." He sighed heavily, knowing their way of life was about to change. "Though the Shadow of Death comes, we will find our strength. Let it be so."

Both masters echoed, "Let it be so."

CHAPTER TWENTY-SIX

SALOME

Salome spent most of the night staring up at the wooden ceiling, waiting for the sun to rise, so she could explore the Hollow. She quietly rolled out of her bed, grabbed her hunting knife, bow and arrows and slipped out of the cozy hovel before anyone noticed she was gone.

The Hollow had an ancient feel to it, as if the trees themselves whispered tales of the past. Mesmerized by the beauty around her, she abandoned the idea of hunting and decided to enjoy a lonely morning walk to clear her head. She inhaled the sweet air that whipped around her and pulled her long wavy curls back into a messy ponytail. This place was intoxicating, unlike any place she had ever been before. She closed her eyes and listened to all the sounds of the forest. Birds chirping, squirrels rustling around, the sound of a twig snapping.

Her eyes opened as she realized she was not alone. She turned to face him. The hooded man was armed with a long sword and walked toward her, noticing she was not armed with a blade.

"Who are you?" Salome stood her ground.

Adonijah held his sword up. "I thought it would take days to find you, but it seems fortune is on my side."

"Find me?" She was confused. "Why would you be looking for me? You must have me mistaken for someone else."

"If you come quietly, I will not harm you."

"It would be best for you to be on your way, stranger," she insisted. Although she had not unsheathed her knife and her bow was strapped to her back, it appeared to him that she had no means to protect herself, so he took a step forward. "Take one more step and I will slit your throat," she drew her knife from the holster attached to her upper thigh, forcing him to stop his advancement.

"Only if you are able to beat me."

"Take another step and find out."

"You are feistier than I expected," he smirked.

"Who are you?" She pointed her dagger in his direction. "What do you want with me?"

He sighed. "As much as I would like to explain everything in detail, love, I am on a deadline."

She started to circle, mimicking his movements. "Do you not understand how to answer questions?"

"I grow impatient, girl."

"As do I," she growled back. "Walk away and I will forget this ever happened."

"I am afraid I cannot do that." He pointed his sword toward her. "Hand over your weapon."

"The only way you will get my weapon is by prying it from my dead fingers," she spat at the ground by his feet.

He shrugged. "Have it your way."

He lunged toward her, but she deflected his attack with her knife. Swiftness was her greatest strength, having practiced with her much larger brother for years. Salome continued to spar with him, ducking and dodging his heavy blows. He left himself open to attack when he lunged too far, and she took advantage. She punched him in the face, hoping to knock him off balance. Enraged by her quickness, he swung his weapon toward her face and while she was distracted, he unsheathed his dagger and swiped at her torso. Retracting his dagger, he landed a powerful blow to her face, forcing her to the ground.

He stood over her as she wiped the blood around her mouth. "Are we finished?"

"Is that the best you can do?" Her dismissive tone signaled round two.

She rolled away from him and jumped to her feet. They sparred once again, evenly matched. Being blessed with the swift ability to read her opponent's pattern, she waited for the precise moment he would lunge forward to slash his chest. As predicted, he launched himself toward her. She cut him across his broad chest and kicked him off his feet. As he fell, Adonijah dropped his sword. She picked it up and knelt on his torso.

With a dagger against his neck she hissed, "Do you yield? Or shall I kick your ass again?"

Adonijah's hood now revealed the bottom half of his face so she could see his mischievous smile. "Not bad... for a woman."

"Stand up," she ordered, careful to keep a weapon pointed at him.

He stood as he was instructed, keeping his hands where she could see them. "Is this when you kick my ass again?"

Salome threw his sword back and he caught it with great confusion. "I never kill unarmed men."

This time he was unwilling to leave their duel up to chance. As they danced around one another, he kicked out his leg and tripped her. The fall surprised her, and she dropped her dagger out of her immediate reach. Adonijah bent down to grab her, but she scooped up a rock and smacked him against the side of his face, knocking him unconscious.

She took a moment to catch her breath. She looked at her attacker and saw his hood had fallen over his head. Adonijah had dark brown hair that fell just above his shoulders. His close-trimmed beard brought attention to his square jawline. She noticed with his eyes closed, he looked almost kind, but she knew better after sparring with him. The hooded man was a skilled aggressor, but she still had no idea why he assaulted her.

Looking through his pockets, she came across two pieces of paper and upon further inspection saw they were wanted posters with her and Crispin's faces sketched for all to see. Without delay, she picked up her weapons and raced back to Harbona's house to warn the others of the Shadows' warrant.

It had been an uneventful morning in Harbona's hovel as the three men lounged in the main room having just finished their breakfast. Crispin was obsessive about his weapons and as was his routine, he began to clean every item he possessed. He knew a soldier was only as good as the weapons he wielded, and he was determined to be at his best at a moment's notice.

Zophar and Harbona sat at the small table smoking their long pipes quietly. The older men were not known to be conversationalists but chose their words cautiously and wisely picked which battles they would fight.

Knowing Salome's routine, Zophar was not at all surprised by her absence when they woke up that morning. She desired time alone most mornings and he knew she would be able to defend herself, if needed.

Salome burst through the wooden door and slammed it behind her holding her bleeding torso. Crispin looked up at his sweaty sister and saw blood trickling down her mouth and jumped up to tend to her wounds.

"What the hell happened to you?" Crispin helped her to a chair.

She threw the wanted posters on the table in front of them. "This. This is what happened to me."

Zophar picked up the papers and saw Crispin and Salome's faces. "Where did you get this?"

"Off the bounty hunter who tried to kill me." She coughed up more blood as Crispin cleaned her stomach wound.

"He did this to you?" Crispin was enraged.

"I am fine."

"Where is he?"

"I handled it."

"You killed him?" Zophar asked after handing her a cup of water.

"No," she shook her head. "He was unconscious; I couldn't kill him in cold blood."

Crispin was furious she had not killed the bounty hunter. "Then what did you do with him? Could he have followed you back here?"

"By the time he wakes up, we will be long gone from here." She defended her decision.

"We had better leave." Zophar looked panicked that a mercenary was able to find them so easily.

"We cannot go together, Zophar." Salome grabbed his arm before he could leave the table. "Everyone is looking for us. Shadows, bounty hunters, greedy peasants; it is too risky."

"You are not suggesting we split up?" Crispin was dumbfounded at the very thought of them not being together.

"I do not see what other choice we have."

"We have never been apart." He refused to listen. "We have always been safer together, Salome."

"Not anymore. They know what we look like," she lifted the wanted posters. "If we stay together, it will be easier for them to find us. We are no longer safe together. At least, not right now."

Harbona, who had remained silent the entire time finally spoke. "She is right, Crispin. Your paths are going in two different directions."

Crispin's chest puffed out. "Where would I go?"

"You and Zophar shall travel south to Numbio to meet with King Osiris. He and your father were good friends," Harbona instructed the young prince.

"And what of me?" Salome asked.

"You and I will find the one they call the Wanderer. He will be an incredible asset to our cause. But we must do this quickly, for if one mercenary found you, then surely more will follow."

Zophar stood up from the table. "I will ready the horses."

"Wait, are we parting ways now?" Crispin was extremely uncomfortable with how quickly decisions were being made for him and his sister.

Harbona rested his hand on his shoulder. "It is time to fulfill your destiny, Crispin. You must walk without Salome for now. Gather your belongings, you have a long journey ahead of you."

When the horses were ready for the four travelers to part ways, Harbona sealed his tree house door and mounted his grey steed. "We must be on our way, Salome."

She turned toward her brother with tears in her eyes. "Please don't do anything stupid, Crispin."

"I make no promises." He smiled to keep from crying. "Take care of yourself." He kissed her cheek.

"We will see one another again," she promised him, knowing he was thinking the same thing she was.

He pulled his slender sister toward him in one last embrace. Fighting back tears he whispered, "I don't blame you for Korah's death. I was silent because in order to save him, I would have had to condemn you. I will never let anything happen to you, Salome. Even if I forfeit my own life in the process. I love you."

She tightened her grip around his waist. "I love you too." Before she had a chance to break down, she kissed his cheek and mounted her horse.

Crispin stared at Harbona. "Watch over her."

"I promise she will be safe in my charge," the Seer assured his prince.

The burly, red bearded man walked over to his young ward, grabbed her hand, and kissed it. "Remember everything you have been taught."

Salome leaned over and kissed Zophar's cheek. "I will."

A sad smile stretched across his pale face as tears filled his blue eyes. "Now, off with you."

As they rode in separate directions, not knowing when they would see one another again, they held on to the hope that their paths would cross again.

CHAPTER TWENTY-SEVEN

NIABI

With her Nephilim by her side, Niabi gazed intently at the skittish scribe that knelt before her throne. The long train of her gown rested gently upon the white stone steps that led to her high-back chair. "Did you get all of that?"

The scribe skimmed through the message he had just recorded and nodded, semi-confidently. "Yes, my Queen."

"Good." She waved for him to leave her presence. "Now, see to it that message is sent to my servant in Myr."

He jumped to his feet and scurried from the throne room. Once he had vanished around the corner, Niabi rose from her throne and motioned for Anaktu to step forward.

"See to it I am not disturbed."

Knowing her orders would be obeyed, Niabi left her Nephilim to do her bidding and made her way back to her private quarters to rest. As always, anyone who was in the hall as she passed by, would bow or curtsy and return to their tasks. The queen did not acknowledge a soul as she glided through the castle, desiring a moment to herself.

Once she reached her door, she suspected someone was waiting for her. Discreetly sliding her daggers from the long sleeves of her dress, she quietly slipped into her chambers. Eyeing every corner of her room, she finally noticed a man standing on her balcony.

"Enjoying the view, Pash?" She hid her knives.

"It is a beautiful view." He stared intently at the mountainous terrain that bordered the Ignacia Sea. "Of course, every window in the White Keep boasts a magnificent sight."

He seemed uncomfortable, as if he were waiting for the right moment to speak his mind.

"Why are you really here, Pash?" She poured herself a glass of wine. "Surely it is not to speak to me about the mountains."

"I know you did not summon me, but I needed to speak with you." He shifted his weight.

"Pash, please -"

"I ask my Queen for permission to speak," he bravely interrupted.

Reluctantly, since she knew what he was going to say, she permitted him an audience. "You may speak."

"I know your story and I have seen your heart broken more than once. I have cared for you most of my life and I will continue to serve you as you see fit," he hesitated, "but you must know, surely you must know, how much I love you."

She took another sip of her drink and nodded her head as she unclipped her black hair. "You know my past, and you have seen my brokenness, so you must know why I push you away. Why I will always push you away." She felt a heavy burden upon her shoulders as she exhaled. "I do care for you, Pash, but we could never be together the way you want us to be."

He was silent for a moment. "Did I do something to upset you?"

She set her glass down and started to brush her long hair, a nightly ritual. "Everyone I love has been taken from me and I do not wish that to be your fate."

She was genuine when she told him she cared for him. She had not felt this way since Dichali. But he did not need to know that. He could not know it.

Pash came up behind her and wrapped his arms around her waist. "You need not fear for me, Niabi."

She closed her eyes, rubbing his arm tied around her. "Why must you make this difficult for me? It may seem I am being cold, but I am doing what is best for you."

She broke away from him and stripped the armor from her left arm, revealing the blackness. He was one of the only people in the entire city who had seen what she hid beneath her custom-made armor and every time he saw it, he realized the decay, the poison, was spreading.

"It is still spreading." He gently grasped her arm to examine it.

"It will continue to do so until it reaches my heart," she spat flippantly as she set her arm band down in its case.

"You could die."

"Does not everyone?"

"A Healer might know how to stop this."

She flashed a serious glare in his direction knowing what he was about to do. "You will do no such thing, Commander. If I am to leave this earth it will be on my terms. I will not be dependent on any healer."

"So," his eyes met hers, "we are back to commander?"

She cupped her hands around his chiseled jaw and looked deep into his eyes. "Find a good woman and marry her before you have grown too old to enjoy her."

"Do you really believe I would listen to that command?" he squinted.

"It is not a command. It is my gift to you." She stepped away from his embrace. "Live your life before it is too late."

He caught her arm and pulled her back. "If I must live this one life, I choose to live it with you. And if you refuse me, then I will live my one life serving you until you change your mind."

"I told you the ones I care for are taken from me -"

"I do not fear Death," he interrupted her. "I fear living my life without you." He tilted her chin up and stared down into her eyes. "You love me too. I see it when you look at me. You may be my Queen, but you are also my lover -"

"Pash."

"Look me in the eye and tell me you do not love me, and I will never mention it again."

Silence overtook the lovers as they stared deeply in one another's eyes. Niabi breathed in the man she had grown to care deeply for and opened her lips to give him her answer.

"I...I..." Her eyes shifted away from him.

"You cannot say it." He leaned closer to her upturned face with the kindest eyes she had ever beheld.

"No," she whispered softly, "because it is not true."

Pash kissed her and this time she did not push him away.

CHAPTER TWENTY-EIGHT

PASH

After several hours alone with her, Pash returned to his quarters with Niabi still on his mind. How he had fallen for the dangerous queen; how he wished their love did not have to remain a secret. It was in these private moments that he genuinely believed they had a fighting chance of having a lasting relationship. Of course, he knew how dark her heart could be, he was no fool, but he also saw the goodness that everyone overlooked.

The commander glanced around his dimly lit chambers to ensure his safety was intact. Every single time he examined the room he was alone, but this time he could feel someone's presence. He unsheathed his sword.

"You love her, but does she love you the same, I wonder?" The raspy female voice echoed through the dark space.

Weapon in hand, Pash turned in the voice's direction. "Who are you?"

With a flick of her tiny wrist, the Old Witch of Endor lit the space with an orb of fire she conjured, revealing herself. "Neither your friend nor your enemy."

"You speak in riddles of which I have no time for." He was leery of the woman who played with fire.

"Tell me, Commander Pash, how did you manage to find yourself in the Queen's bed?"

"You try my patience."

"Does she not scare you as she scares all those around her?" Vilora circled him.

Angrily stepping up to her, Pash spat, "I will cut out your tongue -"

A smirk spread across her weathered face as she waved her hand, forcing him to stop his advance. "Surely you would not harm an unarmed old woman, Pash."

Unable to move, he was frightened. "Who are you?"

"Very soon, you will be faced with a difficult choice to save the one you love most. Will it be her? Or will it be him?"

"Why do you say such horrible things?"

Vilora stepped forward. "I see you are a good man and I wanted to warn you of what lies ahead."

He tilted his head, still struggling to free himself. "You're wrong."

"The Old Witch of Endor only tells the truth."

Once he realized who she was, he was overcome with fear. He had heard tales of her since he was a young boy and knew he would be fortunate to make it out of their encounter unscathed.

"You need not be afraid of me," she assured him. "Your story does not end here."

"Get out," he gritted his teeth.

"Certainly, Commander," she smiled, "but first I have a question."

"Ask your question, witch."

"Are you prepared to die?"

Before he could answer, she waved her hand once more and disappeared, releasing him from his frozen position.

A knock on his door startled him; a guard entered his quarters. "Commander Pash, your presence is required in Her Majesty's throne room."

"I will be there in a moment."

The guard left. Pash looked around his room once more, realizing this time he was alone.

———

The throne room was dark except for bundles of candles scattered throughout the vast and impressive space. A light breeze blew through Niabi's cascading long black hair. It was extremely late, and every occupant of the castle was fast asleep.

When Pash entered, he noticed the grand wooden doors were not being patrolled by her guards and he became concerned: what was this emergency small council meeting about? Pash also realized his father was nowhere to be found. Apart from Niabi, Tala, and the Nephilim guarding the queen, there was one new face in the room he had seen just moments before.

Her white hair glistened in the candlelight, but that was the only softness the Old Witch of Endor possessed. She could not help but smile at the last arriving member. Pash clearly did not trust Vilora and was very confused as to why she was in attendance and his father was not. He marched up to Niabi and respectfully bowed, bringing his arm across his chest.

"You summoned me, my Queen." He sat in his designated seat.

Niabi gripped the armrests of her white throne, clearly something heavy weighed on her mind. "Now that we are all here, there is a matter of great importance we must discuss."

Pash was now certain Gershom was not informed of the meeting. "Forgive me, my Queen, but why is the witch here and your Second absent?"

Niabi glared at Vilora. "I see you the two of you have met."

"Briefly, my Queen." Vilora could sense her irritation.

"What of Lord Gershom?" Pash pressed the issue. "Is he to be absent while she attends?"

"*She* can be trusted," Niabi snarled. "He cannot."

Her words stung.

"But the witch -"

"Has been more honest with me than my own right hand." The irate queen rose from her throne, silencing him. "If you have a problem with my judgment, Commander Pash, then I will deal with you accordingly."

"I beg your forgiveness," Pash diffused the situation. "My intent was not to offend you, my Queen."

"He is right in not trusting me." Vilora's smooth voice calmed Niabi. "Commander Pash does not yet know me, nor does he understand our history. His entire existence is to protect you."

Niabi's eyes softened.

"He is behaving exactly as he should, my Queen." The witch looked at the soldier who seemed surprised by her defense of him.

"*This* is now my small council." The Green-Eyed Raven moved on to matters she wished to discuss. "Gershom has betrayed my trust and now word has reached my ears that he has been secretly corresponding with Southern Lords. His eyes are on my crown and that will be his undoing."

"Let me confront him about these accusations." Pash knew his father was indeed capable of such treachery, but hoped the whispers were untrue.

"Or warn him of our report," Tala spat, arms folded over his chest.

"What is that supposed to mean?" Pash's eyes narrowed.

"You are his son, his heir. How do we know you will not warn him? How do we even know you aren't conspiring with him?" Tala's long black hair blew loosely in the breeze.

Pash leaned forward, elbow on his knee. "Are you accusing me of treason, Lord Tala?"

"Stop it, both of you," Niabi's hiss silenced them. "I want eyes on him at all times. Every move he makes, I want to know about it. Every conversation he has, I want to know about it. Every time he eats, sleeps or shits, I want to know about it!" She slammed her fist on her armrest. "He will not be the only one to rot in my dungeons, but all who aided and entertained him as well."

Pash saw something in her he had not seen since she conquered the North. The vicious and strategic young Niabi had awakened after years of dormancy. Most would say motherhood had changed her for the better, but with her light snuffed out, her darkness once again thrived.

"Gershom is no fool." Pash rubbed his temples. "He will notice a tail."

"He will not be followed by a stranger, Pash." Her tone sent shivers down his spine. "You will be spending far more time with your father."

"Me?" He was shocked by her plan. "You want *me* to spy on my own father?"

"Will that be a problem for you, Commander?" Tala had not taken his eyes off him the entire meeting. "Our Queen has ordered you to report on a Lord accused of treason. If you disagree, say so now."

He had never been put in a position like this before. Gazing up at his queen, he saw by the expression on her face that she agreed with Tala on the issue. Pash was a soldier who had sworn an oath not only to protect the crown, but to do his queen's bidding. His entire life he always followed orders, but now being the queen's lover and being the son and heir to her now suspected rival, he found himself torn. Thinking, but for a moment on how he would respond, he made his decision.

"I swore an oath to protect the crown and that is exactly what I will do."

"We will see," Tala hissed under his breath. "We will see."

CHAPTER TWENTY-NINE

SALOME

"How's my best girl?"

"Lykos!" A five-year-old Salome rushed to him with a smile.

Tightening his grasp around her, he planted a kiss on her cheek. "What are you doing out here?"

"Thinking."

"Thinking about what?" They sat together on a bench in the royal gardens.

"Things."

He had the warmest smile, the kindest brown eyes. "Must be important things."

Her smile faded. "Mother said you're going away."

"I will be back before you know it." He nudged her with his elbow.

"You promise?"

"I promise." He pulled his dark hair back in a traditional Northern bun and took off his pinky ring. "Here."

"But that's yours." She shook her head, refusing to accept it.

"While I am gone, you will need to keep it safe for me." He curled her small fist around the ring. "Can you do that for me?"

She stared down at the silver ring he had entrusted to her care and memorized every detail she could about the intricate piece. That particular *ring had been given to Lykos by their mother after his first hunt. Etched on the inside of the band was the Myridian sigil of an octopus with the words, 'As Deep as the Sea'.*

After a moment to think on his request, she smiled. "I will keep it safe."

"Remember," he lifted her to sit on his lap. "As long as you have this ring, I will always come back to you."

Salome's vision vanished and she was left staring at the dirt path she rode down. She glanced at the ring on her index finger. *Am I going mad?*

"Do you think of Lykos often?" Harbona asked, bringing her back to reality.

"How... How did you know I was...? I was thinking about him?" she stammered.

"I was there the day your mother gave him that ring." He smiled at the ring fondly.

She was silent. "Did you know him well?"

He nodded; eyes now fixed on the road. "He was one of my closest friends."

"I wish I had had more time with him."

"He loved you, Salome." His words bore right through her soul. "I hope you know that."

They were silent for a few minutes before Salome asked, in a hushed tone:

"You said he knew about me?

"Yes." He nodded.

She hesitated, taking a deep breath. "Did he know about my sister?"

"He knew about her, too," he cleared his throat. "But what you actually want to know is: did he know he would die the night he saved you?"

Her weight shifted while riding her horse. "Did... did he know?"

"He knew a few weeks before your sister invaded that Death would come for him."

173

"Why did he not leave with us?" her voice cracked. "He had a chance to live, why didn't he take it?"

"Had he tried to escape with you and your brother that night, it would not have made a difference. Death had called him; nothing could change that."

"Did..." she took another breath to suppress the tears. "Did he suffer... in the end?"

"He went quickly." He returned his gaze to the path ahead but stopped as they came to the bridge that connected The Hollow and the Swamp Lands.

"Is everything alright?" She noticed his hesitation.

"We are not alone," he whispered.

Three men came out of the woods, blocking the path.

"Who are they?"

"Greedy peasants looking for you and your brother," he huffed, trotting toward them. "Let me do the talking, Salome. Perhaps they will not be trouble."

The bounty hunters waited for the riders to get close enough to them before ordering them to halt.

Rozdale, the leader of the group, stepped forward. Shorter than his two companions, the squinty eyed mercenary wiped his dirty mouth, revealing his right hand was missing two fingers. The foul-smelling peasant licked his dry lips. "What was your business in The Hollow?"

"Just passing through," Harbona answered calmly.

"Where are you headed?" Rozdale pestered.

"To my brother's house," the Seer lied.

The dirty gang leader turned his focus on the hooded woman who had remained silent. "And who are you?"

"She is my niece -"

"I asked her, old man," Rozdale cut Harbona off, spitting on the ground. "Now," he drew closer to Salome, "Who are you?"

"I am his niece." She followed Harbona's dishonest lead.

Rozdale squinted his already tiny eyes, not believing a word he heard, but was deciding if he would let them pass. His two associates: Jethro, a tall, gangly man with a fresh black eye, and Morta, a stocky man with a round face who rarely spoke, started to encircle the two riders.

Jethro stood next to Salome and boldly caressed her leg. "I bet you could keep us company." The simple looking man flashed a lustful smile at the first woman he had seen in weeks.

"Do not touch me," she hissed.

Since he was missing a few teeth, Jethro's chuckle was more like a whistle. "Feisty one she is."

"Jethro," Rozdale rebuked. Looking back at Harbona, he stepped out of his way. "You can go."

Salome breathed a sigh of relief as Harbona nodded his head in gratitude. "Thank you." Their horses had barely moved forward, when the three men blocked the path again.

"I said, *you* can go," Rozdale smirked. "She stays with us."

"I am afraid that is not going to happen." Harbona was unmoved by the weapons they now wielded.

Rozdale pointed his sword at him. "I said move along, old man. She belongs to us now."

"Move or be moved," Harbona snarled.

Flashing his decaying smile, Rozdale held up the wanted poster with Salome's picture. "Not without our prize."

Morta and Jethro tried to yank her from her horse, but she expected an attack. She punched Jethro and kicked Morta out of her way. She and Harbona took off over the bridge. The three mercenaries were not about to let their biggest payday get away. They mounted their horses and pursued them. Morta snatched his bow off his back and launched three arrows at the riders.

Salome, who was better with a bow than a sword, shot arrows back at them. Twisting her torso backwards, she released an arrow, piercing Morta in his left arm, just missing his heart. He fell from his horse, but that did not deter the other two bounty hunters from their wild pursuit.

"Harbona, we have to fight them. We will not be able to outrun them much longer."

In agreement, they turned their horses around and charged at them.

The scrappy princess stood on top of her steed, balancing as he stomped along the uneven path. As soon as she was close enough, she jumped from her horse and tackled Rozdale off of his. They both scrambled to their feet; he drew his sword; she unsheathed her dagger. With a loud screech, the leader of the gang rushed toward her, but before he could reach her, she threw her knife, piercing his left thigh. He fell to the ground, squirming in pain. Cautiously, Salome approached her assailant, turned him on his back and retrieved her dagger.

Rozdale eyed his sword which was just out of his reach.

"I wouldn't, if I were you," she warned.

Not one to heed the warnings of a woman, he desperately lunged for his sword, but was stopped short by her knife, which penetrated his already deformed right hand. He screamed as she dug her knee into his spine.

"I warned you." She smashed the blunt end of his sword on the back of his head, knocking him unconscious.

The only one who was left unscathed was Jethro, which Harbona easily handled. Using his staff as a jousting spear, he unseated his enemy from his horse. Terrified, the scrawny man scurried away as fast as he could, hoping they would leave him untouched.

"We must hurry," Harbona insisted. "We do not have far to go."

Salome could barely stomach the smell of the swamp as they dismounted their horses.

"You didn't tell me we needed to take a boat." She stood on the rickety dock, disgusted by the murky water.

"This is no ordinary tavern." Harbona sat in the small rowboat with the weathered and smelly dock master. "Hurry up, we do not have all day."

"What do you mean a tavern?" Her eyes widened. "Are we going to a bar?"

"Bar, tavern, all the same." The Seer shrugged off her concern. "It is there we will find the Wanderer. Now please, get in."

Although Salome knew how to swim, she was leery about the muddy waters, unsure of what may be hiding beneath the stagnant stream. "Perhaps, I should stay here."

"Trust me." He extended his hand.

Reluctantly, she grabbed his arm and sat inside the boat.

The normally quiet dock master began paddling through the swamp. "You said you were looking for the Wanderer?"

Salome glanced up. "You know him?"

"Aye, I know of him." He kept his pace steady. "Dangerous feller, that Wanderer. No one has ever seen his face. It's as if he does not really exist. Like he's a ghost among men."

She scrunched her nose, glanced at Harbona, and whispered, "A ghost among men?"

"You need not be afraid of him." He patted her hand.

"How far is the tavern?" she asked, ready to disembark that small rowboat.

"It's right in front of you." The dockmaster's gruff voice sent shivers up her spine.

"Wait for us." Harbona handed the withering old man a shiny coin. "We will not be long."

The Hidden Tavern was exactly that, hidden. Defying all odds of being considered a solid structure, the bar built on stilts was a popular destination for mercenaries, criminals, and all other undesirables. Walking up the rotting staircase, Salome soaked in her surroundings. She had never heard of this place and was now wondering how Harbona knew about it. As they neared the wooden door, he turned to his young companion and blocked the entrance.

"Make sure to keep your hood on. There are less than honorable men in this tavern who are looking for you and I want to ensure you are safe."

Salome pulled her hood down further, making sure only the bottom half of her face would be visible to suspicious eyes. Once they entered the dark tavern, she glanced around the large room and saw nothing but dirty scoundrels drinking, gambling, and smoking.

"Are you sure about this?" she whispered.

"Why do you doubt me?"

"I do not doubt you. I doubt the Wanderer." She looked around the room. "Is he even here?"

"He is here." He stared at a dimly lit corner. "Do not mention your name; the North has spies everywhere."

She glanced in the direction he was looking and saw a hooded man sitting by himself. Smoke rose from under his cloak from the long pipe he clutched in his fingerless leather riding gloves.

"Would you grab us three drinks?" Before she could object, Harbona started to walk toward the ruffian.

Nearby eyes shifted to catch a look at the old man who dared to approach the deadliest man in the room. The Wanderer sat stoically as he took a sip from his large pint of ale.

"Can I help you?" he asked, unmoved by the unexpected visitor.

"Yes," Harbona lowered his voice, "you can fight for us."

The hooded mercenary set his drink down and smirked. "I guess I can't help you then."

"May I join you?"

"I sit alone, old man."

Harbona sat down anyway.

"You test my patience," he snorted. "Leave me."

"I seek the Wanderer."

"And you have found him, but it doesn't help you."

"Let me introduce myself. I am Harbona -"

"That means nothing to me," the dark figure interrupted the introduction. "You are now wasting my time."

"I do not believe I am wasting your time, Adonijah." He leaned back in his seat with a huff. "And I certainly would not dare waste my time."

The Wanderer was silent. "What did you call me?"

Harbona moved closer to his reluctant host and whispered, "I know who you are, Adonijah, and you were never meant to be a wanderer."

The clearly rattled mercenary pushed into the little bit of light the candle on his table projected, exposing the bottom half of his face. "I chose my path."

"Maybe so," the Seer stared into his shadowed eyes, "but you can redeem yourself by helping us; helping her."

Adonijah looked over at the bar where a hooded woman stood. "And why would I want to help someone I have never met and fight a battle I have no business fighting?"

"On the contrary, you do know her."

Confused, Adonijah once again examined the woman. "I do not know her." He was cautiously confident.

"She is the daughter of Issachar, King of the Northern Lands."

"That is not possible," the young warrior whispered. "The royal family was murdered years ago."

"All but two," Harbona spoke softly. "She and her brother escaped."

"Issachar's *son* still lives?"

"Yes, but I cannot say anymore. It is not safe." The Seer squinted, "It is time for justice; I know that is what you desire most."

"I do not desire justice." Adonijah gulped down his ale. "I desire revenge."

"We need your help, Adonijah."

"I have nothing I can give you."

"It is your destiny."

"You don't need me, old man," the young man scoffed. "I know the old prophecies and I don't bear any mark that would give you victory against the North."

"You are right. You do not bear the sacred mark," Harbona agreed. "But we have the one who does."

Intrigued, Adonijah leaned forward once more. "You have the Hunter?"

"The time has come for the prophecy to be fulfilled and you have a part to play in this war."

"Who is he?"

"Patience, patience, my friend. Revealing their identity would be foolish, especially since the man to your left has been trying to listen to our conversation for some time now." Adonijah turned to look at the eavesdropper, but Harbona grabbed his arm. "We will leave now, and you will get a good look at him. Remember his face because you will see him again."

Adonijah nodded and rose from his seat, casually turning to see the spy as they walked toward Salome. She had just received the drinks she had been instructed to order when he grabbed her arm and escorted her to the exit.

"Time to leave." Adonijah pulled her.

"What is going on?" She stared at Harbona. "I thought you wanted drinks?"

Adonijah set the drinks down on a nearby table where two drunks started drinking them. "No time for questions, we have to leave now."

"Halt!" The spy stood up from his table and walked toward the three fleeing companions.

"Is something wrong?" Harbona turned to face the armed bald man.

"I am placing you under arrest for conspiring against the northern crown by order of Lord Gershom," Ophir declared, eyeing his prize with great delight.

Enraged, Salome pushed past Adonijah and stepped up to Ophir. "May he beg for Death before she takes him," she spat on the ground.

Unsheathing his sword, Ophir gritted his teeth. "Bite your tongue, foolish girl, before I take it from you."

Adonijah stepped forward, shielding Salome. "If you want her, you will have to go through me first."

"With pleasure." Ophir swung his blade at the hooded mercenary with great force. After ducking, Adonijah tackled him to the ground and repeatedly punched him.

Unaware of who started the fight, the drunks in the tavern began fighting one another, tearing the small bar apart. The added raucous caused Adonijah to lose sight of Ophir leaving him vulnerable to attack. Out of nowhere, the older soldier leapt over an overturned table and struck Adonijah across his jaw, sending him flying across the room. Ophir grabbed his sword and stomped toward his younger opponent, determined to slice his throat open. Before he was able to reach him, Salome smashed a wooden stool over his shiny bald head, knocking him unconscious.

The newly banded trio escaped the brawl, jumped into the awaiting boat, and headed back to shore.

As soon as they reached land, the three wanted fugitives paid the dock master and made their way to their horses. The sun was setting; Harbona knew they had to find somewhere to camp for the night, but Shadows and mercenaries were looking everywhere for them, and he had to be sure it was safe to continue traveling.

"Wait here," Harbona instructed. "I will see if anyone is lurking along the roads."

Once Harbona disappeared, Salome looked at her new traveling companion. Adonijah wiped his brow, revealing his face. Her wide-eyed expression caught his attention and they realized they *had* met before.

Simultaneously they cried, "You!"

"You tried to kill me," she snorted, furious at the very sight of him.

"*You* are Issachar's daughter?" His jaw dropped.

"This must be a mistake." She took a step toward him, fingers tickling the handle of her dagger just in case she needed it. "We were looking for the Wanderer."

He took a step forward. "And you found him."

"*You* are the Wanderer?" she rested her hands on her hips, eyebrow raised.

"I am." He seemed amused by her.

She scoffed. "There has clearly been some kind of mistake."

"No mistake." Adonijah leaned up against a tree with a smirk. "You sought me out and found me."

"Why would I agree to travel with you after you tried to kill me?"

"I wasn't going to kill you, love." He rubbed his chin. "I needed you alive to collect the reward money."

She furrowed her brow. "My name is Salome."

"I know what your name is," he hissed.

"Then use it," she fired back.

"Whatever you wish." He shrugged, unbothered.

"And keep your distance, unless you are up for round two." Her blood boiled at the thought of them traveling together.

"Woah, woah. I am on your side now." He raised his hands to the level of his eyes. "I'm not going to turn you in, nor will I harm you."

"I would kill you before you had the chance."

"If you were going to kill me, you would have done it when we first met." Adonijah's crooked smile normally enamored any lady that crossed his path, but she was not falling for his charm.

"I took pity on you," she sneered, stroking her horse's head. "I won't make the same mistake twice."

"Took pity on me?" He snorted. "You cheated me."

"Cheated?" she whipped around with a shriek.

"You hit me with a rock," he reminded her.

"Any skilled fighter knows to use their environment to their advantage. Or did they not teach you that in the Swamp Lands?"

He waved his fingers in the air. "Like a bar stool in a tavern brawl, for instance?"

"You're a quick study, you are," she hissed. "Perhaps you're not as dumb as you appear, Wanderer."

Adonijah extended his hand. "My name is Adonijah."

Salome stared blankly at his hand. "What are you doing?"

"I thought," he stammered, not expecting that reaction. "I thought we could start over since we may have started off poorly."

"May have?" she choked.

"Look," he sighed, "I didn't know who you were when I found you the other day. If I had -"

"You would have done the exact same thing," she interrupted.

"I am trying to make this right."

"You're doing great."

He lit his pipe. "Has anyone ever told you that you are incredibly stubborn?"

"Me? Stubborn?" She placed a hand on her chest, pursing her lips.

"Aye, stubborn," he spat back, mimicking her tone. "Or are you unfamiliar with the word?"

"You think you are far more clever than you actually are."

"All I want is for us to get along." He exhaled in her direction. "Do you think we can do that?"

She swatted the smoke away from her face. "No."

"You can call me Adonijah."

She stared at him until it was awkward.

"Or not," he squinted.

She continued to watch him in silence.

"Hello?" He snapped his fingers in her direction. "Have you finally run out of words to say?"

"I'm thinking." Her eyes narrowed, still staring at him.

"Dare I ask what thoughts are running around that head of yours?"

"I think I should have killed you when I had the chance."

He was unfazed. "If you had, you would've missed out on all the fun."

"I'm still waiting for this to be fun." She crossed her arms over her chest.

"Well, that's a shame." He exhaled another puff of smoke. "I've been enjoying myself."

She scoffed and refocused on her white mare.

"What's her name?" He pointed, sliding down the tree to sit on the ground.

She did not look at him. "Snow."

"Snow?" he muttered disapprovingly. "Why would you name a horse Snow?"

"I haven't seen snow since I left Northwind. I have fond memories of..." Salome furrowed her brow. "Don't."

"Don't what?" Adonijah threw his hands up in the air. "Don't be polite?"

"Don't try to get to know me," she hissed. "Harbona might trust you, but I don't."

"Why didn't you?" He changed the subject abruptly.

"Why didn't I what?" She turned to face him.

"Why didn't you kill me when you had the chance in The Hollow?" his voice softened. "You see, I've mulled over that question since our run in and never thought I'd see you again to get an answer."

"Like I told you before," she eyed him carefully, "I never kill unarmed men."

He wagged his finger with a crooked grin. "I think you're upset because you finally met your equal in both wit and skill."

"You are hardly my equal," she rolled her eyes. "Was one ass beating not enough for you?"

"I already told you." He hopped up and stood in front of her, looking down into her eyes. "You cheated me," he whispered.

Salome was tall, but he still towered over her. She pushed up on her toes and snarled, "I would gladly beat you again."

"Tell me when and where, love."

"My name is -"

"Salome. I know," he remarked flippantly. "How could I forget?"

184

Their faces inches apart, they soaked one another in. For years she had dealt with the unwanted affection and attention of Jacobi, and he was far less irritating than Adonijah.

Why did he bother her so much?

Why was she suddenly uncomfortable being this close to him?

Harbona reappeared. "The path is clear for us to -" His eyes shifted between the two of them. "Is everything alright?"

"Perfect." She broke her gaze to mount her horse.

Shaking his head and muttering under his breath, "Women," he mounted his brown stallion and chased after his new companions.

CHAPTER THIRTY

NIABI

The Green-Eyed Raven stomped through the hallways of the White Keep, focused on one person in particular. With Anaktu closely in tow, Niabi burst through the door that led to Gershom's private quarters. Her unexpected visit stunned the Second in Command, as he was presently entertaining a female companion in his bed.

"My... my Queen?" he stammered, covering himself with sheets.

The young woman, a highly paid prostitute by the look of her expensive clothes, was terrified to see the queen staring at them. "Your Majesty." Her lips quivered as the words left her pouty mouth.

Gershom tried to shove her out of the bed. "Get out."

Niabi lifted her hand in protest. "Stay exactly where you are; my intrusion will be but a moment."

Furthering his discomfort, she sat at the foot of his bed and stared at him intently before she addressed the issue she had come to discuss.

"It has come to my attention that eleven of my Shadows are dead." Every word she spoke was venomous. "Do you have any idea why *my* men were killed in the forests of the Western Lands?"

His gulp was audible. "My Queen, I can explain -"

"Please do," she interrupted with a snarl. "Because the way it appears to me is you abused your power and dispatched my Shadows without my permission. Surely, that is not the case."

Stammering once again, the scruffy soldier pulled himself together. "I assure you, Majesty, I can explain."

"I am listening." She crossed one leg over the other.

"The Shadows I dispatched were searching for your missing siblings and were attacked by rogue fighters," he told a half truth.

"Lies." Her eyes narrowed.

"I swear to you -"

"You dare look me in the eye and continue to lie to me?" she hissed. "You dispatched them before I even knew of their survival, something you were not in the least bit concerned about until I brought it to your attention. I shall give you one last chance to tell me the truth." She unsheathed one of her daggers and laid it on her lap.

Fear blanketed his face, his fingers brushing where his ear used to be. "My astrologer informed me the Year of the Hunter has come and he will come for me, so I sent the Shadows to find him before he could reach the city."

"You are far too superstitious for your own good, Gershom." She shook her head. "No one believes in the Hunters anymore."

"But the astrologer -"

"Believes in what the stars tell him," she laughed. "Only a fool believes in the stars."

"And if the stars are right and he does come?"

"Then let him come," she growled, leaning forward. "I believe in what is in front of me and right now, all that sits before me is a rat."

"My Queen, please -"

"Silence," she whispered through gritted teeth. "If you continue to think yourself mightier than you are, it will cost you your life."

Gershom leaned forward resting his hand over his heart. "I have only faithfully served you -"

"You have served yourself and have become careless in hiding your agenda to usurp me."

"You are mistaken."

Her eyes were cold and vicious. "I would have forgiven your foolish lapses in judgement had your mistakes not cost my son his life."

"Rollo's death was not my fault!" He protested.

"You have gone from friend to foe and as the Almighty is my witness, I shall destroy you with every piece of my broken heart."

She rose from the edge of his bed and glided out of his room.

Gershom was equally afraid and angry by the unexpected visit. He no longer had the appetite for his female companion, and he shooed the hired girl from his sight. All that concerned him now was his own survival.

CHAPTER THIRTY-ONE

ZIGGY

Scurrying out of his quarters, the freckle-faced redhead made her way through the dimly lit underground corridors that led down to the city streets. For the last eight months, Gershom had her sneak in the White Keep so their relationship would remain secret but with the queen now aware of their rendezvous, it was sure to become a problem for both of them.

The second her feet hit the white cobblestone street, she exhaled a huge sigh of relief. Pulling her curls into a messy bun, the petite, fair-skinned escort ensured she was not being followed as she weaved down the alley.

"You're early tonight," a deep voice whispered from a dark corner behind her. "Is something wrong?"

Her blue eyes shifted. "The Queen surprised us."

"Were you hurt?" Nubis stepped into the moonlight revealing his towering muscular frame.

"I'm fine." Ziggy patted his hand reassuringly, exposing the hooked shape scar on top of her left hand. "I need to see him."

The duo slithered through the alleys of Northwind, avoiding all patrols on their way to The Whispering Fox. Once they stood outside the front door, Nubis knocked four times rhythmically. A small rectangular pocket of the wooden door slid open, and a pair of hypnotizing grey eyes stared back at them.

"Nubis?"

"Makada, we must speak to him," he whispered as he looked up and down the abandoned street. The door unlocked and creaked open to allow them entry into the tavern.

"Follow me."

Ziggy and Nubis followed her through the empty bar. Makada had hip long black braids, a curvaceous figure and three hooped nose piercings in her right nostril. Shorter than both of them, the dark-skinned maiden led them down the stairs to Oden's quarters.

"Sit. Wait here," she instructed as she quietly slipped into the adjoining room. A few moments later, the bangle adorned Makada reemerged with Oden following closely behind her.

He sat across from Ziggy and Nubis in his high back chair and asked his spies, "What news do my sparrows bring?"

Ziggy crossed one leg over the other and leaned forward. "The Queen barged into Gershom's chambers unannounced and found us together."

"Were you made?"

"No."

"Good." Oden nodded. "Did they speak of anything of importance?"

"Eleven of Niabi's Shadows were found dead in the Western Lands," Ziggy reported. "At first Gershom claimed he had sent them to find her missing siblings, but then admitted he sent them to find one he called, the Hunter. He did this without her knowledge or permission."

"Did they find him?"

"No, my lord, but the Queen threatened him. She said he was responsible for Prince Rollo's death."

"They are unraveling." Oden looked up and smiled at Makada who stood by his side. "Ziggy, continue to make yourself available to Gershom. Perhaps you will learn more."

"Are you sure that is wise now that the Queen has seen her face?" Nubis protested. "If she is set on destroying Gershom, Ziggy could get hurt."

"A risk we all agreed upon when we joined the Order," Oden brushed him off. "You know your assignments. Nothing changes. Is that understood?"

"Understood." Ziggy and Nubis both nodded their heads.

"Now keep your ears to the ground on the whereabouts of Issachar's children. We need them to lead us to the Hunter before the Shadows find him." Oden rose from his seat. "Be watchful, for the night is long and a storm is coming."

Just like that, their meeting had ended. Ziggy and Nubis saw themselves to the door and stood outside the tavern in silence. The broad-chested Mountain Man stood more than a foot taller than the redhead, making them an odd-looking couple. Normally one could not tell what Nubis was thinking, but when he looked at her, she could see the angst in his face.

"You should not see him again," he broke the long silence.

"Oden is right," she stared into the distance, eyes glossed over. "I knew what I was getting myself into."

"The Queen has seen your face; returning is too risky."

"It has always been a risk being so close to Gershom, but how else would we know what the inner circle is doing?"

"Ziggy, it has gone from being risky to being life threatening. You will be harmed if you do not tread carefully."

She glanced up at him and smiled. "Is that concern I hear?"

"Don't tease me."

"I'm sorry, Nubis." She grabbed his hand and rested her head against his muscular arm. "I promise I will be careful."

"Please don't return to him," he pleaded. "We have already lost so many."

"And if I too am lost, remember me as I am in this moment. To lose my life fighting for the freedom of our own would be an honorable departure." She cupped his face in her petite hands. "If one day you wake up and I am no longer here, know that I lived bravely and died with purpose."

"Ziggy -"

She gently pressed her fingers against his lips and kissed his cheek. "Until we meet again." Before he could protest, she vanished into the darkness of Northwind.

CHAPTER THIRTY-TWO

ZOPHAR

The tiny village of Jannat Sin was a welcome sight. Dozens of tents pitched in the middle of towering sand dunes surrounded the only oasis in Dead Man's Land. Lush palm trees were the only source for shade from the scorching sun.

Crispin and Zophar had traveled through the Sand Lands for days and were in need of rest and supplies. Crispin had done nothing but express his liking for the dry air, endless sand dunes and the sense of adventure, much to Zophar's dismay. Zophar was a man of forests and lakes. The desert did not suit him, and his sunburned skin was proof.

Before parting ways, Harbona told them the people of Jannat Sin were some of the most hospitable in all of Adalore and they would welcome them for three days without asking any questions.

Sheikh Ibrahim was exactly as Harbona had described him. He was a tall man with dark eyes and dark facial hair. His brown skin seemed even darker against his white flowing robes and matching keffiyeh. His smile was warm and his embrace firm, as he ushered the weary duo into his tent where a spread of food awaited them.

"Please, sit," he motioned to the multi-colored cushions scattered on the ground. "Eat, make yourselves comfortable. You must be tired from your journey."

They sat cross-legged on the cushions and ate as the women continued to bring in new dishes for them to try. Lamb, goat, wild berries, bread, dates, and milk. Zophar had not seen this much food displayed at once since he lived in Northwind and although he and Crispin had not eaten food prepared in this manner, they were starving and were excited to put anything in their growling stomachs.

"Thank you for your hospitality." Crispin was so hungry, he swallowed some of his food whole. "I have never seen anything like your village. It's beautiful."

Ibrahim nodded with a smile, "It is paradise."

Zophar cleared his throat, "A friend of ours told us you would allow us to stay the night on our journey to Numbio, if we asked."

"Well, your friend is correct." Ibrahim nabbed a handful of dates and ate them one at a time. "You are welcome to stay as long as you like."

"Thank you," Zophar said, gulping down a mouth full of mutton.

"Is there anything else you will require for your stay?" their host asked, clapping his hands.

"A place to sleep and food to eat is more than generous -"

Crispin's voice trailed off when a woman adorned with bangles on her arms and ankles slowly entered. She wore a sheer black veil to cover the bottom half of her face and a beaded headdress sat upon her long dark hair. Black liner accentuated her dark and exotic eyes. Her robes floated around her as the music began.

Ibrahim grinned, "Entertainment."

The way she danced was hypnotizing. So fluid, so enticing. Even through the veil, they could see the outline of a smile. She locked eyes with Crispin who had not stopped staring at her since she had entered. Zophar nudged him and clicked his tongue.

"Where will we be spending the night?" Zophar asked, doing his best not to ogle like his young companion.

"You wish to retire now?" Ibrahim asked.

"We should get some rest if we are to make it to Numbio by tomorrow," Zophar nodded as he stood and cracked his back. "If that is alright with you, of course."

Ibrahim clapped his hands and the dancer bowed and left. "But of course." He smiled warmly. "Follow me."

As he left the tent, Zophar grabbed Crispin by his sleeve and whispered, "Must you stare like you've never seen a woman before?"

"I've never seen a woman like *her* before," Crispin chuckled, gently elbowing Zophar in the gut. "I love the Sand Lands."

Ibrahim led them to an empty tent, like his, near the water. He pulled back the curtain and motioned them inside.

"There is water inside for you to bathe. Should you need anything else, please, let me know." Ibrahim bowed, "Rest well, my friends."

Zophar and Crispin both bowed, and their generous host released the curtain, enclosing them inside the cozy tent. Crispin was grinning ear to ear. Zophar knew exactly what he was thinking about.

"It would do you well to just forget about her." He shook his head. "Women are not on the agenda."

Crispin sunk into one of the beds and cradled his head in the palms of his hands. "Oh Zophar, how long has it been since you entertained a lady companion?"

Zophar snorted, furrowing his brow. "That is none of your business."

"That long, huh?" Crispin snickered.

It was true. It had been a long time since Zophar had been in the company of a lady. When he was young and still living in the City of Borg, Zophar had a beautiful wife named, Siv. How he loved her. Her red hair, her blue eyes, her freckles, her smile, her warrior spirit, and the two sons she gave him, Bjorn and Ivar. No one, not even

Crispin or Salome knew anything of his life before Northwind, and that is the way he wanted it.

Women in Borg were highly skilled warriors, equal to men in every capacity. Siv died in battle when pirates from Pulau invaded their villages. He gave her a warrior's burial: a fire lit boat sent out to sea. And his sons...

He did not want to think about his family anymore. It was still too painful. But he never took another wife; he never engaged with another woman after Siv's death. She was his best friend and he lost himself when he lost her.

"Zophar?" Crispin brought him back to reality. "Are you alright?"

He forced a smile, wiping the back of his neck with a wet towel. "Just tired is all."

Crispin sat up. "Can I ask you a question?"

Zophar was willing to answer any question Crispin and Salome asked. In fact, he made it a policy once he became their guardian. The only topic that was off limits was his family. He held his breath, hoping that was not what Crispin wanted to know.

"What is your question?" He eyed him in the mirror on the small table in front of him.

"Why was he banished?" Crispin sipped from one of the sheepskins left for them.

Zophar faced him, "Who?"

"I may not know much about the Immortals," Crispin wiped his mouth, "but I know enough to recognize their banishment mark."

Zophar washed his face. "I thought you better than to judge someone before knowing their story."

"So, I should blindly trust him because you do?" Crispin took his sandy shirt off. "He doesn't even have the Immortal glow."

"When he was banished, he lost his aura," he explained.

"What is he then?" Crispin scoffed. "Is he still an Immortal?"

Zophar finished bathing, undeterred by his line of questioning. "Banishment has not stripped him of his identity. Are you any less a northern prince for not living in your ancestral home?"

"One is not banished lightly," the prince fired back. "Why won't you tell me what he did?"

To Crispin's irritation, Zophar dodged answering the question. "It is not my story to tell."

"That is your response?"

"Understand this," Zophar sat down on the pillow-adorned bed, "I would entrust my own life in Harbona's hands. Had I one suspicious thought Salome was in any danger, I never would have parted ways with her."

After a moment of thoughtful silence, Crispin asked, "He said, he knew my father?"

"Aye," he nodded. "He and I served on your father's small council, along with your brother, Lykos, and Lord Maon, his Second in Command."

"Yet none of you knew of Niabi's plan to attack the city," Crispin's words oozed with judgement. "What kind of Seer cannot see a black storm?"

Realizing his tone had turned, Zophar tried to redirect the conversation. "You are clearly under a lot of stress, my young Prince, perhaps sleep -"

"I will have answers *now*," Crispin snorted. "How did a Seer on my father's small council not forewarn of her impending attack?"

"I think you should rest -"

"Tell me what I want to know," he snapped. "Tell me the truth," Crispin stood over Zophar. "Why did he not warn my father?"

"He warned your father," Zophar jumped up from his seated position, "but your father did not listen!" His deep voice frightened Crispin.

Crispin shook his head, bottom lip trembling. "My father would have heeded the warning. He never would have jeopardized my family or our people."

Zophar softened his approach, seeing the confusion in Crispin's eyes. "I begged your father to listen, we all did, but he refused. You were six years old, there is no way you would have understood any of this."

"If what you say is true," he crossed his arms over his chest, "why did my father not listen to Harbona's warnings?"

"Simply put," Zophar rubbed his forehead, "your father underestimated your sister."

"She is *not* my sister," Crispin growled, retreating to his side of the tent.

"Deny her if you like," Zophar shrugged and lit his pipe. "That does not change what is true."

"Then what of Gershom? Surely, he would have known about him."

Zophar exhaled, silent for a moment, reflecting on memories he wished he could forget. But it was time Crispin knew the truth. All of it.

"As I have told you before, Gershom was once the commander of your father's army. He refused to obey one of your father's orders, so your father sentenced him to be executed. There were many soldiers loyal to Gershom, so the night before he was supposed to die, his men freed him from your father's dungeons, and they escaped to the Black Forest."

"So, he waited until he had enough men to attack my father." He paced back and forth, chewing on a date.

"Truth be told," Zophar kicked his feet up on the bed and exhaled a puff of smoke, "Niabi is your father's first born and according to the laws of your ancestors, rightful heir to the White Throne. She has the true claim in Northwind."

"But Gershom -"

"Was a soldier fighting in *her* war."

Crispin was quiet. He closed his eyes deep in thought. "Why didn't he just listen?"

Zophar squirmed, unsure of what to say to ease Crispin. "Your father did not believe she was capable of an attack of that magnitude. Northwind's walls had never been breached. He did what he thought was best."

Crispin started to gather his belongings. "We should press forward."

Zophar clicked his tongue. "I know you want to see King Osiris, but we need to rest. We must regain our strength, or we will never make it."

"We have important matters to tend to." Crispin's stubbornness was in full swing.

Zophar grabbed Crispin's forearm as he passed by, "Important matters that have waited twelve years, one more day will not hurt. Besides, we would not want to insult our host by leaving in the dead of night. We will leave in the morning."

The royal was reluctant to listen, but knew the Westerner was right. "Fine," he snorted, "we will wait until morning."

"Perhaps you should think about that dancer." Zophar exhaled.

"Oh?" Crispin laid on his bed and stared at the ceiling of the tent. "And why's that?"

"Far better dreams with her on your mind."

Crispin half-smiled. "Maybe so."

CHAPTER THIRTY-THREE

SALOME

With his back against a tree, Harbona pressed his lips to his favorite wooden pipe. He inhaled deeply and exhaled a generous puff of smoke toward the small fire Adonijah had started in the middle of their camp.

"Well, that was quite an exit yesterday," the Seer grinned.

Perched in a tree, Salome looked down at Adonijah who sat stoking the flames of their fire. "You're welcome, by the way."

His identity no longer a mystery, Adonijah looked up at the icy princess. "Are you talking to me?"

"A simple thank you will suffice."

"Thank you?" he chuckled. "Thank you for what?"

"What do you find so amusing?" She jumped down from her lounged position and stood over the crouching mercenary.

"You." He did not flinch when her feet hit the ground next to him. "If you are referring to the fight at the tavern, I was fine on my own."

His attitude made her blood boil. "Not from where I was standing."

Adonijah stood up slowly, maintaining eye contact with her. "You expect me to thank you for grabbing a chair?"

Not to be outdone by his sharp tongue, Salome stepped toward the tall, muscular swordsman. "That chair not only gave us time to escape, but also spared your pretty face from being disfigured by your superior opponent."

He clicked his tongue. "I am more than just a pretty face, love," he smirked at his own cheekiness.

"Let me know what that is when you figure it out," she tilted her head, squinting her eyes.

"You have a sharp tongue; I will grant you that." Adonijah lit his pipe and exhaled. "I would have been fine in the tavern without you. I always am."

"Forgive me," she half-heartedly curtsied, "next time, I will just watch you get your ass kicked."

"Please do," he shot back, "you might learn something." Adonijah laughed with each step he took toward her. "I don't even know why you, a woman, would be here in the first place. You're a liability."

"I have more of a right to be here than you do." Enraged, she squared her shoulders to his. "It was my family who was murdered, not yours."

"I may end up losing my life to save you," he leaned over her, "I need to know you are capable of handling yourself. Perhaps you do not know, but there are no chairs for you to use on the battlefield."

Circling around him, she studied him as if he were prey, ready to strike. "Don't flatter yourself, Adonijah. It is you who should be worried about the battlefield. After all, I not only saved you in the tavern, but I bested you in The Hollow as well when you came to collect my bounty. You tell me who is the better swordsman."

"If you are so sure of yourself then what do you need me for?" He stood as still as a statue while she circled him.

"All I need is for you to do what Harbona has recruited you to do and stay out of my way." Salome grabbed his shirt and leaned into his face. "You are a means to an end, nothing more." She released him and pushed past him, stomping into the Swamp Lands to calm down.

He watched as she walked away and once she was out of his sight, he glanced over at the quiet Seer. "Is she always this stubborn?"

Harbona, who had not been deterred from smoking during their heated encounter, finally looked up and said, "Oh, yes."

"Great," he shook his head, "women."

Furious, Salome marched through the Swamp Lands, hoping the walk would calm her nerves. "Who does he think he is?" she mumbled to herself. "He probably won't make it to any battlefield, I might kill him."

The sudden sound of a twig snapping caused her to whip around to see who was following her, but no one was there. This was the type of game Crispin would play when she walked in the woods of the Tree House Forest, but she knew it could not possibly be him. With an eerie feeling she was not alone sending chills up her spine, she reached for the dagger she kept sheathed to her thigh but realized she had left it at their campsite. She knelt to retrieve a small knife she hid in her right boot, when she was struck from behind and knocked unconscious.

After some time, Salome started to regain consciousness and realized she was tied to a large tree. Her three captors were the same men she and Harbona had scuffled with. They were huddled around a slowly dying campfire and appeared to be tending to their wounds from their first encounter. Morta turned to check on their prisoner, prompting Salome to close her eyes, pretending to still be unconscious.

"When is she going to wake up?" Morta grew impatient.

"Well, if you hadn't knocked her out, we wouldn't have this problem," Jethro chimed in, spitting on the ground.

"Oh, so now this is my fault?"

"All I'm saying, Morta, is there was no need to hit her that hard."

"Now let me tell you something, Jethro -"

"Jethro, Morta, would you two shut up!" Rozdale huffed. "She'll be awake soon enough and then we'll hand her over to Ophir."

Morta clenched his teeth, "And that's another thing. Why is Ophir not working with us? He should do his own dirty work."

"Watch your tongue," Rozdale hissed, hands over the fire. "Ophir is our master, and we shall do his bidding."

"What if she wakes up before he arrives?" Jethro picked at his few remaining teeth with his knife.

"Then we question her about the whereabouts of her companions," Rozdale spat on the ground.

"And if she doesn't answer our questions?" Morta furrowed his brow.

Rozdale unsheathed his dagger with a smirk. "She'll answer one way or another."

Jethro's stomach began to growl loud enough for his companions to hear. "I'm hungry. When are we going to eat? We haven't eaten all day."

Grabbing his axe, Rozdale rose to his feet. "Fire is about to go out. I'll chop some more wood."

As he left, Morta reached for his bow and arrows. "I'll get you something to eat; anything to stop your whining."

"What should I do?" Jethro never liked being left alone.

"Watch the girl." He disappeared.

Salome slowly opened her eyes to assess the situation and saw only Jethro remained, and he foolishly had his back to her. Keeping a watchful eye on the sulking bounty hunter, she sliced through her binds with the small knife she wiggled out of her boot. Conflicted as to whether to kill her captor or just sneak away, she carelessly stepped on a twig alerting Jethro of her impending escape.

"Oi!" he shouted as she sprinted. "Rozdale, Morta! She's getting away!"

Light on her feet, she easily kept a safe distance between them as she weaved in and out of the trees. As she ran downhill, she avoided the bogs and ducked behind a bald cypress. She looked around and saw a fallen tree limb and bent down to grab it. Once he ran up to her hiding place, she swung the branch with all her might, knocking him backwards.

Jethro scurried to his feet with his sword drawn, only to see Salome running toward him with a knife. He swung his weapon, but he was not fast enough. She easily dodged the incoming blow and swept him off his feet with a low kick. Jethro backhanded her to buy himself some time. She lunged for her dagger, which flew out of her hand when he slapped her, but he tackled her to the ground before she could reach it. Sitting on top of her with his sword to her throat, he believed he had neutralized her.

"You have caused me more trouble than you're worth," Jethro gnashed his teeth as blood oozed down the side of his dirty mouth. "You'll regret trying to escape once Rozdale gets ahold of you."

She managed to stretch for her dagger without him noticing and with a swift motion, plunged her knife into his neck, killing him.

Knowing it was only a matter of time before the other two goons found her, she pushed Jethro off her, grabbed his sword and placed her dagger back in her right boot.

"There she is!" Morta caught sight of her.

"Get her." Rozdale charged toward her, weapon drawn.

Frustrated she had been found so quickly, she started running through the wooded swamplands hoping to escape them once and for all.

Morta launched arrow after arrow at her and she managed to dodge several of them, but one of his arrows landed near her foot and tripped her. Closing in on her, she flipped to her back and began to crawl away from them. The sword she had swiped from Jethro was now beyond her reach, and her two captors had caught up with her. She glanced at the sword and hoped she might be able to snatch it in time.

"Ah, ah, ah," Rozdale clicked his tongue with a triumphant grin. "I wouldn't try that if I were you."

"She killed Jethro," Morta growled.

"And she will pay dearly for it. You should not have tried to escape. Especially after we took such good care of you."

"Took care of me?" she hissed, unafraid of the blade she now faced. "A horse could have taken better care of me than you three idiots."

"Get up," Morta ordered.

"No."

"I said, get up!" Morta viciously pulled her to her feet, shoved her toward Rozdale, and they led her back to their camp.

Knowing she still had her knife hidden in her boot, her mind raced to formulate a plan to escape when Adonijah stepped out in front of them with his sword drawn.

"Who goes there?" Rozdale addressed the man who blocked their path.

"Release her and I will not harm you." Hooded, Adonijah's tone was chilling.

Rozdale laughed the deepest laugh a man could laugh and directed Morta to, "Kill him."

"With pleasure."

Morta stepped up to the mercenary and the two swordsmen began to duel. Rozdale firmly restrained Salome and held a knife to her throat, just in case, anything happened to his last remaining companion. The two men sparred quickly and ferociously, both knowing the one to fall had much to lose. In the end, Morta was no match for Adonijah, who was far superior with a blade, and was stabbed through the chest.

Turning his focus to the lone bounty hunter, Adonijah issued one last warning. "Release her and I will let you live."

Rozdale swiftly sliced Salome's upper right arm, hoping to show his enemy how serious he was. "Drop your sword or I'll kill her." His voice trembled even though he clearly had the upper hand.

"Don't listen to him!" Salome ordered as blood trickled down her arm.

"Don't test me." Rozdale shoved the knife deeper against her neck, drawing blood. "Drop your sword or I'll kill her."

"Don't do it!" Her eyes were filled with a rage that surprised Adonijah.

Unwilling to risk her life further, he dropped his sword. "I've done as you asked. Now let her go."

Rozdale cackled, "Did you really think I would let her go?"

Never without a knife clipped to the back of his pants, Adonijah slowly moved into a position to throw it. "I thought you would be a man of your word."

"I am collecting the bounty on her head and if you try to stop me, I'll run you through."

"Suit yourself."

Adonijah launched his knife at the unsuspecting goon, and it sliced into Rozdale's forehead. Rozdale fell to the ground dragging Salome down with him.

Adonijah rushed over and knelt next to her, wiping the blood from her cheeks. "Are you alright?"

"I'm fine," she breathed heavily.

Focused on the deep cut across her right arm, he began to examine the damage. "It could be worse."

Not liking the attention, she shrugged off his concern. "It's just a scratch."

He applied pressure to her arm.

"Ah!" She winced and pushed him away. "Why would you grab my arm?"

"Only a scratch?" He tried to wipe the dirt and blood from her face, but she slapped his hand away. Once again, he turned his attention to her arm. "Let me take a look at that cut."

"I said, I am fine," she insisted, twisting her shoulder away from him.

He squinted his eyes at her. "That is a deep gash and if it's not cleaned, it could get infected."

"I can take care of it," she once again refused his help.

"Salome" he said softly, "let me help you."

"I said not to worry about it."

"I think you might be the most stubborn woman I have ever met," he rubbed the back of his neck. "Just let me help you."

"No."

"I promise I will be careful."

They stared at one another silently, for the first time truly taking one another in. His dark eyes, which she once found menacing, were actually quite warm and kind. He too, found himself in a daze, soaking her in until he noticed she released her arm and allowed him to clean her wounds.

"Who were they?" he asked, eyes focused on her arm.

"Bounty hunters Harbona and I had a run in with earlier." She grimaced as he fiddled with her wound. "They were waiting for a man named Ophir."

"Ophir?" Adonijah stopped what he was doing and stared at her.

"Do you know him?"

"I have heard the name before, but I haven't met him," Adonijah refocused on her arm. "From my understanding, he is one of the founding Shadows."

"That is who they were going to hand me over to; they called him their master."

"We should be heading back to camp before he arrives and finds you here." He wrapped her arm with a piece of fabric he had torn from the edge of his cape.

"Thank you."

He was surprised by her gratitude. "You're welcome."

They walked back to their camp site, exhausted and hungry.

After a moment of silence, he looked down at her and smiled, "I won't hold rescuing you over your head." He tried to lighten the mood with his version of a joke, which surprisingly, rendered a smile from his stubborn companion.

"I am sure you won't."

The weary duo finally laid their eyes on Harbona's friendly face. The Seer leapt to his feet and welcomed them back to camp. "Are you hurt?" His eyes examined her blood-stained clothes.

"Just some cuts and bruises." She smiled at him as he exhaled a sigh of relief.

"Thank the Almighty One you are safe."

Salome turned to the hooded figure that followed her. "I am glad you found me in time."

He was waiting for her to finish with a snarky comment or break out into laughter, but she didn't.

"You're welcome," he fumbled over his words. "I should have thanked you earlier for what you did for me in the tavern."

"Don't mention it." Perhaps, she could trust him after all.

CHAPTER THIRTY-FOUR

OPHIR

As the sun set, Ophir rode up to where his minions had set up camp, but upon inspection, realized it had been abandoned. Dismounting his horse, the Shadow looked for any clue that would lead him to the three bounty hunters who had disappeared. Finally finding fresh footprints, he followed where they led; his horse closely behind him. Not far from the campsite, he found Jethro's dead body. Now suspicious, he unsheathed his sword, in case he encountered any mischief.

Continuing forward, he found Morta and Rozdale lying on the ground in pools of blood; the sight frustrated him.

How could this have happened? He had given them the simple task of capturing a woman, but even they turned that into a life and death ordeal.

About to mount his horse once again to leave, he heard a faint cough escape Morta's beaten body.

He coughed up blood. "Master."

Ophir knelt next to him, keeping a watchful eye on his surroundings, "What happened?"

"We failed you."

"Tell me who did this." The bald Shadow was enraged.

"We captured the woman just like you asked, but she got away."

"*She* did this to you?"

"She killed Jethro." His pale face, stained with blood, now had tears streaming down his cheeks. His friends were dead and now it was only a matter of time before he too slipped into the afterlife.

Ophir grimaced at Rozdale's disfigured face. "Who killed Rozdale?"

"There was a man that came for her," he gasped for air.

"Did you find out what their names are? Where they were headed?" Ophir milked him for any information he could get, knowing there was nothing he could do to save him. Not that he would have bothered in the first place.

Having great difficulty breathing, he managed to whisper, "Salome."

The name sent a shiver up his spine, knowing exactly who she was and how dangerous the situation had become. "And the man? What was the man's name?"

"Forgive me, Master," the dirty bounty hunter cried. And with one last breath, the last member of the trio died.

Ophir released his limp arm, brushed himself off, and mounted his horse. A proper burial would not be necessary in the swamp. There were far more creatures living in the wetlands than even he knew about. Their bodies would be gone within three days, leaving no memory of their existence.

CHAPTER THIRTY-FIVE

PASH

Pash marched to Niabi's chambers unsure of why she had summoned him. Oddly, four soldiers were standing guard outside her door.

"Is our Queen alright?" he asked.

"She has been expecting you, Commander Pash." One of the guards stepped in front of him. "Follow us."

He was escorted inside, which had him on high alert. She was standing in the threshold of her balcony staring at the city below, sipping a glass of wine. She did not bother to turn when he entered.

"You sent for me?" he bowed.

At the snap of her fingers, her guards encircled him with pointed spears.

He raised his arms showing he was unarmed. "What is the meaning of this?"

"Seize him." They obeyed her orders. "Wait! I have changed my mind. Release him." They let him go. "Leave us."

"Niabi -"

"Did you notice how they obeyed my orders? Listened to my voice?" She whipped around, glaring at him indignantly as they walked out of her chambers.

Pash was confused. He brushed himself off, his fingertips grazing the handle of his sword. "What is going on?"

"If you ever consider obeying your father's voice again, remember mine. I am your Queen. I have the power to give life or take it," she growled. "My Shadows are never to do Gershom's bidding again or I promise it will cost you your head."

"Niabi -"

Eleven raven sigil pins hit the floor at his feet. "They are only of use to me alive."

He exhaled deeply. Losing men was never acceptable. "I never thought they would be in any danger."

"You are their commander, but I am their master," she grated her teeth behind tightly sealed lips. "It would do you well to remember your place. From this day forward, I expect to know every time my birds set flight."

"Do you not trust me after all my years of loyal service?" He boldly stepped forward.

"A man cannot serve two masters, Pash. To truly serve me, you cannot do your father's bidding."

"As I said before, I did not believe they would be in any danger."

"Slaughtered!" She shouted, shattering her glass against the wall behind him. "They were slaughtered by peasants!"

His voice cracked, "He is my blood."

"Blood means nothing. They are often the very ones to betray you." She walked over to him and cupped his face in her hands. "You are a fool to think he wouldn't do the same to you, given the opportunity."

"You speak of him as if he were some sort of monster," he whispered, eyes locked on her.

Her fingers slid from his face to the decanter of wine on the table behind him. She poured herself a fresh glass.

"Monsters are not figments of our wild imaginations. No, no. You see, the truth about monsters is they are real. They are those we once loved, once trusted, and maybe still even care about. They will stop at nothing to steal our happiness. They play on our fears, exploit our weaknesses, and plot our ultimate destruction. Monsters are not just creatures in fairytales told to frighten children at night. They are people. And if not careful, we could become the very creature we fight." Her glassy eyes homed in on him. "If your father should require your services again..."

"You are my Queen. In life or death, I serve you and you alone." He knelt before her with his arm crossed over his chest.

"Mind your steps." Her eyes narrowed, running her fingers through his hair. "I will not show mercy again."

"Niabi -"

"That will be all, Commander."

Dismissed, Pash bowed and left, unwilling to risk angering her any further. After her door closed behind him, he saw Tala round the corner with a smug look on his face.

CHAPTER THIRTY-SIX

TALA

"It would appear you have once again failed our Queen," Tala cooed. "I would tread lightly, if I were you."

"Is that advice or a threat, Lord Tala?"

"What good are threats from me, when you are your own worst enemy?" The Andrago smirked. He no longer hid his animosity for him.

"You have always envied me."

"You confuse distrust with jealousy, Commander."

"What is your issue with me?" Pash spat.

"I will not stand by and watch you betray her as so many others have."

"She is just as much my Queen as she is yours. We are on the same side."

"You are more like him than you even realize." Tala circled around him; arms secured behind his back. "You think she does not see it? You believe she can truly trust you, while you defend him?"

"Spying on my father and executing him are vastly different." Pash stood very still as the Andrago circled him.

"Both of which you object to, or am I mistaken about that as well?" He stopped and faced him.

"I will do as my Queen commands."

"And when she demands his head?" Tala asked the question he truly wanted answered.

"What is it you would like me to say?" Pash shot him a vicious look. "That I would execute my father for her if she asked? She is my Queen. I swore an oath to serve and protect her. I know my duty."

"Did you not also swear an oath to serve your father's house? To wear his sigil?" Tala pressed, knowing he was getting under Pash's skin. "Yet I see no symbol of the bear on your arm. It would seem you are good at swearing oaths of loyalty, but following through, that remains to be seen."

Pash's eyes narrowed. "You sit on her small council and hold a high position among the Andrago, do I question your loyalty?"

"The difference between us is the Andrago have not failed nor betrayed her." Tala stepped up to him and hissed, "If your father should ever think of attempting to usurp her authority, I wonder where your allegiance would fall. One day soon, you will have no choice, but to truly pick a side. Will it be her or him?"

"What did you just say?" Pash had heard those words before.

"You look pale, Commander. Perhaps, you should consult a Healer." Leaving Pash in the hallway, he entered the queen's chambers for a private audience of his own.

She sat in her chair, sipping from the glass of wine in her hand.

"I heard about your Shadows." He closed the doors behind him.

She looked at the eleven raven pins scattered on the floor. "Gershom is a fool."

"Yet you let him live." He crossed his arms over his chest.

"You know that my hands are tied," she growled, staring at the silver scar running across her right palm.

"He cannot be trusted and therefore -"

"He must die," she interrupted. "I know the Andrago way."

"He still lurks in your halls," he looked at the shelves filled with boxes, "more of a threat now than before."

215

"You heard about his ear, I gather." She smiled and looked up at the box containing his ear that she proudly displayed on her shelf.

He sat across from her. "Is it wise to poke a sleeping bear?"

"If only to watch him dance." Her tone of voice could not disguise her delight.

"He is dangerous." Tala cautioned, preferring Gershom dead than agitated. "He should be dealt with."

"When his time has come, he will suffer greatly before Death takes him. But until then," she leaned back in her seat and stared out the window, "he is not to be touched."

Tala cleared his throat and whispered, "Would you have already executed him if you and the Commander were not involved?"

"You know about us then." She set her goblet down. "You think me to be weak?"

"I believe your mind is clouded." By the wrinkles in his forehead, she could tell he was worried about her.

"You took no issue when I murdered my own father on account of Dichali."

"Your father had to pay for his crimes," Tala poured himself a glass of wine, "as does Gershom."

"You are my most trusted friend and advisor. Your opinion bears much weight, but I ask you to trust me now, as you trusted me all those years ago." She reached for his arm, looking deep into his sunken brown eyes. "It takes great strength to allow your enemy to live, knowing he still serves a purpose."

After a slight hesitation, he nodded his head in agreement. "Tell me what to do and it will be done."

She leaned back in her chair and smiled. "Gershom has been sneaking a red headed prostitute into the castle. Find her and bring her to me unspoiled. She and I have much to discuss."

CHAPTER THIRTY-SEVEN

SALOME

"Why are you crying, Salome?" Lykos asked. "Were Elias and Mosgalath picking on you again?" She nodded her head, affirming his suspicions. He picked her up, sat her on his lap and kissed her forehead. "You should not be sitting here crying."

"I shouldn't?" Her chest rose and fell with rapid breaths.

"No," he wiped a tear from her cheek. "You should defend yourself."

"How?" She fidgeted with her ringlets.

"I will show you." He flashed the training sword he had been practicing with. "I will teach you everything you will need to know."

Wide-eyed Salome shook her head, refusing to take the weapon. "Girls are not allowed to fight."

"Women of the North should know the way of the sword."

"But father -"

"You learn how to fight," he interrupted; the sternness in his voice surprised her. "A woman can fall to a sword just the same as a man."

She hesitated. "Am I a woman?"

"Of course, you are," Lykos smiled. "Just a short woman." He extended the sword to her, and she accepted it. "Lesson one: never underestimate your opponent."

He noticed her admiring his dagger with the handle carved in the shape of a wolf, so he unsheathed it from his hip and handed it to her.

"Take it."

"But father gave it to you," she protested.

"It is mine to give to whom I please and I could think of no one worthier than the North's first female warrior."

The vision faded away and Salome was left holding the unique gift in her right hand. She had spent years training herself not to dwell on the memories of those she had lost, but for some inexplicable reason, she found herself unable to stop the visions. They felt so real. As if she had stepped back in time to relive that moment. *But why? Why was it happening?* She did not understand, but perhaps it was best that way.

Jarred from her quiet moment by the sound of approaching footsteps, she threw the knife. The dagger struck a tree, barely missing Adonijah, who had come to check on her.

"That was close." His eyes darted toward her.

"What are you talking about?" She rolled her eyes and grunted, "I missed."

He pulled the knife from the tree. "I have never seen a blade like this."

"It belonged to my brother." She took the knife from him and sheathed it in its holster on her thigh.

By the tone of her voice, he could tell she did not want to speak of him any further and decided to let it go.

"Harbona sent me to find you. We must cross the Enchanted Swamp before dark if we are to reach Port Daelon in two days."

<hr>

The three companions travelled as quickly as they could through the wetlands. Usually, travelers avoided the Enchanted Swamp due to the countless people who went missing. Harbona knew the risks of the misty lands, but knowing they were being hunted by the Shadows, decided to take his chances.

Although dark in the swamp, Harbona had a small orb that he kept in his breast pocket. Whenever he needed a light to guide him, he would breathe on the orb and it would float in front of him, glowing so the path would be easy to follow.

Salome never imagined anything so remarkable possible. She was tempted to ask him a bunch of questions about the orb but seeing how focused he was on getting them through the swamp unscathed, she held her tongue.

"Tell me again why we are going deeper into the swamp." Adonijah kept a steady eye as he walked beside his skittish horse.

"It is the quickest way to Port Daelon, and Shadows avoid the swamp, fearful of what might be lurking," Harbona answered with a shortness.

"That I understand." Adonijah's eyes dropped to the murky water.

Harbona whipped around and hissed, "Do not look at the water. Focus on the lit path and we shall make it through."

Craving to know why they should avoid looking at the water, Salome once again wrestled with whether she should ask about it or just obey and press forward. She decided on the latter but felt she would burst if anything else spiked her curiosity.

Even with the orb leading them, the further they walked, the darker the Enchanted Swamp became, making it difficult to see what was before them. That is when Salome's foot caught the top of a thick root protruding from the ground, causing her to fall. Adonijah knelt to help her up when they both noticed their odd, warped reflections in the cloudy water and instantly disappeared.

"No!" Harbona's risky trek through the Enchanted Swamp backfired; he knew if he wanted to see them again, he would have to find *her*.

Adonijah and Salome were swept into another dimension of the Enchanted Swamp and although they had both peered into the mysterious waters, they were not sent to the same place.

Salome found herself in a meadow filled with tall grass that swayed in the light breeze. The wildflowers that adorned the field were familiar to her; they were lavenders, her mother's favorite flower. Suddenly, as if thinking of her mother made her appear, she saw her standing across the field. Dressed in a billowing white gown and a crown made entirely of lavender flowers, she extended her hand to her daughter. Without any hesitation, she sprinted toward Bilhah, but as she approached the former queen, she stopped a few feet short, not knowing if she was real or not. Her mother handed her a flower and upon taking it, sniffed it. As soon as a familiar comfort set in, a dark storm tore through the peaceful meadow, leaving an evil aura all around her.

Salome blinked and saw she was now atop a high mountain, encircled by her deceased family members. "Mother? Father?" Tears welled in her eyes at the sight of her loved ones.

"Avenge us," Issachar instructed his daughter.

"Avenge us," Bilhah echoed.

"Avenge us. Avenge us." Her four brothers joined her parents' chant.

It was then that a masked warrior dressed in black from head to toe, walked toward her carrying a bloody sword with blood-stained hands. Frightened, she backed away, unsure of what she was supposed to do.

◄———◄

Adonijah was walking through the wheat fields of the Farmlands, north of Gomorrah, when he saw a small, wooden farmhouse in the distance. He recognized his childhood home and entered the front door expecting to find his mother inside, but no one was there. Walking around the humble abode, he caught sight of his old toys, his mother's favorite quilt and a battered vase of fresh flowers sitting on the wooden table in the center of the common room. He closed his eyes and heard his mother's breathy voice singing a lullaby she used to sing to him every night. He opened his eyes when he heard footsteps behind him, and he drew his sword. He turned around and found himself face to face with a Shadow.

Harbona had never moved so quickly before, but he knew he had a limited amount of time to save his companions from a brutal and excruciating fate. Nestled in the misty clearing was an old wooden and metal bungalow with a rickety front porch. On the eastern side of the small house was a body of murky water and a raft anchored to the dock. The Seer finally saw the woman some believed to be a myth. What was unanimous amongst all Adalorians was whether she existed or not, she was to be feared.

The Enchantress of the Swamp sat on her front porch with her large, black boxer resting loyally at her feet. Upon seeing the visitor, Reaper alerted her of his arrival with a deep howl. Her beautifully hydrated brown skin showed no sign of her age, but her white, hip-length long braids revealed she had walked Adalore for many years. Her petite, curvaceous figure was adorned with gold jewelry and her round nose boasted an ornate septum ring.

She stood with a smirk plastered across her square-shaped face as soon as she saw him. "I have been expecting you, Harbona."

"Where are they, Odelia?" Having known her for quite some time, he was not in the mood for her games.

"No proper greeting?" She shook her head. "Is that any way to greet your hostess?"

"I will not ask you again. Where are they?"

"Somewhere in the swamp." Her voice was smooth as honey and could hypnotize just about anyone who would listen. "But you already knew that."

"Release them."

"You are in no position to demand anything of me, Harbona. The last time I saw you, my hair had not yet turned white."

"Is that what this is about?" he roared. "Because I left?"

"Do not flatter yourself," she brushed him off with a chuckle. "This is the Enchanted Swamp. You know what happens when you look into the murky waters."

Feeling completely helpless, he appealed to her good nature. "Surely there is something you can do to save them."

"Rules are rules," she shook her head and stroked Reaper's muscular chest. "The only way you will see your companions again is if they defeat what they fear most." Odelia walked inside her dark house and waved her hand over a black metal cauldron. "Come, see for yourself."

Harbona realized all he could do at that point was watch.

Salome's family did not stop chanting for her to avenge their wrongful deaths, all the while the assassin circled her. She drew her sword, trying her best to look confident. The fighter initiated their duel and Salome realized she was no match for her skill level. Salome caught a glimpse of the mercenary's green eyes through her mask. Distracted, she left herself open to attack and her left thigh was sliced. Salome crumbled to the ground, writhing in pain. The warrior raised her sword, dripping in Salome's blood, and was about to strike her down when Lykos broke from his chant.

"Salome," his voice was warm, just like she had remembered it, "you are greater than your fear."

"I am greater than my fear," she whispered his words under her breath. "I am greater than my fear."

With the little bit of strength, she still possessed, she rolled away from the impending strike and swung her sword with all her might, cutting her enemy's head off. Her mark began to sizzle, burning her eye. She had never felt pain so excruciating in her entire life. She covered her left eye and watched her family members, one by one, fade from existence.

"No," she whimpered, reaching out to them, "do not leave me again."

Lykos knelt in front of her and smiled. "We never left." And he faded away.

Anger swept over Adonijah at the very sight of the Shadow standing in his mother's house. He began to fight the intruder with a ferocity he had never exercised in battle before. Landing blow after blow on the Shadow's shield, Adonijah hardly noticed the Shadow was not putting up much of a fight. Swiftly knocking the warrior clad in black to the ground, holding his sword against his throat, Adonijah ripped the mask from the soldier's face to reveal his identity. The face staring back at him was his own. Terrified, he stabbed him in the chest and screamed in pain as if he felt the brunt of the blow.

Following their encounters, Adonijah and Salome both reappeared in the Enchanted Swamp where they had last seen Harbona. They were both trying to catch their breath, just a few feet away from one another.

He crawled to her. "Are you alright?" He wiped sweat from his forehead.

"I will be," she leaned against a tree. "What happened?"

He hesitated, kneeling in front of her. "I came face to face with what I fear most."

"I did, too." She was somewhat relieved to know they had experienced the same thing.

He leaned against the same tree, sitting next to her. They sat in exhausted silence for what seemed like an eternity but was only about a minute.

"What did you see?" She pulled the loose strands of her curly hair back into a ponytail.

He shook his head, "I can't say."

"Can't or won't?"

"Both," he spat. "What I fear is between me and the swamp."

"Feared," she corrected. "What you feared. You must have conquered it. How else would you have made it back?"

"Then why am I more afraid now, than I was before? What was the point of this?"

"That is your answer." Odelia walked up to them with Reaper by her side and Harbona following closely behind. "The girl is wise beyond her years. Everyone fears something or someone, but only a few face them."

"Who are you?" Salome was not in the mood for any more surprise encounters.

"I am Odelia," she smiled, "Enchantress of the Swamp."

"So, it is *you* we have to thank for this?" Adonijah hissed.

Odelia bent in front of him with a tight-lipped grin. "It is not *I* who peered into the murky waters, Adonijah, the Wanderer. But it is *I* you have to thank for your enlightenment. Now come, you both must be hungry, and we need to take care of your wounds."

Both of them stared at her, still unsure if she could be trusted.

"You need not fear me." Odelia motioned them to follow her. "You are now my guests and will be treated as such. Now come."

CHAPTER THIRTY-EIGHT

CRISPIN

Crispin stood in awe of the limestone walls that soared thirty feet into the sky. Two giant, black alabaster statues guarded either side of the main gate of Numbio. One of the protectors was fashioned in the likeness of the late Queen Zulu and the other was carved in the image of King Osiris.

The city appeared to be one large marketplace, filled with a constant flow of people buying and selling goods. The Southern people were not afraid to dress in attire that showed skin. Crispin had never seen such beautiful and vibrant colored fabrics before. He and Zophar were definitely noticeable standing in the sea of brown smiling faces with their dull, worn-out clothes and Zophar's fiery red hair.

It did not take the weary travelers long to notice the majestic palace in the distance. Weaving through the markets, they passed the crystal clear Umpoco River where fishermen brought their hauls back to the docks. They finally found themselves at the bottom of what had to be a hundred stone steps up to the front doors of the palace of Osiris.

"I am too old for all these stairs," Zophar huffed as they neared the top.

"I never thought I would hear you admit to being old."
Crispin flashed a smile at him.

"I am not too old for battle," he fussed, "but I am too old for climbing these steps."

Crispin could not help but chuckle. Once they reached the top, they were met by four guards and one elderly attendant of the royal court.

"Who comes before the throne of His Majesty King Osiris?" the feeble man asked in a gravelly voice.

"I am Crispin, son of Issachar, and this is Zophar, son of Nen. We were sent by Harbona the Seer to have an audience with King Osiris."

The attendant stared at the two dirty men and with a slight nod of his head, he entered through the two large doors, leaving them with the fearsome guards.

"Wow!" Crispin turned to admire the view of the bustling kingdom. "I've never seen a city like this. It's beautiful."

Zophar was eyeing the steps they had just climbed and shook his head. "So many steps. Why? Why so many steps?"

Crispin patted him on the back reassuringly, "You made it though, old man."

"Barely, my boy." He leaned as far back as he could and cracked his lower back. "Barely."

His focus returned to the palace. "I hope this works," Crispin whispered.

"It will." Zophar nodded. "Trust Harbona."

"But -"

"It has to work," Zophar interrupted and pointed downwards. "I don't intend to touch those steps again, until absolutely necessary."

The attendant reappeared and motioned them to follow him inside. "His Majesty will see you."

Crispin and Zophar followed the old man as he led them into the royal throne room. They were in an open courtyard with no roof, surrounded by ten colorful columns documenting the history of their ancestors.

At the end of the long courtyard, King Osiris sat stoically on his golden throne with a black onyx and ivory scepter in his right hand. Even in a seated position, Crispin could tell he was tall with wide shoulders and powerful arms. His elaborate gold crown sat upon his dark bald head and his white goatee highlighted his strong chiseled jaw. Osiris' wide nose sat evenly between his dark brown eyes that bore neither kindness nor fear. He had been King since he was nine years old; nothing and no one intimidated him.

To his right stood an equally impressive royal, his son and heir, Heru. In his physical prime, the tall, broad chested prince wore colorful robes that draped over his left shoulder, exposing his toned brown abdomen. His black beard was perfectly manicured to compliment his dark hair. Although the prince facially appeared to be the exact image of his father, his kind hazel eyes were given to him by his late mother.

Queen Zulu had married Osiris when they were teenagers and bore him two sons. Their youngest son, Duale, died two years ago in a chariot racing accident during Numbio's Festival of the Fallen, an annual celebration honoring their ancestors. Having lost her son was more than she could bear, and her mourning manifested into a disease their healers could not cure. Heru was by her side until the very end and he now wore her favorite jade necklace in her honor. Everywhere you looked in Numbio, you could see statues, paintings, and other pieces of art erected so the people would always remember the beautiful and compassionate queen who spent her whole life serving her people.

"Your Majesty," Crispin bowed.

"Rise." Osiris' deep voice boomed as he rose from his golden seat and descended the steps. "So, you are the son of Issachar; you have his eyes. Your father was my friend, his death was difficult to bear. Harbona told me to expect you." He extended his arm, "Welcome to Numbio."

"Thank you," Crispin grasped his arm.

"I feared his children dead. Though, I had heard rumors that one of his sons had escape." Osiris could not hide his curiosity.

"My sister and I escaped with Zophar by means of an old tunnel."

"Three very brave and blessed people. The Almighty One has surely smiled upon you." He motioned for his son to step forward. "This is my son, heir, and commander of my army, Heru. The old man lurking in the shadows is my advisor, Memucan."

Crispin turned toward the feeble old man who stepped out from behind one of the colorful columns and hobbled his way to his King's side. With a slight nod, he showed the visiting men respect.

"It is an honor to meet you, Prince Crispin." Heru extended his arm for Crispin to grasp.

Crispin had not been referred to as a prince in a long time and it felt weird to hear the title before his name. He grabbed Heru's arm. "The honor belongs to me, Prince Heru."

"Why have you come to Numbio?" Osiris asked, taking a cup of wine from his cupbearer.

Crispin took a deep breath. Confident. He had to be confident. "I intend to challenge Niabi for my father's crown."

"War with the North?" Heru's eyes darted back and forth between Crispin and his father.

"I have come to ask for your aid." Crispin locked eyes with the king.

"You are indeed your father's son." Osiris gripped the arms of his throne as he sat back down. "I understand your desire to avenge your family and take back your home, but to battle the North, to battle the Green-Eyed Raven, is suicide." He lowered his head. "Many have tried, and all have failed to assassinate her and that rat of a Second, Gershom. Those taken alive by the Northerners paid the price for their rebellion." Osiris sighed. "Your father was one of my dearest friends, but I cannot risk anymore of my people's lives for this crime."

"What if there *is* a way to defeat them?" Crispin was not deterred by the ruler's first response. Harbona had instructed him not to take 'no' for an answer.

"A sure way to defeat a monster is wishful thinking." Osiris sipped his wine.

"What do you know of the Hunters?" Crispin asked.

"The Hunters are a myth at best," Memucan chimed in with a snarl. "Besides, no one has even seen one of these so-called Hunters in over two hundred years."

"That is true, no one has seen one for quite some time," Crispin pressed on, determined to win Osiris over. "But if I told you I have seen the Hunter of our age; would you join my cause?"

Heru and Osiris glanced at each other, unsure of how to respond.

"I cannot guarantee men will not fall," Crispin furthered his plea, "but I swear to you on the blood of my ancestors, I *will* take back my father's throne."

Silence. Five men said nothing for what seemed to be a lifetime.

Heru stepped forward, arm pressed across his chest. "I will join you, even if our army does not."

Osiris cleared his throat, furrowing his brow at his son. "You have seen the Hunter's mark?" His attention fell back on Crispin.

He nodded. "I have seen it."

King Osiris's stare was so intense, Crispin almost felt like he could read his mind. *Does he think I am lying?* Crispin did not blink. He held his breath, maintaining eye contact with Osiris. *How can I get him to believe me? What else do I need to say to convince him?*

"Harbona came to me many years ago and spoke with me about this day," Osiris broke his silence. "Years before you were born, your father saved my life, and I was never able to repay him. Even though he is gone, perhaps now, I can repay my life debt." The king crossed his scepter over his chest. "The Numbio will join you."

Lord Memucan did not even attempt to disguise his contempt for Crispin. Before the prince was able to express his gratitude, the hunchback advisor shook his bald head. "Your Highness, we have no quarrel with the North. Why stir up conflict when it is not in our best interest?"

"We have no quarrel with the North. But we have no allegiance to the North either." He focused once more on Crispin. "With him as King, we can rekindle the alliance. I have no daughter of which to bond our peoples in marriage, but we can be bonded in blood, like your father and I were many years ago." Osiris lifted his right palm where a scar sat.

Crispin extended his right hand. "Then let us be bonded."

Osiris smiled. "So much like your father."

"Majesty," Memucan stepped forward, "with all due respect, can you honestly believe what this Northerner says, to be true? Should we not see this Hunter with our own eyes?"

"Bite your tongue, Memucan," Osiris barked. "I am the rising and setting sun. What I say is final and I have spoken." His furrowed brow softened as he looked at Crispin. He lowered his head an inch to show respect once he rose from his throne. "I shall retire for now. Heru will make sure you are taken care of."

Crispin bowed, "Thank you, Highness."

"I, too, shall take my leave as I have matters that require my attention." The shriveling old man eyed Issachar's son as he left the room.

"I would be delighted to show you around, but I know you both need to rest after your long journey across the desert." Heru suggested with a smile.

"You will hear no arguments from us." Crispin noticed a woman standing in the shadows of the throne room but was unable to make out her face before she disappeared.

Heru waved his hand and one of his attendants stepped forward. "See to it our guests are given the finest rooms and have new robes sent to them." The servant bowed, obedient to do his master's bidding. "I shall see you both tonight."

CHAPTER THIRTY-NINE

HERU

The wide palace hallways were decorated with beautifully painted images of Numbio royalty and the history of their ancient people. Columns of alabaster supported open archways looking onto the Umpoco River, the Golden Temple, and the hustle and bustle of the city below. Light linen curtains swayed in the dry breeze as Heru weaved his way through the endless hallways. He passed a courtyard with a pool surrounded by lush palm trees on his way to the last door on the right. Not bothering to knock, he made sure no one was nearby to see him enter the Apothecary.

Once inside, his eyes rested upon a curvaceous, dark skinned woman mixing potions on an enormous wooden table in the middle of the airy and bright space. Half of her ceiling was open to the light blue sky which allowed sunlight to beam down on her, highlighting the gold and turquoise beads she had clipped in her midback length braids. Her white robes billowed as he approached her. She did not bother to look up; she knew who had entered.

"I thought that was you in the throne room." Heru stood across the table from her and noticed her unwillingness to look up from her work. "You heard?"

She nodded her head. "Will you go with him?"

"It is my duty."

"You are the heir to your father's throne," she glanced up at him. "What happens if you do not return? What of your people? What of your father?"

"Is that concern for your future king I hear?" he teased.

"You know my concern for you runs deeper than that."

Heru rounded the table and wrapped his arms around her from behind. "I will return to you," he whispered.

"You should not promise such things," she fought back tears.

He gently kissed the back of her head. "Why not?"

"War claims many lives. It does not discriminate between soldiers and their generals."

Heru turned her around to face him and held her chin in his hand. "Rayma, do you trust me?"

"You know I do."

"Then know, I will return to you." He kissed her lips. "I'm sorry I can't stay longer but I must make arrangements for our Northern guests. I will see you tonight."

"I am going with you," she blurted.

He stopped in front of the door and turned, hand still on the knob. "What?"

"When you leave Numbio, I will be with you."

"The battlefield is no place for a woman, Rayma," he frowned. "It is far too dangerous."

"I do not go to the battlefield as a woman. I go to the battlefield as the best healer in the Southern Lands." She stepped up to him. "You cannot deny my skills."

She made a valid point. She was the best healer in Numbio. He had told her so on many occasions. She had been an apprentice for years under the former Royal Healer before his untimely passing and took his place. A year ago, Heru had fallen from his chariot and broke several ribs along with his arm. She eased his pain and helped him heal faster. During their short visits, he fell in love with her: her beauty, her intelligence, her fiery personality. She did not fear him, and she did not treat him differently because he was royalty. She kept him in line; she helped him grow up.

But to let her go into battle… He shook his head. "I cannot allow you to come."

"Give me one valid reason." She popped her hip to the side and crossed her arms over her chest.

"I don't want anything to happen to you." He clenched his jaw. "What if I am not there to protect you?"

"What if I am not there to protect you?" She cupped his face in her hands. "I would rather die by your side, than live in the shadow of your memory."

He knew she was not going to relent. "Before I say yes to you," he rested his hands over hers, "I must ask you something."

She narrowed her eyes. "What is your question?"

"When this war is over and we return," he took a deep breath, "will you marry me?"

"Ma… marry you?" she stammered, taking a step back. "You will be King one day and I am not of royal blood -"

"Our people need a queen again, and I can't think of anyone more suitable than the woman I love." He ran his fingers along her jawline. "So, when we return will you be my wife?"

"I will," her voice cracked.

Grinning from ear to ear, he kissed her. "I must go." He pecked her forehead. "I will see you tonight, my love."

<hr />

Rayma busied herself mixing potions. Her blissful moment would not last long, A feeling she was being watched forced her to look up toward her door. Hunched over just inside her space was Lord Memucan, and she was not at all pleased to see him.

"That was quite the performance, Rayma," he cooed. "I almost believed you love him."

"What do you want?" she growled.

"I have not come to discuss what I want, but what we have agreed upon." The shriveled old man hobbled up to her table. "You know what must be done. The Northerners will not deter our plan."

"Do you not trust me to accomplish my end of the bargain?" She snarled, uncomfortable with him standing so close to her.

Memucan had a certain odor. At first, she thought it was because he was old, but that was not it. For years she could not place the smell, but as he stood there it finally hit her. Cheese. He smelled like cheese. When she thought about it, she realized he always had a board with cheese on display in his chambers. Her nose crinkled.

Memucan ignored the face she made. "I am afraid you have actually grown fond of our young Prince and that might cloud your..."

"Judgment," she finished his thought.

"Loyalty," he corrected with a hiss.

"You ask me to play the part, now you are worried I am too convincing," she scoffed, stopping her work. "Make up your mind. I grow tired of your games."

"You are in no position to speak to me in that manner," he snapped at the healer. "*You* are the one who has everything to lose, not I."

"Heru has agreed to let me accompany him when they leave Numbio, and I will report to you what I learn."

He glared at her. "Bantu will be going as well."

"You are sending your spy to watch me!?" Her eyes narrowed and her nostrils flared. She hated Memucan. But she hated Bantu even more. Sniveling little rat.

"It is for your own good, Rayma. Just in case you believe you can outwit me." He shuffled back to the door and halted for one last word. "Remember, I own you."

"How can I forget when you remind me daily."

Memucan smirked as he left. She grabbed the nearest glass vile and threw it across the room, shattering it against a column.

CHAPTER FORTY

NIABI

Niabi made her way down to the damp dungeons where Tala and Anaktu were waiting for her outside a cell door. Leading her into the small space lit by several torches, she sat down at the table in the middle of the room. Tala removed the sack that covered Ziggy's terrified face.

"Leave us," Niabi ordered. Her haunting gaze fell upon the red head. "What is your name?"

Her throat was so dry, she could only answer once she had gulped her own saliva. "Ziggy, Majesty."

"You are from Borg." A safe assumption from her features. "Yes."

"How did you come to live in Northwind?"

"My parents were killed when pirates from Pulau invaded our village. They took us girls and sold us to the highest bidder. My master lived here in Northwind." Ziggy explained, breathing heavily.

"Slavery is illegal in the North."

"Illegal," Ziggy nodded, "but exists."

"And who is your master?" Her eyes narrowed, wanting a name.

"He was a ship builder named Bronn." Ziggy told the queen a truth most of her companions did not even know.

"Did he hurt you?" Niabi's voice cracked, she could not hide the compassion in her question.

Ziggy shifted in her seat. "I have lost count of all the scars on my body."

Niabi pointed, "Is that how you got that scar on your hand?"

She rubbed her hand, pulling it back from the table. "I tried to run away the night he bought me, but he found me easily. To remind me not to try to escape again, he sliced my hand open."

"How old were you?"

"I was twelve." Ziggy's eyes met the floor.

Niabi placed her elbows on the table and clasped her hands together. "Are you still his slave?"

Ziggy shook her head. "He went to a tavern one night a few years ago and after losing all his money playing cards, offered me up as payment. The man who won me gave me my freedom."

"And what of your former master?" Niabi pressed. "What happened to him?"

Ziggy hesitated. "He had an accident."

The queen leaned in closer, intrigued. "You mean to say you killed him?"

"He drank himself into a stupor and took a tumble off the dock." Ziggy's eyes showed no emotion.

"You didn't answer my question." The queen twisted a ring on her index figure absentmindedly. "Did you kill him?"

"My only regret is that I didn't do it sooner." She spat indignantly. She noticed a smile spread across Niabi's face. "Might I speak freely, my Queen?"

"Please do."

"Why am I here? Surely it is not to learn of my childhood."

Niabi leaned back in her seat. Ziggy was clever. She liked that. "I have suspected for quite some time now, that Gershom might try to usurp me." She paused. "You are his only female companion, so clearly he trusts you."

"What are you asking?" Ziggy mirrored the queen and sat back in her seat.

"Continue to see him and report to me what he confides in you."

The tone of the queen's voice frightened her. "You want me to spy on him?"

"Yes," Niabi confirmed.

"What if he finds out?" the red head's voice quivered.

"Anaktu and Tala have been instructed to keep a watchful eye on you." Her fingers tapped rhythmically on the table.

"Will Gershom not find their hovering odd?"

"So many questions," the queen growled.

"Forgive me, my Queen," Ziggy shrank in her seat. "I am nervous. I have never done anything like this before." She lied.

"Tell me everything he says and does." She rubbed her hands together, her eyes flashed. "Nothing is insignificant. Trust that Anaktu and Tala will protect you."

"Yes, my Queen." She agreed.

"Good. Now be off before someone notices your absence." As Ziggy stood to leave, Niabi grabbed her arm. "And if you betray me, Ziggy of Borg, I will give you to my Shadows until there is nothing left of you to be had. Do I make myself clear?"

"Yes, my Queen."

Niabi released her from her tight grasp, and she bowed once more before scurrying out of the queen's presence.

"You think this will work?" Vilora slithered around the corner. "What if she has feelings for him?"

Niabi's mouth curled into a smile. "She fears me more than she cares for him."

Vilora twisted a lock of her straw like hair, sitting in the seat Ziggy had occupied. "And your promise to protect her?"

"To ensure her loyalty." She stood up and looked down at the witch. "Her life means nothing to me. We are all pawns in someone else's game; I choose to be the one controlling the pieces."

CHAPTER FORTY-ONE

ODELIA

The trio sat at the large wooden table in Odelia's bungalow after eating one of the best stews they had ever had. Reaper stretched out underneath the Enchantress' chair, keeping a watchful eye on the front door. Harbona and Adonijah both lit their pipes and silently puffed, filling the small space with a hazy smoke.

"You look just like your mother." Odelia broke the silence as she stared across the table at Salome.

"Did you know her?" Salome's eyes softened as she set her cup down.

"Not personally," the Enchantress sipped some of her hot tea. "I knew her Aunt Vilora." Harbona glared at her. She knew by the look on his face that she should not say anything more about the witch.

"I'm afraid I don't know much about my mother's family or their history." Salome wiped some of the dirt from her face with the wet towel Odelia provided.

"You will learn about all of that very soon," Odelia smiled. "Is that not right, Harbona?"

Salome's eyes darted to the Seer who continued to smoke his pipe. "I thought we were going to Port Daelon. Are we going to the Isles of Myr?"

"I have arranged for us to have safe and secret passage from Port Daelon to Myr," Harbona confessed. "Your grandmother, Queen Nym, will be eager to finally meet you."

"Why did you not tell me before?" her voice cracked.

"I did not know how you would feel about going to your mother's homeland and it is vital we speak with your grandmother. Trust me." He exhaled a puff of smoke.

"How can you tell me to trust you, if you aren't honest with me?" She pushed back from the table. "I am used to being the hunter and now, I am the hunted. If we are going to be successful, or even make it through the night, we need to be honest with one another."

"You are right." He set his pipe down. "I should have spoken with you about my plans and from this point on, I will. For now, I ask you to accept my counsel and know that I will not lead you astray."

"You need not be afraid, Harbona," Odelia chimed in, knowing what was truly bothering him. "She is Issachar's daughter, not Issachar himself."

"What does that mean?" Salome glared at Odelia.

"Do not be offended, child." Her smooth voice brought a sense of ease with every word she spoke. "Your father did not listen to Harbona's warning and it cost him his life. He may not show it, but he is afraid of failing you."

"Harbona, what is she talking about?" Her shoulders tensed.

Odelia noticed how uncomfortable Harbona was, clearly unwilling to discuss what she had purposely brought up. Adonijah noticed Harbona's demeanor and leaned forward, now interested in knowing what he was hiding.

"Harbona?" Salome set her spoon down. "What are you not telling me?"

"Harbona was a member of your father's small counsel and before your sister attacked the city, he warned your father of her plans." Odelia spoke on the silent Seer's behalf. "He did not heed

239

Harbona's warnings nor listen to the pleas of his small counsel to take necessary measures to protect not only the city, but to protect the royal family from certain death."

"That's not true," she stood up, shaking her head.

"He thought your sister to be weak," the Enchantress persisted. "He denied her. He underestimated her. Because of his stubbornness, he failed to act on the visions, and it cost your family their lives."

"Stop speaking lies!" The princess slammed her fist on the table. "It's not true." Her voice ebbed into a raspy whisper; repressing the tears that burned her eyes. She turned her gaze toward the quiet Immortal. "Tell me it's not true."

"I only hope you can trust me as your father could not. His death was not easy to bear." His eyes were filled with grief.

Silence enveloped the small bungalow.

Adonijah set his pipe down and eyed Salome. "I could use some fresh air and think it best not to walk the swamp alone. Walk with me?"

She nodded and left with him.

"How long have they known one another?" Odelia watched them descend the creaky porch steps.

"Not long at all," he answered, wearily. "A couple of days."

"Not long at all and yet he cares very deeply for her." She had a soft spot for potential romance.

He closed his eyes and rubbed his forehead. "I know he does."

"Curious, is it not, how two people can go from strangers to so much more in such a short time." The Enchantress sipped her tea with a coy smile.

"Everyone was once a stranger to another." Harbona shooed her romantic notions. "Such is life, Odelia."

"You know something." Her brown eyes danced with curious delight.

"I know a lot of things." He wiggled his back against his chair to satisfy an itch. "You will have to be more specific on what I supposedly know."

Her eyes rolled. He had not changed. "You know something about their future."

"I see many futures, you know that. It is my blessing and my curse." He exhaled a large cloud of smoke.

"You are not going to tell me, are you?" She leaned back in her chair, already knowing the answer to her question.

"There are many possibilities," he looked up at her, "their futures are not yet set."

"Yet you brought them together?" She tilted her head with a grin.

He narrowed his eyes with a sigh, "He was always destined to protect her."

"And what is *her* destiny?" she pried.

"To be his light in a dark place."

CHAPTER FORTY-TWO

ADONIJAH

Outside, a short distance from Odelia's bungalow, Adonijah and Salome sauntered aimlessly around the swamp. Reaper had followed them out and settled down on the creaky front porch where he kept watch. They welcomed his presence because it gave them a sense of safety in the strange terrain.

"Thank you," she said, now composed.

"For what?" He looked over at her, curious.

"It is not easy to speak of my parents. I didn't know them as others did." She rubbed her hands against her thighs. "I just have so many unanswered questions."

"Perhaps, travelling to the Isles of Myr will give you some answers." He comforted her as best he could, but his face flushed, and he immediately regretted his effort.

"Have you found the answers to your questions?"

"What do you mean?" He cocked his head, looking her up and down.

"I have lost many loved ones, Adonijah. I can see you too have suffered a similar loss." He stared at the ground. "You don't need to tell me what happened but know that you are not alone. I understand your pain." She reached for his hand and squeezed it, then headed toward the old wooden house.

"I found the answers I sought." His whisper stopped her where she stood.

"And?"

"The answers are just another form of pain." He glanced up at her, pulling leaves from a twig he picked up. "It did not bring those I loved back. It did not ease the ache in my heart. It did not bring me peace." He dropped the stick and sighed heavily. "I was reminded of how powerless I was to save them. It showed me how much hatred still fills my heart."

"I don't believe I could feel any more powerless than I am already. That I could hate my enemies more than I already do."

"You would be surprised at the depth one can hate another. You will see," he leaned against a tree and crossed his arms over his chest. "Myr will give you the answers you seek and break your heart all over again."

CHAPTER FORTY-THREE

SALOME

Early the next morning, Salome sat on the front porch and listened to all the unfamiliar sounds of the misty swamp. The day before, she found the wetlands abhorrent, but staying with Odelia and getting to know her better, made the spooky swamp seem quite nice. The land was truly alive with its own personality. The air was so thick, you felt you had walked into a wet cloud. She could see why Odelia loved it. It was quiet, peaceful, and private; every quality she held dear.

"I thought I was the only one who rose this early in the morning." Odelia's sudden presence surprised her. "Sorry, child, I didn't mean to startle you."

"It's alright." She smiled, noticing Reaper sat down next to the Enchantress' rocking chair, as if he were on duty. "I always wake up early to have time alone to think."

"And what were you up so early thinking about?" She plopped into her chair and rocked softly.

Salome shrugged her shoulders and changed the subject. "Why did you name him Reaper?"

"Because he is the Reaper of Lost Souls, of course," she smiled widely. "When the Swamp claims a soul, Reaper collects them. How else could he live to be forty-three?"

"Reaper is forty-three?" She did not know if she believed her tale.

"Aye, child, forty-three." Odelia nodded her head as she patted him on the head. "And as long as people continue to lurk into the Enchanted Swamp and look into the murky waters, he will keep on living."

He did not look menacing, but Salome looked at the enormous black dog with a newfound fear.

"Does he frighten you?" Odelia wiped the bubbling beads of sweat from her hairline.

She half-shrugged, "Normally, a dog wouldn't scare me but - "

"Not Reaper," Odelia interrupted. "Your male companion."

"Adonijah?"

"Aye, girl." She chuckled. "Does he frighten you?"

She shook her head. "No."

"Your eyes tell a different truth." Odelia's eyes danced.

"And what of your eyes, Odelia?" Salome sassed, bringing her legs up to her chest. "I see how you look at Harbona. Who is he to you?"

The Enchantress grinned fondly as she played with one of her dreads. "A memory."

"Now, it is *your* eyes that tell a different truth," Salome teased, finishing her tea.

"It is a pity you must leave so soon," Odelia cooed. "Me thinks we would have gotten along quite nicely."

Adonijah shuffled outside with his pipe pursed between his lips. "Ladies," he greeted once he noticed them and sauntered toward the horses to ready them for their journey.

Salome could not help but giggle. "He definitely doesn't frighten me."

"He *should* frighten you." Odelia's tone sent chills up her spine.

"Why?" Her eyes narrowed as she planted her feet on the ground.

"If I had a man that handsome look at me, the way he looks at you, I would find myself in a heap of trouble." Her eyes softened as Harbona stepped outside.

Salome stood and excused herself, knowing Odelia would want to say goodbye privately. "I will try to keep myself out of trouble."

"Or not." Odelia winked.

Odelia smiled as Reaper followed Salome down the steps. "She's a spitfire. Reminds me of myself when I was her age."

"You were far sassier." Harbona's eyes squinted as he flashed a warm smile her way. "You have not changed a bit."

She eyed the banished Seer, her tone serious. "I looked into her future, and it is not what I expected."

His gaze fell to his feet. "Odelia, you shouldn't have -"

"Harbona, if she should fail -"

"I know what would happen," he interrupted, rubbing the nave of his neck.

"Death will come for her," her voice cracked.

"I know," he whispered, eyes meeting hers. "Death comes for us all. But if she focuses on her own mortality, she will not live to see her victory."

The Enchantress could tell how much the mortals meant to him. He had advised many of them throughout his thousands of years walking Adalore and buried even more of them. But this mortal seemed to mean more to him than all those before her.

"It was good to see you, Harbona, after all these years." Odelia cleared her throat. "Perhaps, do not wait so long to visit me again."

He looked at her with deep regret. "I never should have left the way I did. You didn't deserve that."

"Ah!" she waved her hand in the air. "That was a lifetime ago."

"I *am* sorry, Odelia." He grabbed her tattooed hand in his. "When this is over -."

She gently caressed his cheek and examined his face. She did not know him before his branding, but the banishment mark did not cause her to treat him any differently. Although, it had been nearly three decades since she last saw him, his grey eyes were the same, except for the crow's feet around his eyes. His long platinum blonde hair pulled back revealed he had lost the glow of the Immortals. Emotions she had not felt in years flooded her heart as she stared at the man who held a special place in her heart.

"I will see you when I see you," she kissed his cheek. "May the Almighty One protect you."

She waved as they rode away and patted Reaper who had rejoined her on the porch.

"That man will be the death of me," she sighed.

<hr>

The trio road through the rest of the swamp silently, simply because they had nothing to say. After hours of trotting through the misty wetlands, they finally arrived at the mouth of the Valley Pass, a narrow road nestled between two opposing mountain ranges. It was the only way to reach Port Daelon, which was at the very end of the pass. Any traveler who wished to survive the dangerous road, remained vigilant and made sure he made it to the city before nightfall or strange creatures, it was said, would attack.

"What is that?" Salome halted her horse to listen to a distant noise that sounded like the beating of a drum.

After listening to the echoing sound, Adonijah recognized the rhythmic beat and jumped off his horse. "We need to get out of sight. Now!"

Salome and Harbona both dismounted their steeds and pulled them behind a large cluster of boulders. Once they were securely hidden, she peered around the rocks to catch a glimpse of the incoming travelers.

Two men on horseback turned the corner and right behind them was a group of nearly two dozen chained men and women marching in single file, prodded by five slavers armed with whips, maces, and knives. All seven men were tall and broad-chested with unnaturally, bulging muscles and deeply scarred, bald heads. Their bodies were covered in white ash with black paint around their soulless eyes.

Salome could not take her eyes off their pointy ears and equally sharpened teeth, both filed in those distinct shapes by their masters. They only wore black, high-waistbands and loin cloths. The only armor they sported were spiked chest and shoulder pieces.

"The Thrak," Adonijah identified in a hushed voice. "Slaves to the rulers of Gomorrah, with one purpose: to hunt and enslave the Stormcrags."

"The Thrak of Gomorrah?" she whispered; eyes still glued on the villainous creatures.

"The very thought of that unholy city is more than I care to think about," Harbona spat on the ground.

"And the prisoners?" Her gaze switched to the men and women that marched through the Valley Pass in chains. They were of mixed racial backgrounds; clay and shades of blue and purple paint were splattered across their faces, arms, legs and chests to show which warrior clan they belonged to. Piercings adorned their faces, and their hair was left wild and untamed.

"Stormcrags. They are one of two rival tribes of Mountain Men, dwellers of Fennor of the Bone Mountains," Harbona explained.

"Sons and daughters of criminals," Adonijah said with contempt.

248

"They are known for their brutal attacks on caravans that travel around the mountains," Harbona continued. "To capture a Stormcrag is a difficult task, but there is a large price on their heads if brought back to Gomorrah alive. For hundreds of years, their peoples have battled, every attack becoming more sadistic than the last."

"What will happen to them in Gomorrah?" She spotted a small child among the prisoners, and it tugged at her heart.

"They will be questioned on the location of Bone City and their temple, Tears of the Gods, and when they refuse to answer, they will be tortured to death in the town square for all Gomorrians to witness."

Every word Harbona spoke weighed heavily on her. "We must help them," she declared, without a second thought.

"That is too risky," Adonijah protested, "Have you ever seen the Thrak in action? Because I have and -"

"You would rather have them tortured to death?" she cut him off with a snarl.

"They are none of our concern. If we are overrun and you are captured by either side, you will be lucky to have a quick death." Adonijah stood his ground.

"It is a risk I am willing to take," she fired back in a raspy whisper. "No one should be enslaved and brutalized for the pleasure of another."

Harbona finally added his input, "If we succeed in freeing the Stormcrags, they will owe us a life debt, something they take very seriously."

"But the Stormcrags are a vicious people." Adonijah continued to protest. "Who knows if we could truly trust them not to slit our throats in the middle of the night."

"The Stormcrags honor their word, unlike the Krazaks, who offer anyone up to the Thrak for sport." Harbona eyed Salome. "The Krazaks would slash our throats, no doubt."

"We have to help them," Salome insisted.

Adonijah was reluctant but knew he had been outvoted. "If we are going to do this, we must act quickly." He and Harbona unsheathed their swords and Salome nocked her arrow, ready for a swift strike. "On my mark, we will attack." Once Adonijah saw the Thrak had completely passed their hiding spot, he nodded his head. "Now!"

Salome jumped up and launched her first arrow toward the nearest Thrak, striking him between his shoulder blades. She ran to the fallen slaver and stood over him as he tried to crawl away. Clutching a mace in his right hand, he turned to strike her, but was met with a second arrow that pierced his thick neck, killing him instantly.

Adonijah found himself fighting the largest Thrak of the lot whose weapon of choice was a double-sided mace with spikes as long as knives. He had seen his fair share of fights but had never seen a weapon like that. At first, his main focus was defending himself as the Thrak swung the mace around in sporadic movements; ducking and dodging until he finally noticed a pattern and became the aggressor. With swift and determined thrusts of his sword, Adonijah finally bested his ashen opponent, cutting his leg out from under him and stabbing him in the stomach.

Salome noticed a Thrak charging Adonijah from behind and shot him down. He turned and saw the dead Gomorrian face down in the dirt and nodded his head to show her his appreciation for her having his back. She caught sight of a ring of keys attached to the waistband of the slaver she had just killed and realized one of those keys had to unlock the prisoners' chains. She swiped the keys and started to free the Mountain Men.

"Go!" she shouted once their chains had been unshackled. "Run, you're free!"

Harbona had not been in true hand to hand combat longer than he cared to admit, but thankfully, he was not having difficulty in defending himself. Immortals were known for their agility and grace on the battlefield and although he had been banished, he still moved like an angelic being. The enormous Thrak grew tired as he swung his

250

wooden spiked club toward the Seer and once he slowed, Harbona took the opportunity to strike. He slammed his staff on the ground causing the slaver to fly back and land on his back. Now disarmed, Harbona ended him quickly by slashing his throat.

As soon as Salome had finished freeing the last prisoner, she turned in time to see one of the horseback riding Thrak stampeding toward her and she dove out of his path. Instead of turning around to finish her off, he rode away to escape the Valley Pass. Harbona hopped on his horse and chased after the Gomorrian. If he were not caught, their whereabouts would be reported.

"You've cost me dearly, woman," the second Thrak on horseback hissed as he dismounted his steed.

She tried to hurry to her feet, but unable to scramble away, he kicked her ribs as hard as he could. Writhing in pain, she once again attempted to stand up, but he unsheathed his knife and slashed her face.

Adonijah was dueling the last Thrak and saw Salome was in trouble. He fought the ashen warrior as quickly as he could swing his sword, but this Thrak was armed with two swords and moved swiftly despite his large size.

Adrenaline kicked in and Salome grabbed her wolf blade from the holster on her thigh and blocked his incoming blow. She knew she was no match for him size-wise, but she knew she could beat him on speed. She swung her leg around, knocking him off his feet. Still in excruciating pain, she slowly stood to her feet watching to see what he would do next. To her surprise, he flipped up, drew his whip from his hip, and cracked it against her leg. He flung the whip back with every intent to strike her again, but Salome threw her hand in the air in a desperate attempt to halt the impending lash and grabbed hold of the end of the leather whip. The tip wrapped around her hand, stinging her, ensuring he could not rip it out of her possession. The Thrak cackled as he forcefully pulled her toward him, dragging her the entire way.

Adonijah whacked one of the swords from the Thrak's hand and took the opportunity to launch an aggressive assault. He whipped his sword around, knocked his enemy's second blade out of his grasp which exposed his stomach for Adonijah's kick. As he fell backwards, Adonijah took his knife from the holster on his back and threw it, slicing into his neck. He quickly retrieved his dagger and sprinted toward Salome who was a good distance away.

Struggling and failing to get to her feet, the Thrak pulled her closer to him. His eyes were crazed, almost possessed; she had never seen such blackened eyes. While being dragged on her belly, she tried to release her hand from the whip she was entangled in, but by the time she freed her bleeding hand, the Thrak had wrapped his calloused fingers around her neck.

"Now you die." The Thrak raised her off the ground.

Her feet dangled as she tried to pry his hand from her neck; now losing consciousness. Just before she blacked out, she dropped to the ground. When she opened her eyes, she saw the tip of a sword protruding from the Thrak's chest. The Thrak fell; he was dead. Standing before her, she saw her savior. It was one of the Stormcrags she had freed.

"Who are you?" She felt the loss of blood taking its toll on her. Instead of answering her question, he sprinted away.

"Salome!" Adonijah swept her in his arms and was instantly drenched in her blood. "Stay with me."

Salome's eyes fluttered as she woke, and a rush of pain flooded her body. When she was able to focus, she noticed all the bandages wrapped around her hand and leg.

"You're awake," Adonijah breathed a sigh of relief.

"How long was I out?" She eyed the makeshift camp as she rubbed the back of her head.

"A couple of hours."

Sure she had been drooling, she wiped the sides of her mouth when he turned to stoke the fire. "Where's Harbona?"

He rotated the rabbit he had caught over the flames, "One of the Thrak escaped. He chased after him."

She attempted to sit up, but the pain shot through her body. She grabbed her torso, wincing from an aching ribcage. Adonijah knelt in front of her and touched her non-injured hand.

"I feel like my ribs are broken," she scrunched her face.

"Not broken. But you took a beating." She eyed him before lifting her shirt to see bandages wrapped around her torso. "I had to bind your wounds. I'm sorry if that makes you uncomfortable," he explained.

She stroked her face and felt a nasty cut.

"Aye," he nodded with a grimace, "he got your face as well."

"I'm sure that will scar nicely," she mumbled. "Is it bad?"

"Since I tended to your wounds quickly, it should not be as noticeable. And even if it is, it will suit you fine." He hesitated before he said, "You have many scars."

She became uneasy. "No more than others."

"Where did you get this one?" He pointed at a small scar on her left forearm near her six lined tattoo.

"I was thirteen," she tugged at her earlobe, "I fell from a tree."

"And this one?" He motioned toward her collarbone.

"Crispin bested me during training a few years back. I think he did it on purpose after we got into an argument."

"And the one across your stomach?"

"I have you to thank for that one." She remembered that one distinctly from their first encounter in The Hollow.

"I'm sorry about that." He broke eye contact with her.

"It's alright." She pointed at a fresh scar on his chest. "I returned the favor."

"I suppose I deserved that." He smirked and cocked his head. "How many scars do you have?"

"Too many." She stood up with great difficulty.

"Where are you going?" He remained in his crouched position.

"I need to walk around," she breathed heavily. The pain was worse standing up than sitting down. "I need to clear my head." She leaned against one of the boulders their camp was hidden behind.

"You need to rest, Salome."

The way he said her name sent a tingling sensation through her body. It was just her name. She had heard it countless times over seventeen years, but it sounded different coming from his lips.

"I will be fine." She limped away from him keeping her hand against the rocks for support.

"Has your eye been like that since birth?" He scratched his beard, rising from his crouched position.

Her breath quickened. "Why do you ask?" The question fumbled out of her mouth.

The way he looked at her made her heart skip.

"Why are you looking at me like that?" She pressed her fingers to her lips, uncomfortable with his question.

"I know who you are." The words oozed from his lips.

She tried to hide the panic in her voice. "I am Issachar's daughter -"

"You are the Hunter, aren't you?" Their eyes met.

She lunged for her sword and pointed it at him. "Don't come any closer."

"What are you doing?" he flinched.

"I said, don't come any closer." She tightened her grip on her weapon.

He lifted his hands to where she could see them. "I swore an oath to protect you."

"A promise you made before you knew the truth." She felt trapped, cornered like a wild animal trying to escape its cage.

"I mean you no harm," his voice was silky, warm. "Please, lower your sword."

"I can't."

"Do you trust me?"

"I want to." She was sweating, unsure of what to do.

"Then trust me."

"This could be a trick."

"If I were going to kill you, would I have gone through the trouble of binding your wounds? Surely that counts for something." She still clutched her weapon. "I am the same Adonijah who swore to protect you."

"I am not the same Salome you swore to protect." Tears filled her eyes, her bottom lip quivered.

"To me, you are the same." He knelt before her and gazed into her shifting eyes. "You need not fear me, but if you do not trust me, take your sword and end me now. I will not live one more day with you fearing me to be your enemy."

She stared deeply into his caring brown eyes and lowered her sword with tears streaming down her cheeks. "I didn't want this."

"Are you afraid?"

Her nostrils flared, she whispered, "I am."

"I am too."

They stared at each other silently.

She sat on the ground across from him. "What do you fear?"

"Myself," he finally admitted out loud.

"Why?" She watched him intently.

"I fear I will become like my father. His blood runs through my veins, his weaknesses, his failures. I am afraid that if I let myself, I will live as he did, and I would rather be dead than be what I hate."

She rested her sword in her lap. "What did he do that frightens you?"

"He has brought more pain and sorrow than I dare talk about." Adonijah tore his eyes from her and stared at the ground.

"Who is he?" she asked, but as she expected, he remained silent. "Is that what you saw in the swamp?"

"Know your secret is safe with me." He rose from his seated position. "Nothing changes between us."

"Adonijah -"

"Stay down," he silenced her and ducked. Hearing horse hooves fast approaching, he readied himself for a possible altercation, but saw the rider was Harbona.

"Did you catch him?" Adonijah threw him a sheepskin filled with water.

"I tried my best – nearly followed him into Gomorrah itself – but it was as if he had wings." Harbona jumped from his exhausted horse and drank the refreshing water.

"It will not be long before the Gomorrian Lords set a bounty on our heads." Adonijah knew exactly what would be headed their way if they did not make it to their ship quickly. "The Thrak will not rest until they find us. We must reach Port Daelon by nightfall, or we may never make it to the Isles of Myr."

CHAPTER FORTY-FOUR

MATILDYS

Racing through the dirty streets of Gomorrah, the Thrak that escaped Harbona swiftly made his way through the overpopulated kingdom that smelled of soot and manure, toward the menacing Black Tower that stood in the center of the circular city.

Gomorrah was completely enclosed by a black stone wall. Originally, the wall was a light color, but with the blacksmiths working on the outskirts of the city, it turned the structure black with dirt. Throughout the city hung the mangled bodies of tortured Stormcrags for all Gomorrians to mock as they passed by. An unhygienic people by nature, they were perfectly satisfied living in filth, if it meant they did not have to abide by any laws. All that was required of Gomorrians was that they honor and protect the crown.

Although the cannibalistic Thrak were considered barbaric to the rest of Adalorian cities, Gomorrians worshipped them and gladly committed their firstborn sons to the enslaved order. Thrak were not given names but were known only by the numbers that were branded into the back of their necks as children. Completely lacking in empathy, they were the perfect soldiers for King Cyler's army.

King Cyler was of the purest blood. Following the Gomorrian custom, a ruler could only reproduce with family. His blonde hair and blue eyes were his only redeeming features. He suffered from a plethora of diseases and the bulging hump on his back further weakened his feeble frame, forcing him to rely heavily on his wife and sister, Maltidys, to take care of daily affairs.

Maltidys was oddly beautiful and healthy for being a product of incest. Her wavy blonde hair cascaded to the middle of her back and her sunken, icy blue eyes were haunting. The queen's high cheekbones, narrow nose, and thin lips were the envy of all Gomorrian women. Because she never left her tower, her skin was extremely pale, and she appeared almost corpse like. Black and gold were the only colors she would wear, and she always fashioned her hair in the traditional Gomorrian way: half of her hair was twisted in two side buns, accentuating the squareness of her face, and the rest of her hair would lay flat across her back.

Most people in the Ten Kingdoms feared their kings, but in Gomorrah, everyone knew King Cyler was no true threat. Maltidys, on the other hand, was not only feared, but adored for her ruthless demeanor. She was their true leader and was grooming her fifteen-year-old twins, Thanos and Ranalda, to be just as merciless.

From their infancy, her son and daughter would watch as the captured Stormcrag men, women, and children, would be tortured for hours until there was nothing left of them to mutilate. After years of watching merciless torture, they had become just as cruel as their mother. Both Thanos and Renalda were in the dark throne room with their parents when the Thrak numbered 62198 appeared on bended knee before them.

"62198, your task was to find and capture Stormcrags for questioning, but it appears you have returned empty handed." The queen's chilling voice echoed through the circular stark room. "Why is that?"

The Thrak's black eyes darted around the room, not sure where to focus. "My Queen," his deep voice gurgled, "we captured many Mountain Men -"

"Then, where are they?" Maltidys interrupted with a shriek.

"We… we were attacked," he stammered. "I am the only Thrak to survive."

"Who would dare kill the Thrak of Gomorrah?" she wheezed in disbelief.

"There was a woman, highly skilled with a bow -"

"A *woman* did this to you?" Prince Thanos scoffed in disbelief.

"Hush, Thanos." The queen's eyes darted toward him, infuriated by his outburst. "A woman withstood the pain to birth you and if underestimated, a woman can easily take your life." She refocused on the Thrak. "Finish your tale of this skilled woman."

"She was not alone, my Queen. She had two men with her. One bore the banishment mark of the Immortals. They killed the Thrak and freed the prisoners."

Maltidys stroked her husband's bony hand in her own. "What do you think of 62198's report, my love? Should we believe him?"

The sickly king's hollowed eyes slowly lifted to stare at the Thrak who had returned empty handed. His hoarse voice whispered, "He knows the penalty for failure."

"Exactly what I was thinking." She eyed the quivering slave and flashed a sinister grin. "Take him to the Square."

Two Thrak grabbed their comrade and dragged him from the throne room down to the Square at the entrance of the Black Tower. A deep resonating horn sounded throughout the entire city alerting the people that fresh meat had arrived. Excitement pulsed through every citizen who rushed toward the infamous Square. The royal family made their way to a covered balcony two stories above the wooden platform which was quickly surrounded by eager civilians. Thrak 62198 was forced to his knees in front of an executioner's block while Maltidys stood to address the blood thirsty Gomorrians.

"Gomorrians," her shrill voice echoed. "Thrak 62198 returned to our great city having failed in his mission to capture our enemies." Her eyes fell on the condemned Thrak. "Gomorrians, what is the penalty for failure?"

"Death! Death! Death!" The crowd erupted in a thunderous roar as they pumped their fists in the air and stomped their feet.

"And Death he shall receive," she smiled.

With the slight nod of her head, the executioner swung his gigantic sword, claiming the disgraced Thrak's head to the delight of the dusty people.

Seeing her husband was exhausted from the day, Matildys motioned for her son to stand up. "Thanos, take your father inside. He needs to rest."

Obedient to his mother's commands, he helped his ailing father inside, leaving his sister and mother alone to watch the elated crowd.

"Ranalda, what is our creed?" Maltidys asked the elder twin.

"Kill, steal, destroy, but keep the blood pure," she beamed with pride. Ranalda had her mother's beauty, but she was not nearly as intimidating. Her rosy cheeks and boyish figure left her lacking the confidence her mother had.

"Very good." Her mother patted her thin fingers. "One day you will rule all Gomorrians -"

"But, mother, Thanos will be King, not I."

Maltidys smacked her daughter across the face. "Do not interrupt me again."

"I am sorry, mother." She rubbed her cheek, trying to hide the tears that welled in her eyes.

"Listen to me, Ranalda," the queen quickly moved on, "Thanos is weak and as long as I have anything to say about it, he will never rule our people."

"But our law states only a male can be -"

"You think your *father* rules the Gomorrians?" she hissed. "Do not be so naïve. He may bear the crown, but it is my voice the people obey. When I am gone, you shall take my place."

Ranalda was confused. "What of Thanos?"

"You want to be queen, do you not?"

"Of course, Mother."

"And queen you shall be. Thanos will pose no threat to your reign."

Before Ranalda could ask another question, Thrak 47134 bowed before them with a rolled-up parchment. Matildys snatched it and shooed him away as she read the papers.

"What is it, Mother?"

"The North is offering a hefty bounty if these two criminals are found and delivered to them alive."

Ranalda inspected the posters of Crispin and Salome. "They killed Queen Niabi's Shadows? How could peasants massacre such deadly mercenaries?"

Maltidys tapped her lips, deep in thought. "There must be more to this than meets the eye. No one would offer such a sum for peasants and insist they be captured alive." She examined Salome's poster once more and remembered what Thrak 62198 claimed. "A skilled woman..." A smile stretched across her pale face. "*She* killed the Thrak and released my prisoners. Ranalda, order Thrak 47314 to take a band of twenty to Port Daelon to find her."

"She may not be there."

"Tell him whoever brings her to me alive and unspoiled will be given their freedom." Maltidys could not tear her eyes from the poster. "She stole from me, and she will pay the price."

"But if you kill her, we will not receive her bounty," Ranalda pointed out.

"Revenge before riches," the queen glared at her daughter. "Revenge before riches."

CHAPTER FORTY-FIVE

PASH

Gershom wiped the beads of sweat that dripped down his forehead. Breathing heavily, he was clearly exhausted, but refused to take a break from practicing with his sword. Any who watched could not deny he was highly skilled and even in his late years of life, he was still deadly. The Bear sparred with his personal guards daily for a minimum of two hours. Most thought he was trying to prevent old age from setting in, but Pash knew the real reason he kept himself trained was because he was always concerned someone he had wronged would one day come for him.

Pash had entered the room virtually unnoticed and watched as his father sparred. As fearsome a warrior as he was, he knew the true lethal threat was Niabi. After watching silently for several minutes, Gershom finally noticed his son lurking in the shadows of his private training room.

"What do you want?" Gershom hissed as he dismissed his guards.

Pash stepped forward. "I came to talk to you about the Queen's Shadows."

"Oh, she sent you, did she?"

"She does not know I am here," he lied. "Tell me how to help you."

"Why should I believe you wish to help me when everyone knows where your loyalties lie?" he scoffed. He sheathed his weapon in its holster and set it on the table.

"She never should have harmed you." He stared at the hole where his father's ear used to be. "Had I known what she had planned, I would have stopped it."

"It is the last thing she will ever take from me," Gershom growled.

"Tell me how I can help you and I will do it."

He stared at his son suspiciously. "I wish I could believe you, Pash."

"I know I have not lived up to your expectations, but you are my father, and blood is everything. You have been careless in your dealings with the Shadows, but with me behind you, commanding them, she will never know of my betrayal."

Before Gershom could answer, the Nameless Rider entered the private grounds. Crossing his right arm to his left shoulder, the Shadow began to report his findings. "My Lord Gershom, Commander Pash, I have returned from the village where our men were slaughtered."

"What has been done to those bold and reckless villagers?" Gershom fumed.

He grinned. "Most of them are dead, my lord."

His words struck Pash like a dagger. To think of the innocent being murdered did not sit well with him.

"Most?" The Second in Command eyed the Shadow in frustrated confusion.

"We spared one villager, Jacobi the Baker, who has given us detailed information about the two villagers responsible for the Shadows' deaths. He has proven himself useful. For now."

"Do you mean to tell me the two villagers responsible escaped you?" If Gershom still had his sword, he would have struck the Shadow down.

"They fled the night before we arrived."

"You have come all this way to tell me of your failure?" Gershom hissed.

"No, my lord." The Nameless Rider handed him the two wanted posters of Crispin and Salome that were circulating around Adalore. "To show you these."

"What do I care of their faces?" Gershom threw the two pictures on the ground without looking at them. "Find them!"

"We will find them, my lord," the Nameless Rider assured him.

Pash picked up the posters and examined them further. "Their names are Crispin and Salome."

"And what do I care what their names are?"

Pash glanced at him. "Those are the same names of the two children who escaped you twelve years ago."

Gershom snatched the pictures and immediately saw their resemblance to Issachar. "It cannot be," he muttered. "It cannot be." The longer he stared at them, the paler he became. "The villagers who killed the Shadows are Issachar's children?"

"We have posted these throughout the Ten Kingdoms. It is only a matter of time before we capture them," the one-eyed Shadow stated confidently.

"You will not find them in the Western Forests or the Swamp Lands." Ophir's voice echoed as he entered, still dirty from his long journey.

"What are you talking about?" Gershom whipped around to see his younger brother approaching.

"I don't know the boy's whereabouts, but the girl was headed toward the Enchanted Swamp." Ophir set his belongings on the table and poured himself a glass of wine.

"And how would you know that?" Gershom grimaced as he watched Ophir wrap his dirty fingers around the crystal decanter.

Ophir grabbed Salome's poster. "I saw her with my own eyes. And upon hearing her companions' plans to gather an army, I ordered my men to capture her."

Gershom's eyes brightened; he clapped his hands together. "Finally, some good news. Bring her to me."

Ophir cleared his throat, "She escaped."

"She what?" A vein in Gershom's neck protruded.

"By the time I made it to their camp to retrieve her, all of my men had been killed." Ophir tried to hide the worry on his face. Gershom was known for having a short temper and was always eager to strike down anyone who failed him.

"Am I only to receive reports of failure?" Gershom shook his head as he stroked the shaved sides of his head.

"There is one more thing they spoke of that you need to know," Ophir hesitated, fiddling with the now empty wine glass.

"Well," Gershom growled. "What is it?"

"The men she was with claimed to have the Hunter."

The Bear turned ashen white and stumbled to lean against the wall. "Are you quite certain?"

Ophir nodded. "On my life, I speak the truth."

As Gershom's eyes darted around the room, eyeing the three men that stood before him, a servant cautiously entered carrying a message sent by courier pigeon from Lord Memucan.

Pash took the piece of paper and handed it to his father. "A message from Numbio."

After reading the note, Gershom crumpled the parchment and threw it on the ground. His eyes raged. His breathing slowed. His teeth gnashed together.

"What news from the South?" Pash asked, offering him a glass of much needed wine. He tried to mask his disappointment that the rumors about his father corresponding secretly with foreign Lords was true.

He snatched the glass and drank every drop. Wiping his mouth, he said, "Crispin, son of Issachar, has arrived in Numbio seeking aid from Osiris." Gershom closed his eyes as he dropped into a chair, pale and feeling ill.

"Surely, they would not be so foolish as to join him." Pash's eyes darted between his father and his uncle.

Gershom rubbed his temples in a circular motion. "Osiris has pledged allegiance to him."

"Where did you say the girl was headed?" Pash turned his attention to Ophir.

"Into the Enchanted Swamp." Ophir sat in a chair opposite his brother. "If they find a way through, they could reach Port Daelon much faster than using the main roads."

"Why Port Daelon?" Pash joined them in a seat of his own and crossed one leg over the other. "That's Trader's Bay. Only merchants and seafarers travel there."

"Because -"

"They will seek aid from her grandmother, Queen Nym in Myr," Gershom interrupted Ophir with an exhausted sigh. "They must be stopped. Crushed before they can muster anymore hope." He leaned forward, elbows on his knees, "Find them."

"It will be done." The Nameless Rider crossed his arm over his chest and took his leave.

"I will send word to our assassin in Myr and have them handle our problem." Ophir was confident this would work.

Pash was taken aback. His father had an assassin living in the Isles of Myr? Was it possible his power stretched that far? This only confirmed Niabi was right to be suspicious of him. While collecting his thoughts, he sensed someone was watching him. Glancing up, he saw his father staring at him intensely.

"What would you have me do to help you?" If his father could read his thoughts, he would have struck him down where he stood.

Gershom shifted in his seat. He appeared reluctant to accept Pash's help. "These are trying times we now find ourselves in and I have run out of options, Pash." He sighed, "I believe there is something you can do for me."

CHAPTER FORTY-SIX

HERU

"We are to meet my sister at the abandoned fortress, Oakenshire, in the Black Forest to regroup." Crispin pointed at a large map of Adalore spread across an enormous table in the heavily stocked armory.

"It will be difficult to march our soldiers that distance without detection." Heru stared at the map and crossed his arms over his chest.

"What do you suggest?" Crispin glanced his way.

Heru inhaled, deep in thought. "I suggest we send a fleet by sea to the outer banks of Oakenshire off the coast of the Ignacia Sea."

"When could they be ready to leave?"

"It will take a couple of months before the ships could leave our port."

"We cannot wait that long to start our journey," Crispin shook his head. "My sister will be expecting us sooner than that."

"What if we take a small company of your fiercest warriors by foot and send the rest by sea?" Zophar proposed as he smoked his favorite pipe.

"When would we be ready to travel?" Crispin looked back at Heru.

"Give me a week and we will be ready to march." Heru nodded his head, flashing a proud smile.

"Then it is settled." Zophar scratched his red beard as he sat at the exceptionally wide table. "Do you suppose we could eat now?"

"I have never seen a man eat as much as you do and not get fat," Crispin laughed, stretching his back.

"We Westerners are fine specimens, indeed!" Zophar winked and patted his belly.

Heru discovered early on that Zophar was proud of his burly chest and hairy exterior, as was every Westerner. They ate plenty, loved often, and fought until Death took them; they were truly a people to be both feared and admired. And Heru was excited to have finally met one of them.

As the three men kicked up their feet to eat, a young servant hid in the shadows behind a large column with his bow drawn. He squinted one eye to aim at his target in the distance. Breathing slowly and methodically, he pulled his arrow back against the side of his cheek and exhaled as he released the arrow. The assassin watched as the arrow sliced through the room and pierced the prince.

The prince grabbed his chest as he fell to the ground; the arrow had pierced him directly above his heart. "Zophar..." he whispered, as blood oozed out of his chest.

"Guards! Guards!" Heru yelled as his soldiers rushed to search the palace. He caught one of them by the arm. "Bring Rayma."

Zophar covered in Crispin's blood, continued applying pressure to the wound. "Hold on, Crispin."

His eyes fluttered as the loss of blood began to take its toll on him. "Don't let me die," he whispered in Zophar's ear.

"Hush, my boy." Zophar gently patted Crispin's head. His eyes burned fighting the tears that slowly streamed down his cheeks. "You'll be alright."

"Please," a tear escaped Crispin's eye, "don't let me die, Zophar."

Rayma sprinted into the room with a bag full of potions and bandages. "What happened?" she asked as she tended to Crispin's wound.

"There is an assassin in the palace." Heru was enraged and on high alert. "Will he be alright?"

"He has lost a lot of blood," she examined him, "but I believe the arrow missed his heart."

"So, he will live?" Zophar wiped his face and held the prince tightly in his arms.

"Yes," she nodded her head. "I can heal him."

"See to it Prince Crispin is taken care of," Heru ordered as he stomped away.

"Where are you going?" she asked before he disappeared.

"I must speak with my father." His nostrils flared as he growled every word. "There is a traitor among us."

Heru found his father in his private chambers, heavily guarded due to the assassin running loose in the palace. The prince rushed toward Osiris and bowed before him.

"Father."

"My son," Osiris stood up as he entered. "Is he dead?"

"No."

Osiris exhaled, relieved, "Thank the Almighty One he still lives."

"I think it best we speak in private." Heru's eyes shifted to the guards.

The king waved them all out of his chambers.

"What is it, Heru?"

"Someone in the palace tried to assassinate Crispin."

"Surely it was not one of our servants." Osiris shook his head in disbelief. "They are all loyal to the crown."

"Which crown?" Heru spat harshly. "Someone has either been bought by the North or serves them willingly and we must find out who. What if there are more like him?"

"Our guards will find the perpetrator." Osiris patted his son's shoulder. "I will have Memucan investigate this matter. If there are more like this traitor, he will find them."

"Can Memucan even be trusted?" Heru hardly found the old advisor of upstanding character. "He was adamantly against us aiding Crispin."

"His duty as my advisor is to ensure the safety of our people, even if that means disagreeing with me."

"What if *he* is with the North?" Heru snorted.

His distrust of Memucan stemmed from his mother's dealings with him. Queen Zulu never liked him, and it was a fact she did not mask. She would always tell him, '*He's a serpent, my son. He is crafty and charming. But his words are coated with poison. Best to cut off a snake's head before it strikes.*'

"He has been a loyal friend and servant for many years, Heru." Osiris returned to his seat. "He would never betray the Numbio."

One of the Captains of the Royal Guard marched in and bowed. "Majesties, we found the assassin."

"Bring him forth!" Heru whipped around with a growl, fingers tapping the handle of his sword.

"He is dead, my Prince."

"Dead?" Osiris' voice boomed. "How?"

"We cornered him as he attempted to escape through a window, but instead of surrendering, the coward jumped to his death." The soldier shook his head, "There is not much left of him."

Osiris waved him off and turned once again to his son. "Whoever he was loyal to will remain a secret for now. This is one of many attacks that may cross Prince Crispin's path. Be vigilant, my son, for those who stand for their beliefs will surely be challenged to defend them."

CHAPTER FORTY-SEVEN

ADONIJAH

The beaten and weary trio arrived in Port Daelon just as the sun set. Under Harbona's advisement, Salome covered the bottom half of her face, just in case, her wanted poster had circulated through the enormous port. Ships from almost every kingdom in Adalore found their way to Port Daelon, for if there was trading to be done, it was done in Trader's Bay. Nestled in the mountains were a few local inns, taverns, and brothels at the disposal of sailors and merchants to help them relax and do business in the seaside village.

Salome and Adonijah followed their Immortal guide as he weaved around the dark and nameless floating dock streets with their horses in tow. Adonijah kept a watchful eye to ensure they were not being followed or recognized by bounty hunters. To his relief, the sea farers were too consumed with their liquor and female companions to even notice them passing by.

"We're here," Harbona announced as they stood before a large wooden vessel designed to transport spices.

"The Golden Rose." Salome read the ship's name aloud.

"Who goes there?"

Harbona looked up at the man who had called out to them. "Has it been so long that you do not recognize me, old friend?"

"Harbona?" The captain squinted his almond eyes, surprised to see him.

"Hello, Diron."

Diron waved them to come aboard his vessel. "I see you have not come alone this time." The middle-aged sea farer brushed his stringy dark hair out of his sun kissed face.

"These are my traveling companions." He embraced the captain and whispered, "We need passage to the Isles of Myr."

The narrow-eyed captain stared at a partially masked Salome with great curiosity but knew better than to ask about Harbona's affairs. "Then you are in luck. We are sailing for Myr at first light." He once again focused on the Seer. "Any chance someone might come looking for you?"

"Discretion would be appreciated."

"Follow me." Diron led them below deck, but instead of showing them to a room, he walked to the end of the hall and gently pressed the top corner of the wall and it opened. Inside was a cozy room equipped with two small cots and several shelves. "I hope this will be adequate for your journey."

"Thank you." Harbona extended a bag filled with gold coins, but Diron declined the payment.

"Consider us now even." He turned to leave. "I will see to it your horses find their way below deck. Rest, my friends."

As soon as the door closed, Adonijah eyed the Seer as he sat on one of the cots. "How did you come to be owed a favor from a smuggler?"

"He's a smuggler?" Salome uncovered her face.

Harbona nodded his head. "Diron was much younger when our paths first crossed. He had escaped from his cruel master in the Eastern Lands and asked to be hidden from his soldiers. I kept him safe for several weeks until he decided to sail with a crew based here in Port Daelon. Most know him as a spice merchant, but his true mission is to smuggle those who wish to be free from their oppressors to safety."

Salome sat on the opposite cot and rubbed her knees. "And his crew?"

"All slaves he helped free," he smiled. "He is a good man and will make sure we arrive to Myr safely. You both should rest. I want to smoke up on deck."

Once Harbona had left the small room, Adonijah laid down and stared at the planked ceiling. Noticing Salome was still sitting upright, with her eyes glued to the floor, he said, "You should get some rest."

"How can someone believe they have a right to enslave another?" she whispered. "That their life is somehow more valuable than another's?"

"You mean to tell me your father did not have slaves?" he yawned, rubbing his tired eyes.

"There are no slaves in the North." Salome lifted her eyes. "We are all free."

He was surprised by that. "But those who work in the castle - "

"Are free men and women who are paid for their work. In Northwind, it is not only an honor to serve one's king, but it is a paid profession."

He turned on his side and propped himself up on his elbow. "You realize that is not the same in most kingdoms."

"Were you born free, Adonijah?"

"Aye," he nodded, "I was born free, but too poor to matter."

Salome propped herself up on one of her elbows, mirroring his position, to face him. "Where are you from?"

"The Farmlands north of Gomorrah." No one had asked him that in a long time.

"Why did you leave?"

The way she looked at him; it felt like she could read his thoughts, see right through him. Her eyes. Those beautiful eyes that stared at him were filled with compassion. He was used to hiding under a hood, not letting anyone make eye contact with him, fearing what they would be able to see. She was not intimidated by him and that is what made him uncomfortable.

"It's complicated." He laid back down. "You should get some sleep."

She laid down and within a few minutes she had fallen asleep.

Her eyes fluttered as the rocking of the boat stirred her from her slumber. As she rubbed her eyes, she heard an odd noise. She turned and saw Adonijah was gone and Harbona had taken his place. Careful not to wake him, she grabbed her knife and sheathed it against her thigh and went to investigate the sounds she had heard.

She found a staircase that led to the lowest level of The Golden Rose and upon her descent, she realized it was completely dark. She lit a lantern hanging by the entrance, being careful not to set the boat ablaze. The noise had stopped, but she continued forward. She came upon their horses.

She pressed her face to Snow's nose. Maybe it was just the horses she had heard. But then, she sensed someone was watching her. She was not afraid; she was confident she knew who was standing behind her.

"I never had the opportunity to thank you for coming back to help me." She slowly turned to face the shadowed Stormcrag who had saved her from the Thrak.

He stepped into the light; his tan skin was smeared in clay and blue war paint. His appearance would normally frighten anyone who laid eyes on him, but his soft brown eyes were kind and Salome was not like most Adalorians. Salome stood at five feet, eight inches, and he was not much taller.

"You have been following us." She stepped toward him, but he lurched back, unsure of her advances. "Don't be afraid."

"I am not afraid," he said.

She tilted her head. "What is your name?"

"My name is of no importance."

"Your name is the one thing no one can ever take away from you." She stroked Snow's face. "Are you hungry?"

He did not respond, but by the look in his eyes, he was starving.

She motioned for him to follow her. "Come with me."

As she passed him, he said, "My name is Cato."

"Cato," she repeated with a smile. "I am Salome."

Adonijah stood above deck, he had never sailed the seas before and found himself to be quite seasick. Doing his best not to vomit, he clutched the railings as if his very life depended on it. He had not slept at all and his weary eyes were all anyone who looked at him noticed.

Diron patted him on the back, startling him. "A bit jumpy, aren't you?" The belly toting sea dog laughed the deepest chuckle Adonijah had ever heard. "First time out at sea?"

He nodded his head, "Aye."

"Take deep breaths and keep your eyes on the horizon," he pointed.

Adonijah burped. "Does that really work?"

"A lot better than staring down at the rippling waters." He chuckled once more and leaned against the railing. "Is she your wife? The woman you are traveling with."

"No." Adonijah did not like Diron asking questions about her.

"I meant no harm," the captain sensed he overstepped. "I noticed how protective you are of her and assumed she was your woman."

Adonijah was far too ill to try to intimidate Diron. He cleared his throat, eyes fixated on the horizon hoping it would help. "We had a run in with some less than desirable folk."

Diron nodded, "Understood."

Salome ascending the steps caught the captain's eye. Her presence was met with a friendly smile until he saw an unregistered passenger following her.

"Who is that?" Adonijah saw him, too.

"I do not know." Diron furrowed his brow as he approached them. "Who are you?"

"This is Cato." Salome stood between them. "He is one of the prisoners we freed from the Thrak on our way to Port Daelon."

Diron's mouth dropped in disbelief. "You *stole* from the Thrak?"

"If by steal you mean freed a person who was enslaved by his oppressors, then yes." Salome's eyes darted toward the captain. "We stole from the Thrak."

Diron scratched the stubble along his jawline. "To steal from the Thrak is unwise. They will surely be hunting you."

"You of all people should understand why we did, what we did." Salome held her ground.

Diron's expression softened as Harbona came into sight. "So, he told you."

Salome nodded, compassion in her eyes.

He whispered, "Aye, I do understand but -"

"But what?" she interrupted.

"The Mountain Men are the sons and daughters of exiled criminals," Adonijah said what Diron was thinking. "Their ancestors, Stormcrags and Krazaks alike, established a city built on the bones of both their enemies and the innocent."

"Should he be judged for the sins of his ancestors?" she quipped. "When I was in need of help from a Thrak that had bested me, this man saved my life. Surely that counts for something."

"He is right about us," Cato found the courage to speak. "The Mountain Men are a harsh people, but if we are not vicious, then all who wish to kill us would succeed. We are not hunted by only Thrak, but by the Krazaks, as well. It has been this way for as long as I can remember." His voice softened, "I lost both of my parents to the Gomorrians and my sister to our rival tribe. Without you," he turned to Salome, "my life would have been forfeited, and in order to truly repay you for your deed, I wish to join you on whatever quest you find yourself on."

"Join us?" Adonijah's words dripped with disapproval as he clutched the railing.

"When you return to the mainland, the Thrak will be searching for you," Cato warned. "I know their routes, patterns, and way of thinking. I also know my way around the Bone Mountains and can lead you where you need to go undetected. The Stormcrag owe you a life debt."

"If you know the Thrak so well, how did you come to be their prisoner?" Adonijah attempted to stand straight despite the queasiness in his stomach.

"I underestimated the Thrak." Cato's eyes shifted to his feet. "A mistake I do not intend to repeat."

"I believe he would be a great asset." Harbona stepped forward, resting his hand on Cato's shoulder.

Adonijah and Diron glanced at each other. Adonijah knew they would be fighting a losing battle, so he nodded reluctantly.

"Captain," Harbona lit his pipe with a satisfied grin, "perhaps, we could find some clean clothes for our new friend below deck?"

Diron nodded his head and muttered, "Aye," then followed Harbona and Cato down the creaky wooden steps.

Once they left, Adonijah leaned over the railing and stared at the horizon, breathing deeply. He closed his eyes and inhaled the fresh sea air. Suddenly feeling a presence, he opened one eye and noticed Salome standing next to him, eyeing him unapologetically.

"What did I do now?" his mouth twisted. From the look on her face, he already knew what she was going to say.

"Is Cato joining us going to be a problem?" Her tone was icy.

He rolled his eyes, gripping the railing tightly. "You and Harbona are the only Adalorians I know who seem to have a soft spot for the Mountain Men, and I cannot understand why."

"An entire people cannot all be bad -"

"For all you have suffered, Salome, you are far too trusting of men." He let go of the railing to light his pipe.

"And you aren't nearly trusting enough," she fired back. "There is more good in the world than you know." She rested her hand on his and whispered, "You told me you don't want to become like your father -"

"That is different." He ripped his hand away from hers, irritated she would bring that up.

"Is it different, Adonijah?" she asked softly. "You do not wish to be judged for your father's sins, so why do you judge Cato for the sins of his ancestors?"

He pondered her question. He had an inexplicable desire to argue with her, to fight her tooth and nail the remainder of their journey if he had to. But he knew she had trumped him by using his own past, his own fears, against him. There was nothing he could do or say to change her mind. She had won this round.

"Give him a chance." She leaned against the railing next to him, their arms touching. "He may surprise us."

"That is what I am afraid of," he whispered, exhaling a puff of smoke.

CHAPTER FORTY-EIGHT

CRISPIN

Crispin opened his eyes and felt the pain from his wound surge through his body. His shoulder and chest had been carefully cleaned and wrapped by Rayma while he had been unconscious. The weary prince turned his head to the right and saw Zophar sitting in the corner of his room, smoking his pipe. The dark bags underneath his eyes indicated he had not gotten much sleep, choosing instead to keep watch over his injured ward.

"You look terrible," Crispin winced as he sat up in his bed.

Zophar forced a smile, "Not as terrible as you." He placed the sword he had on his lap to the side of his chair and stretched as he walked over to the prince's bed. "How are you feeling?"

"Like I've been gutted." Crispin cleared his throat, "How long have I been out?"

"Three days."

"Three days?" Crispin grunted as he put his feet on the floor.

"You are not safe here," Zophar whispered.

"It would seem I am not safe anywhere anymore." He was now fully aware of the danger he was truly in but forced a smile to ease Zophar's frayed nerves.

"We must not stay here any longer." Zophar rubbed his bloodshot eyes. "Whoever sent that assassin will not hesitate to send another to finish the job."

"Good thing I have you to protect me." He winked, but Zophar did not laugh. He did not even crack a smile.

"I was not able to protect you from the arrow that narrowly missed your heart." His voice cracked so he cleared his throat. "We are not among friends."

"You worry too much. That's why you're starting to get those white hairs."

"Aye, and you do not worry enough," Zophar clicked his tongue, looking at his reflection in the mirror. "If I do have white hair, it's because of you."

"Me? And not Salome?"

Zophar pointed to the wrinkles around the corners of his eyes. "These are from Salome."

Crispin laughed, slowly standing to his feet, clutching his chest. "Glad to see we both gave you something permanent."

"Where do you think you are going?" Zophar huffed.

"I need some fresh air," Crispin muttered.

"Then I am going with you."

Crispin patted the burly man's shoulder. "I will be alright, I promise."

"Have you not heard a word I said?"

"Every word," he sauntered to the door. "Go to sleep. I will be back before you wake."

"Cheeky boy. Has a head as thick as they come," Zophar muttered under his breath, fighting the long overdue sleep that slowly overtook him.

Crispin shuffled through the hallways of the palace and gained strength the longer he walked around. He stopped at an enormous room filled with thousands of scrolls shelved from the ceiling to the floor. As impressive as the library was, the view from the three floor-to-ceiling windows nearly took his breath away. He never dreamt he would ever be standing in the great palace of

Numbio, yet there he was. He could see the port on the Umpoco River and watched for several minutes as the seamen and tradesmen conducted business. When he was a young boy, he did not value the majestic view Northwind boasted, but being in Numbio, and after living most of his life in the Tree House Forest, he finally attained an admiration and appreciation for large cities.

Out of the corner of his eye he saw a figure pass behind him, sending him into high alert. "Who's there?"

"Walking the palace alone so soon, Prince Crispin? Are you not concerned for your wellbeing?" The mysterious voice spoke with a smoothness that made him feel at ease, even though he did not know who was speaking.

"Should I be?" His eyes darted around the library, hoping to catch a glimpse of the person the voice belonged to. "Who are you?"

"Why do you wish to know?"

"You know who I am, I think it only fair to know who you are."

"My Lord, life is not fair."

"Why not at least tell me your name?" He finally caught sight of a shadowed figure in a dark corner of the room.

"I am Amunet."

Still unable to make out her face, he said, "Step into the light."

After a moment's pause, Amunet stepped from the shadows into the bright light that poured through the windows. Crispin was in complete awe. She was beautiful and tall with wild tight curls. Attention was drawn to her hazel eyes by golden paint streaked around her eyes and cheekbones.

"Is this better?"

Crispin was rendered speechless but caught himself staring and pried his eyes from the dark-skinned beauty. "Who are you?"

"Follow me and all of your questions shall be answered."

Crispin hesitated only a second before he followed her down the hallway. Her long arms were adorned with gold jewelry that would be the envy of any royal in Adalore.

After several minutes of walking in silence, Crispin's curiosity got the better of him. "Where are you taking me?"

Amunet did not respond, but his question was answered as soon as they turned the corner. The Golden Temple was nestled between the palace and the Umpoco River and was easily the most stunning structure in the city, since it was constructed purely of gold, onyx, and ivory.

"You are a priestess?" he guessed once they entered the holy place.

"I am Amunet, the High Priestess of the Golden Temple."

Crispin was confused. "Why did you bring me here?"

"For this." She glided to an oversized golden mirror and ripped off the white linen sheet that covered it. Careful not to step in front of it, she waved Crispin forward. "What do you see?"

He stood before the mirror and silently stared at his own reflection. He shrugged, "I see my reflection. Is this a trick?"

"Look closely." Her serious tone amused him, and he once again stared into the mirror. "Tell me what you see."

This time, the mirror began to swirl until he was looking at a sinister version of himself. He watched as his heart slowly turned black, and in a panic, stared at his reflection's eyes and saw his brown eyes fade into total darkness. Every second that passed, his reflection grew more evil which terrified him. He tried to pry his eyes away from the horrific image, but found he was completely powerless.

"Make it stop!" Crispin yelled.

"Tell me what you see," the high priestess demanded, unmoved by his cries.

"I do not wish to see anymore."

"Now is the time your questions receive answers. There is more you must see before the mirror will release you." The mirror showed Crispin his homeland of Northwind and the White Throne he had coveted since his youth. "From the ashes, one will rise; to the ashes, one will fall."

Crispin found himself face to face with Gershom in the middle of a crowded and bloody battlefield. He remembered Harbona's warning but did not heed his instruction. The prince sprinted toward his enemy and with great force, swung his sword, initiating their duel. After a hard-fought battle, Gershom disarmed him and stabbed him through the heart. He could hear his sister's screams as his eyes faded to black.

Finally, the mirror released him, and he fell to the ground, clutching his heart. "What dark magic is this?"

"You have seen your future, my lord." She stood stoically as she looked down at him.

"That is not my future." His breathing was heavy. "The mirror lies."

"The mirror never lies. People lie." Amunet draped the linen over the mirror once again and turned her attention to the sweating prince. "If you do not accept it is not your destiny to battle Gershom, your life will be forfeit." Crispin sat on the ground, overwhelmed with the vision. "I see I am not the first one to warn you of this." She knelt in front of him and lifted his face toward her. "Your heart is fading, Crispin of Northwind. Do not let the evil that has consumed your enemies, fill your heart. Let your hatred go."

"My hatred is all I have." Tears filled his tormented eyes.

"If you lose yourself, then you have already been defeated."

Crispin shot up, "No! Stop saying such things."

She stood before him and gently rested her slender fingers on his chest. "You will be the leader of thousands. They will follow you into battle, but if you do not rid your heart of the poison that consumes it, you will not live to rule them."

He felt a deep and immediate connection to the priestess when she touched his chest and rested his hand on top of hers. "Come with me."

She shook her head. "I am needed here."

"I need your guidance."

The priestess unhooked her long pendant necklace and placed it around his neck. "As long as you wear this, I will be with you. May this be an everlasting reminder to follow your path and not wish for another's."

"I feel like I know you." He stared deeply into her warm hazel eyes. "As if I have seen you before."

"Perhaps, you have."

"Will I see you again?"

"When the time is right our paths will cross again." Her words brought him much needed comfort. "Now you must return to the palace before you are missed.

CHAPTER FORTY-NINE

PASH

On the same day for the last ten years, Pash drank himself into a stupor just to numb the pain of his mother's death. Shortly after Northwind had been conquered, his mother, Oona, was found dead in her chambers. There was no physical evidence of how she was killed. A full investigation was launched into her murder, but no one was found responsible and inevitably she was forgotten by nearly everyone in the city, except for him. Not a day went by he did not think of her, and wished she were still walking the halls of the castle, bringing joy to everyone she crossed paths with.

As he poured himself another glass of wine, he stared with teary eyes at a portrait he had painted of her. Oona had large round brown eyes, luxurious black hair that cascaded down to her hips and dark brown eyebrows. Her pointy nose and tawny skin tone had been passed down to him as were her long limbs. A smile was always on her freckled face and he could vividly remember she had the voice of a celestial being. As a child, he would only agree to go to sleep once she had sung him a song of her Southern ancestors, although now he could no longer recall any of the lyrics.

Oona had been sent on behalf of the Numbio to serve as their Ambassador to Northwind during King Issachar's reign. Due to

Issachar's insistence of Gershom finding a suitable wife, the marriage between Gershom and Oona was arranged and blessed by both kingdoms. Pash would not describe their marriage as a happy one. His father had a wandering eye and dubbed monogamy a hindrance. But Oona had Pash, and that was enough.

"I miss you," his voice cracked as he glanced over her portrait with sad admiration.

"Has it been another year already?" Ophir startled his nephew. "Your mother was a wonderful woman, rest her everlasting soul."

"What do you need, Uncle?" Pash did not look up.

"I knocked; you did not answer. I wanted to make sure you were alright."

"Much troubles me, Uncle, but they are my burdens to bear. You need not worry about me. I will be fine by morning."

Ophir watched him guzzle the last bit of his drink and drop his goblet on the floor. "How much have you had to drink, Pash?"

"Why does it matter?" His eyes were glassy, his speech slurred.

"You are the Commander of Her Majesty's Shadows and the Second in Command's heir," Ophir reminded him. "You have a duty to conduct yourself in a manner befitting your titles or you will lose more than just your rank."

"Neither the Queen nor my father care if I live or die," Pash spat. "I am just a pawn they use at their convenience."

"Be quiet before someone hears you," Ophir whispered. "I know better than most, that something spoken in secret can cost you what you value most."

"Let them hear me!" he whipped around and shouted from his balcony. "Let all of Northwind hear my words!"

Ophir hushed him, trying to pull him back inside. "Think of your life, boy."

"I don't care for my life anymore." Pash ripped his arm from his uncle's grasp. "It has never been mine to begin with." The spitefulness in his voice did not go unnoticed.

"If you are not careful, your father will surely make you suffer."

Pash tapped both of Ophir's ears. "Are you not listening, Ophir? I no longer care. Let him take my life," he snarled as he leaned over his balcony. "It would be the first act of kindness I ever received from him."

"Pash -"

"I will never be good enough in his eyes." Pash's voice softened, tears in his eyes. "You of all people should understand."

"I do understand." Ophir poured himself a glass of wine from the decanter. He sat in a lounge chair and sipped his drink. "I helped my brother rise to his position of power and I will die to keep him there. It is our duty."

Pash turned around, fury in his bloodshot eyes. "You would let your own brother mistreat you and remain silent? After everything you have done for him. After years of loyal service. After everything you've lost?"

"He is my lord first and foremost, my brother second. You are his soldier first and son second. Learn this Nephew, it will do you well."

Pash stood only a few inches taller than his uncle but made a point to step in front of him to intimidate him. "What have you gained by selling your soul to the devil?"

"A home, wealth, power." Ophir was not fazed by the question.

"Do you sleep at night?" Pash's voice cracked. "Because I don't. I cannot sleep anymore."

"If you cannot sleep, then perhaps, you should consult a healer."

"What have we gained serving him?" Pash was on a warpath. "What has my father ever given us other than contempt and blatant disrespect? He has taken everything from us! Everyone we have ever loved."

"Pash, be silent," he hissed. "You need to collect yourself. You are coming unhinged."

"And what of Satara?" Pash knew by the mere mention of her name, he would get an honest reaction from Ophir. "Do you mean to tell me she meant so little to you that you would continue to serve him?"

Ophir's bald head turned a shade of red Pash had not seen before. Defensive and now enraged, he barked, "Never mention her name again!"

"You loved her, and my dear father took her for himself."

"Stop it, Pash."

"And when he had tired of her, had her killed." Pash would not relent. "And you did nothing to stop him."

"Pash, you are drunk -"

"I know my father had something to do with my mother's death." Pash paced the room, like a caged animal waiting to be set loose. "One day, I will learn the truth, and I swear before all the gods in the Ten Kingdoms of Adalore, that I will have his head for it."

"Enough, Pash," Ophir nearly shouted. "You speak of high treason."

"Why do you fear him?" Pash furrowed his brow as he faced him. "*He* is the one who should be afraid."

"Watch your tongue."

Pash scoffed. "Look at you, Ophir. You are just a shadow of a man I once respected. It is no wonder he took Satara from you. You're weak."

Ophir punched Pash, knocking him to the floor. "One day, Pash, you will push me too far."

Ophir retreated from the room, leaving Pash to sleep off his drunkenness alone on the cold floor.

CHAPTER FIFTY

CRISPIN

Once night had fallen upon the vibrant city of Numbio, all the citizens donned their finest clothes and began to celebrate in the city streets, at the same time, King Osiris' banquet was underway in the palace. Having had limited time to organize the festival for his warriors, Osiris was pleased with the splendor of the great hall. The Southern Kingdom was known for their elaborate celebrations and Crispin was excited the tales were true.

"It is most unusual for pale ones to be included in our festivities," Memucan interrupted Crispin's moment of admiration. "I remember when your kind were forbidden from our halls."

"Your city is one I greatly admire, Lord Memucan, and your people are some of the finest in Adalore." The old man was visibly impatient with him. "Out of all the men and women I have had the honor of meeting, you have been the only one to show contempt for my presence. Why is that?"

Memucan showed no sign of embarrassment by the foreign prince drawing attention to his behavior.

"Prince Crispin, if I should even call you by that title," he sneered. "You have come to my city asking for the Numbio to fund your war against a queen who has done us no harm. The blood of *my* people will be sacrificed for a tragedy that most have nearly forgotten." The shriveled advisor hobbled closer to Crispin so only he could hear his whispers. "Let it be known that Memucan, son of Wentu, spoke against this alliance and opposed this war. The Numbio's blood will be on your hands. The wails of their widows and tears of their children will be on your head. Remember them as you command their husbands, brothers, fathers, and sons to fight your enemies. Remember them, for they will surely remember you."

Crispin did not know what to say. He watched silently as the advisor disappeared into the jubilant sea of smiling faces.

"There you are!" Zophar patted Crispin on the back as he ate some type of meat off the bone. "Why do you look so glum? This is a celebration, not a funeral."

Crispin mustered up a smile to please his friend, but deep down all he could think about was for some of these joyous warriors, it was their funeral.

Osiris stood from his throne silencing the music and the people in the room. After a deep inhale, the king's booming voice echoed through the vast space.

"Many years ago, I lost one of my friends. To know his life had been taken; that his murderers had claimed his throne and tainted the halls of his home was difficult to bear." With his gaze now fixated on Crispin, he continued. "Today, we have hope that a terrible wrong will now receive justice. By the grace of the Almighty One, Prince Crispin escaped the hands of his enemies and now seeks to sit on his father's throne. We remember the dead, and celebrate the living, who are willing to do what is right." Osiris lifted his golden cup in Crispin's direction; every guest followed suit. "Whether in life or death, we are with you, my brother."

Crispin drank with them, but he felt as if his eyes had been opened. All he had considered was himself, his family, his dead. In truth, he had not thought about anyone else. He had not weighed the gravity of the role he was assuming: Leader. The responsibility of that word gripped his heart. For years, this is what he wanted. Now that he was in the midst of it, he was unsure how heavy a price he would pay for victory.

←———▪

After the king's speech, the jubilee resumed, and Rayma slithered through the crowded hall searching for one face in particular. Unable to find him inside, she knew exactly where Heru would be hiding. Out on a secluded balcony that overlooked the city, she spied him quietly observing his people dancing in the desert streets.

"Surely you must know I am not the only one looking for you." He turned his head toward her, smiled and extended his hand. She grabbed it and he pulled her close to him. The sound of his heart soothed her to the point she found herself closing her eyes to fully enjoy the rhythmic beat. "Why are you out here alone, Heru?"

"I have never left Numbio before and I am afraid that I may forget the sight of her."

"What you see is merely buildings constructed by men. That is not Numbio." She glanced up at him and placed her hand on his bare chest. "Numbio is here and that is something you will never forget."

The prince gently kissed her forehead and held her tightly. "If something should happen to me -"

"Do not speak of such things," she interrupted.

"Rayma," his strained whisper hushed her. "I need you to do something for me, if I should fall."

"Do not ask me to do what I cannot bear to think about."

"Please, just listen." He sweetly lifted her chin so he could see her face. "If I should fall, bring my body back home to my father so I may be buried with my ancestors."

Tears streamed down her cheeks upon hearing his request, but she mustered the strength to nod. "If you should fall, I will do as you ask."

The following day, just before the sun began to set, the band of elite warriors made their final preparations before setting out on their long journey across the desert. Heru stood at the top of the palace steps that overlooked the caravan. He had been standing there for nearly an hour, mentally preparing to leave his homeland for the first, and possibly last time. Osiris joined him and watched Crispin ready his horse for the long trip.

"He looks just like his father," the king broke the silence. "Let us hope he is wiser."

Heru exhaled, "I will protect him."

"I do not worry for him, my son." Osiris embraced him. "Fight hard, Heru, and may the Almighty One bless and protect you."

"I will return," he saluted his father. "You have my word."

The war horn of Numbio sounded throughout the entire city, alerting all who heard that their warriors were about to depart. Every man, woman, and child lined the streets from the palace to the main gate to pay their respects. As the caravan made their way through the city, Crispin noticed all the people were dressed in red and held their left fists in the air with their right hands resting on their hearts.

"Why do they stand that way?" Crispin asked Heru who rode beside him.

"When we send our warriors from our homeland, we pay respect by lifting one hand to our Creator to ask for his protection and the other hand on our hearts to ask for his blessing. We wear red to signify that whether in life or death, we the Numbio, will forever be warriors."

Crispin was once again humbled by Heru's mighty people and realized how great a sacrifice they were making for him to reclaim his father's throne, to take back his home.

"To glory, my brother." Heru crossed his hand over his heart.

"To glory," Crispin touched his heart.

After travelling through the night, the sun peaked above the horizon signaling the caravan of an imminent stop. Ready to rest, the soldiers welcomed the dawn. Heru raised his hand and the Numbio stopped in unison.

"We shall camp here until nightfall," Heru announced.

Every member of the caravan knew their responsibility and began setting up their camp without further instruction.

Rayma pulled an apple from her bag and fed her exhausted horse, while the soldiers set up the campsite.

"You always spoil that horse." Bantu slithered up next to her, startling her.

"You know we are not supposed to be seen together, Bantu," she chastised Memucan's servant. "What do you want?"

"The master wanted me to give you this." The sunken eyed servant discreetly handed her a glass vile.

"Does he truly not trust me to -"

"No, he does not trust you," Bantu interrupted her. "Pour this in his drink at the right moment and the master will do as he has promised."

"And how do I know I can trust him?" She lifted an eyebrow. "Or you?"

"You don't." He smirked. "That is part of the fun."

"Get away from me before someone notices you," she spat.

"Remember," he taunted, "he is always watching you." Amused, he walked away with a grin spread across his dark face.

On the other side of the campsite, Crispin observed the endless miles of sand that laid before them.

"What do you see?" Zophar squinted in the direction Crispin was staring.

"Nothing," he replied, eyes still glued to the horizon. "Nothing at all."

"You make it sound as if that is a bad thing," Heru chimed in. Crispin's silence confirmed his suspicions. "What troubles you?"

"Something is coming. I can feel it."

"You have not slept well in days," Zophar drank water from his sheepskin. "You should rest while you can. I will take first watch."

At that moment, the entire caravan heard a thunderous rumble south of them. Staring toward the scorching desert, Crispin spied a billowing sandstorm headed directly for them at a frightening pace.

"Sandstorm!" Heru shouted.

Scrambling to their horses and camels, the group of travelers sprinted away from the determined storm. The winds whipped ferociously as they tried to escape. As the raging wall of sand neared them, Crispin could have sworn he heard a man's voice chanting in the distance.

◄─────◄

His feeble arms stretched wide, Memucan's eyes were tightly shut as he chanted his incantation. On the table behind him sat a large black book filled with dark magic spells. Determined to destroy both Issachar's heir and Heru, he continued to recite the incantation passionately, knowing the more focused he was, the larger the storm would become. Despite his incessant shouting, he oddly started to feel weaker the longer he spoke. It seemed as if an opposing force was combating him, and he had no idea who it could be.

◄─────◄

Feeling Crispin was in danger, Amunet stood in the Golden Temple and began praying for the warriors. She had never felt such evil before and feared her light magic would not be strong enough to defeat the unknown sorcerer. With her arms stretched wide, she closed her eyes and continued to fight for the Numbio's survival.

⬸━━━━━☪

They swiftly galloped away, hoping they could outrun the storm, but they came to realize it had grown larger and was picking up speed. Crispin fought to keep his eyes open as sand swirled around them. He mumbled a quick prayer under his breath, hoping for some kind of miracle.

"We can't outrun the storm!" Heru yelled.

Crispin looked forward and caught sight of the mouth of a cavern. "Get to the caverns!"

The southern warriors rode toward their refuge. Sand continued to swarm them as they urged their horses onward. The storm claimed three warriors' lives, but the rest of the caravan made it safely into the cave.

⬸━━━━━☪

Memucan raged when he saw the vision of them escaping and screamed, which sent a bolt of lightning down to strike the rocks above the cave's entrance. Cascading boulders fell and completely covered the opening, trapping the remaining Numbio inside.

CHAPTER FIFTY-ONE

RAYMA

"Where are we?" Zophar lit a torch and looked around the vast cavern.

"Some sort of cave." Crispin ran his hands on the rocky walls.

"This is no ordinary cave." Rayma joined the leaders. "This is the Cavern of the Undead."

"Cavern of the Undead?" Crispin repeated slowly.

She could tell by the way he looked at her, he had no idea what she was talking about.

"Out of the countless men who have dared to enter this place, only one lived to tell of its mysteries and he died from his madness," Rayma's words induced dread. "We must leave this place before it is too late."

"The way is blocked," Zophar reminded her.

"We must unblock the entrance," she insisted.

"That could take us far too long, Rayma." Heru rested his hand on her shoulder.

She gasped, "You cannot possibly be suggesting we go deeper into the cave." Her eyes darted from Heru to Zophar to Crispin. *They do not understand. If they did, they would be tearing those rocks apart.*

"That is our best option." Heru turned to Crispin who had been examining the blocked entrance. "What say you, Crispin?"

After a minute of weighing their options, Crispin agreed with Heru. "We must travel through the caverns."

"Forgive me, my lord," Rayma insisted her voice be heard once more, even though she knew her tone was dancing on the line of sounding disrespectful. "You don't know what creatures lurk in the darkness."

"I know that path is uncertain," Crispin acknowledged, "but that is our best chance for getting out of here alive. We do not have the tools necessary to remove these boulders and we need to conserve our strength for what lies ahead."

"Prince Crispin has spoken." Heru eyed Rayma in such a way that she knew fighting would be futile, so she reluctantly agreed. "We march forward," he announced to the warriors. "Stay alert."

⊰────────⊱

The city of Numbio had suffered some damage from the storm that had originated from their borders. King Osiris dispatched his soldiers to ensure the citizens were taken care of and their kingdom walls were secure. While they followed his instruction, the king rushed to the Golden Temple and upon arrival, he saw Amunet lying on the ground in exhaustion. He knelt next to her and helped her sit up.

"What happened to you, Holy One?"

"Someone has the Book of Noot," she gasped for air. "I have never felt such powerful dark magic."

"The Book of Noot?" Osiris exclaimed. "That cannot be. The book was destroyed."

"The book survived," she whispered, "and its servant is here in Numbio."

"Why would he conjure a sandstorm?" As soon as the question escaped his lips his eyes widened. "My son? Is my son alright?"

She nodded as Osiris rested her against the wall. "He is alive."

"Bless the Almighty One."

"My King," Amunet's weakened voice halted his celebration.

"What is it, Holy One?"

"They took shelter in the Cavern of the Undead."

"But that means..."

She mournfully grimaced, "They are beyond my sight. I can no longer help them."

"Rest easy, High Priestess." Osiris stood and looked out over Numbio. "We shall find the traitor who used dark magic in our city."

<hr />

Cautiously, the caravan pushed forward through the caverns for hours. Exhausted, they desperately searched for a safe place to set up camp, but the narrow winding pathways made that impossible. If they had not been concerned with remaining vigilant to a possible ambush, they would have been completely amazed by the wonderous beauty that surrounded them.

Rayma was still opposed to Crispin's decision and had kept to herself the entire time they journeyed through the unknown territory. Heru rode up next to her when he saw the path had widened.

"He did what he thinks is best," he whispered.

"Best for who?" Her tone was dripping with venom. "Why is he the only one making decisions for the Numbio? That is *your* responsibility."

"I pledged to fight with him," Heru looked at her, still speaking in a hushed tone. "I am not weak because I choose to follow. I am strong because I understand my place in this journey."

"He will lead us to our downfall," Rayma angrily disagreed.

"A leader is only as strong as his weakest soldier. He will not always make the right decisions, but he will never be victorious, if he must always battle his own."

"So, you wish him not to be questioned or his choices challenged?"

"Speak when you must, Rayma, but never undermine." Heru touched her hand as discreetly as possible and smiled. "You will make a great queen."

Before she could respond, a warrior cried out, "Water!" A short distance before them was a winding river.

"The River of Lost Souls," Rayma muttered under her breath.

Bast, the only man to have escaped these caverns, told tales of the creatures that lived in the darkness. The river that flowed through lured mortal men in, but it ultimately led to their doom. He told anyone who would listen, what he had seen; what he had endured. But the Numbio laughed at him. Called him mad. She was just a little girl when she saw him running through the streets in tattered clothes, a ghost of who he once was. Everyone mocked him, but she always believed. He died a broken and lonely man. All she could think about when she was growing up, was if she would suffer the same fate.

"We will set up camp here, until we have rested enough to continue," Crispin declared to the delight of the weary travelers.

Not having all of their resources because the sandstorm claimed their last campsite, the Numbio shared what they had and took shifts watching for the creatures that supposedly inhabited the caverns.

CHAPTER FIFTY-TWO

CRISPIN

For the first time since Crispin left the Tree House Forest, he felt at ease. Even though, the unknown of the caverns frightened everyone else, he did not mind it. He was used to the "on edge" feeling. Never knowing if the villagers would learn who he really was or if Niabi and Gershom would finally discover they had escaped. But most importantly, he knew if he showed any sign of fear, those who followed him would feel hopeless.

Most of the camp fell asleep quickly after their long day. There were a few warriors guarding their slumbering companions, although, they did not expect an attack.

Zophar passed out the moment his bushy red beard hit the cot. His snoring could keep anyone up but having spent most of his life under the same small roof with the Westerner, Crispin was immune. Unfortunately, the young prince laid in the tent, wide awake; his mind was consumed with far too many thoughts to allow him to rest. He decided since sleep eluded him, he would relieve one of the nightguards. At least one of them would enjoy a restful night's sleep.

As he looked around the cold and damp caverns, he realized if there were any creatures out there, he would have no way of knowing they were there. The only light came from the campfire in the center of their encampment and that is where he spotted Rayma going through her apothecary bag.

"Can I safely assume you could not sleep either?" He broke her concentration as he approached.

Although she did not look pleased to see him, she politely responded, "I never sleep much, not even in Numbio."

"I have nightmares most nights," he sat down to warm his hands. "I have learned not to rely heavily on sleep."

She nodded her head and returned her focus to her bag.

"I have heard you are one of the best healers in all of Adalore. I am truly honored you are with us -"

"You may save your flattery, Prince Crispin," she interrupted. "I am not here for you, but for my people, who will more than likely need my services."

He smiled warmly. "You are not too fond of me, I gather."

Rayma softened her tone but remained bold. "I am sure you are a good man. There is no denying you have suffered greatly, but the North has no quarrel with us. I do not want Numbio blood spilled over a war we do not belong in."

Crispin nodded his head, having heard those words before from Memucan. "I agree with you."

"You agree with me?" Rayma was stunned.

"A few weeks ago, I was living in a humble tree house with no real hope of reclaiming my homeland. Then in a matter of minutes, my entire life was once again, turned upside down." Their eyes met. "I never wanted anyone to risk their lives for me. I just wanted someone to believe this wrong should be righted. That my family had not been forgotten by their friends. I am not a perfect leader, Rayma." He cleared his throat, "Is it alright if I call you Rayma?"

She nodded approvingly.

"Rayma, I will make many mistakes. But I will never ask any of you to do something I am not willing to do first." He hesitated before he continued. "I also know you are opinionated, and I value honesty. Crave it. My desire is that every member of our troop will one day soon, return home. I know you will help me make that happen."

"I am afraid I misjudged you." She reached out to him. "Although, I am against our involvement, the Numbio will always aid our friends in need. Just know if I need to speak up, I will."

He smiled. "I wouldn't want it any other way."

The horn of Numbio suddenly echoed through the caverns. Crispin and Rayma ran in the direction of the sound and saw a tall, pale, bone thin creature attacking the lone look-out. The hunchback assailant swung his sword, made from bones, with swift fury. His arms were as long as his legs and made running on all four possible. The soldier fought the pointy eared goblin as he continued yelling for back up. Crispin quickly joined the soldier and helped subdue the long, curved-nose devil. As they tied their prisoner, he growled, showing rows of jagged teeth.

"They are more frightening than I could have ever imagined." Rayma could not tear her eyes away from the beast who looked as if he used to be human.

Zophar and Heru rushed over to help and were shocked by the unsightly cavern creature.

"Hell!" Zophar could not believe his eyes. "What is this foul beast?"

"They are the Wagura," Rayma answered in a raspy whisper. "And I can guarantee you if it found us, its horde will not be far behind."

"It's a scout?" Heru asked.

Crispin knelt before the bound Wagura and stared into its yellow eyes. "Where is your horde?"

The creature cackled, "You stand no chance against the Wagura." His demonic voice was chilling.

"You underestimate us." Crispin showed no sign of fear, although, he was terrified of the nightmarish sight. "This is the last time I will ask. Where is your horde?"

"They are already here." It let out an unearthly howl signaling the awaiting horde to attack.

"To arms! To arms!" Heru shouted as a thundering swarm of Wagura charged at them from the darkness.

The captured cavern dweller howled once more, this time even louder. Fearing he would alert more creatures than they could handle, Crispin slit his throat and was surprised to see a green liquid ooze out of him instead of red blood.

Unlike the scout, the warrior Waguras towered over the tallest Numbio by nearly a foot. Even though they were bone thin, they were incredibly agile and strong. The Numbio fought with swiftness and great skill but there were so many creatures, they were concerned with being overrun.

Zophar sliced a creature across its chest and was splashed with green goo. Noticing Heru battling three Wagura, he let out a war cry and jumped to the prince's aid. The eight-foot-tall enemy squared up to the Westerner, who stood between him and his original prey. Enjoying every second of his first battle in over a decade, Zophar gritted his teeth and then cried, "Come closer, so I might send you back to hell!

Once Zophar evened the odds, Heru began striking down Waguras. Adrenaline pulsed through his veins. Unlike Zophar, a veteran, Heru had never faced an enemy in battle and was in survival mode. From the corner of his eye, he saw Rayma tending to the fallen Numbio, unaware of a Wagura rushing at her from behind.

"Rayma!"

He slashed his last victim and sprinted to save her. Making it in time to shield her, he took the blow. His arm was sliced, and blood gushed.

"Heru!" Rayma cried in horror as he yelled in pain.

Unable to shy away from his present clash, Heru switched his sword from his dominate, but injured arm, to his weak hand. Determined to protect Rayma, he battled through excruciating pain. The prince swung his sword and sliced off one of the creature's pointy ears, but it showed no sign of anguish, despite the flow of green goo pouring down the side of its weathered face. Heru dodged an incoming blow and quickly rolled behind the Wagura and stabbed it in the back.

Rayma was clearly shaken by the duel and threw her arms around Heru's neck, tears streaming down her face. "I thought I had lost you."

"I did too."

Near the River of Lost Souls, Crispin found himself covered in green 'blood', but unscathed. His eyes fell on the largest member of the horde stomping toward him wielding a five-foot-long bone sword. Its body was scarred from head to toe and it was the only creature who had black paint markings on its arms and chest. Crispin assumed the creature covered in human blood was the commander of the horde and prepared himself for the duel of his life. He was no longer practicing with Salome in the forest. This battle had consequences should he fail to defeat his foe.

The Wagura commander circled the young prince with a soulless glare. Crispin was trying to remember all the lessons Zophar had taught him as he stared at the demonic creature. Without warning, the Wagura swung his impressive weapon down on Crispin who sidestepped the blow. The ground shook where the large sword landed. Using his speed to his advantage, Crispin danced and skirted around the much stronger combatant.

Crispin grimaced when the creature's blade finally caught him, slicing his right thigh. He no longer had a choice, he had to become the aggressor, or this would be the end of him. Stumbling to his feet, he swung his sword and sliced off one of the Wagura's arms. He capitalized when he saw an opening and plunged his sword deep into the creature's chest.

Growling, the demon pulled Crispin toward him, and in a desperate attempt to kill the human, plunged them both into the rushing River of Lost Souls. The prince unsheathed his knife as he fought to keep his head above the icy water, and once the Wagura was close enough, he slashed its throat, nearly severing its head.

Zophar saw when Crispin was dragged into the river and ran as fast as he could down-stream to catch him before he disappeared into the dark cavern. Crispin was able to grab ahold of a large rock that protruded out of the water. Zophar extended his hand to him.

"Take my hand." They stretched for one another, but he was just out of Zophar's reach. "Reach, Crispin!"

"I cannot reach you," Crispin's tone was solemn.

"Don't you do it." The red bearded warrior saw exhaustion in Crispin's eyes. "Don't you dare let go!"

"Tell Salome, I'm sorry." His fingers slipped and the river claimed him.

"No!" Zophar watched as he disappeared into the darkness.

Heru approached him with his arm in a sling. The horde was defeated, and Rayma was tending to the injured Numbio. "Where is Crispin?"

Eyes glossed over as he watched the waters rush downstream, Zophar whispered, "He's gone."

CHAPTER FIFTY-THREE

NIABI

Two torches lit the dark crypt. Niabi sat on the white stone bench in front of her son's final resting place. For hours she stared at his statue in silence, remembering him as a young boy. They had many wonderful adventures together – memories she was terrified she would one day forget. He had been her light when darkness consumed her, and with him gone, her past self, resurfaced. The queen faithfully visited her son, twice a week, but she found herself speaking to him less and less.

If Rollo could see what she had allowed herself to once again become... she cared not to finish that thought. He knew her as the best version of herself and that was all that truly mattered. She heard someone turn the corner.

"Your Majesty," Leoti stopped. "I'm sorry. I didn't realize you were going to be here."

Niabi patted the empty space next to her. "There's room for one more."

Leoti accepted the queen's invitation and sat down. She mumbled a short prayer under her breath.

"You still mourn him?" Niabi eyed her black ensemble.

"I will always mourn him. He was my best friend."

The queen looked at her son's statue again. Her smile was filled with sadness. "He was the sweetest child. My reason to continue living after Dichali..."

Leoti hesitated. "My father speaks of them almost daily. He misses them too."

Niabi grabbed Leoti's hand without looking in her direction. "Thank you."

"For what, my Queen?"

"For loving my son." She held back tears, gulping loudly, a knot in her throat. "I could always tell when he had been with you. You brought him so much joy." She turned toward Leoti who wiped tears from her cheeks. "My son may be gone, but you will always be my daughter."

Leoti's lip trembled, "I miss him so much."

"I know." Niabi nodded, fighting back tears as she held Leoti in her arms. "I know." She stroked Leoti's hair, fire raging within her, thinking about why her son had been taken from them. "Those responsible for Rollo's death will be dealt with."

The queen's gravelly whisper fueled Leoti. She leaned back and locked eyes with Niabi. "Yes," her tone deepened, "yes, they will."

Niabi was taken aback by Leoti's response. *What did she mean by that? What exactly did she know? What was she not saying?* Niabi noticed Pash standing at the end of the hallway and pushed the questions to the back of her mind. Maybe it was better if she did not know what Leoti was plotting.

She kissed Leoti's forehead and whispered, "If there is ever anything you need, you come to me."

She saluted her son's crypt and met Pash outside the entrance of the tomb.

"My apologies for interrupting -"

"Did he believe you?" she cut him off.

He nodded. "Yes."

"Good." She wrapped her black shawl around her shoulders. "What have you found out?"

He retrieved two folded up pieces of paper and handed them to her. As she examined the wanted posters, she intuitively knew who they were.

"He has Issachar's eyes." She flipped back to Salome's picture. "They are wanted by the Shadows?"

"It seems your brother and sister are the peasants who killed your Shadows in the Western forest."

Her hair was down without ornamentation for the first time in years. No crown, no jewels, just her natural self. The way he soaked her in did not go unnoticed by her. She felt him touch the tips of her raven black locks as they flowed lightly in the cool breeze. No one saw her in her natural appearance, except him. But that was only when they were alone. His eyes were filled with a longing that was undeniable. *He misses me,* she thought.

"What do we know?" She handed the pictures back to him, emotions now secondary to business.

"Your sister was spotted near the Enchanted Swamp," he cleared his throat, eyes shifting away from her. "Ophir returned with his findings when I was with my father."

"He found Salome?" Niabi's eyes beamed. "Is she here?"

"No, she escaped Ophir's men before he was able to retrieve her." The news irritated her, but he continued. "She was travelling with two men, neither fit Crispin's description. One appeared to be a mercenary for hire, while the second bore the banishment mark of the Immortals."

"Harbona," she whispered and tapped her lips. "So, the Seer is helping her. Where are they now?"

"Ophir believes they were going to Port Daelon."

"She is going to see Nym. Clever girl," the queen smirked. "Salome is not the only one with allies in Myr," she rubbed her hands together. "My sister is not my main concern. Find Crispin and she will come to us." She stepped toward the lookout point and together they gazed upon the White City.

"Crispin was last seen in Numbio with one companion."

"And how do we know of his whereabouts?" her eyes narrowed. "*I* have no servants in the Sand Lands."

He tilted his head. "It appears my father has allies in the South."

She straightened; a smirk crept across her face.

"You look... pleased?" He shifted his weight.

"Oh, I am." Her look pierced his soul. "You see, my suspicions of his misdeeds are now confirmed. Not only will he reap the benefit of these misguided alliances, but I too, will know everything he does. After all, knowledge is power."

"There have been no other sightings of Crispin." He rested his hand near hers on the white stone wall. "Without a lead, it may be difficult to find him."

"Do I look worried?"

After a moment of silence, he asked, "Do you trust the witch?"

"For now." She did not hesitate.

"For now?" he repeated. "How can you trust someone for a moment?"

"There was once a time I trusted your father." Her response was cold, but she had no problem speaking the truth.

Pash turned his gaze to the kingdom. The sun had just begun to set behind the Mountain of Kings and the White City was ablaze with the sun's orange glow. "What if they do come for the throne?"

"I sold my soul to take Northwind, and if necessary, I will fight until my very last breath to keep it. Let them come," she hissed, "I am ready."

ACKNOWLEDGEMENTS

First and foremost, I want to thank God for leading and guiding me to this point in my life. Without Him, I wouldn't be here.

To my husband, Brad, without your constant belief and encouragement, I probably would have given up years ago. Thank you for supporting me and for pushing me to be everything you already knew I could be.

To my daughter, Remi, thank you for telling me everyday how much you love me. You will never know how much your love means to me.

To my son, Archer, thank you for your random hugs throughout the day. They are my favorite interruptions.

To my daughter, Roux, thank you for smiling at me, for no particular reason whatsoever. Those smiles feuled me.

To my Mom, thank you for raising me to be the woman I am today; for being my first fan and my loudest cheerleader. Thank you for being my second pair of eyes, reading everything I sent you, and for helping me mold it into the finished product. There is no me, without you.

To my Dad, thank you for encouraging me to pursue my dreams and imparting in me your love of history and reading.

To Potter, the goofiest boxer and my best furry companion. Though some would say you're just a dog, you are more loving and loyal than most human beings. You have seen me through life, my dear, and it means the world to have you cuddled up by my side.

And to anyone who gave me a word of encouragement, a nudge in the right direction or kept me in their prayers, I express my gratitude and send you all my love.

MEET THE AUTHOR

Morgan Gauthier lives in East Tennessee with her husband and best friend, Brad, and with their three children, Remi, Archer, and Roux (who are 4 years old and younger!). If five people wreaking havoc in the same house wasn't enough, Morgan also has three dogs, Potter, Skye, and Bubba, and one grumpy bird named Titus.

Her first book, *Wolves of Adalore*, was published in 2021 and is the first book in a YA Epic Fantasy Trilogy. The second book, *The Red Maiden*, was published in 2022, and the third book, *The Raven and the Wolf*, is due for publication in 2023.

Morgan also published *Aloha, Seattle* in November of 2021. It is her first Contemporary Romantic Comedy and she is planning on writing more in the genre.

If Morgan isn't writing or reading, she can be found binge watching Netflix shows, playing video games, attempting to cook like Gordon Ramsay (not even close to his level), and practicing archery.

You can follow her on:
Instagram: @morgan_gauthier_
Facebook: @authormorgangauthier
Website: www.morgangauthier.com
Goodreads/Amazon: Morgan Gauthier
Pinterest: Morgan Gauthier
TikTok: @morgan_gauthier_

Made in the USA
Monee, IL
24 May 2022

96974562R10174